Gareth Clarke

WHEREVER THERE IS

HZPublishing

HZPublishing

Wherever There Is

Govanhill

1

Early summer in Govanhill. Heat rebounding off the streets. Familiar shapes, reflections, white light, colours, glinting off tenement windows, shop fronts, car windscreens, side windows. The smell of spices, beer, meat, fish and chips, exhaust fumes, discarded rubbish.

This place he loved. This at least remained familiar, comforting. Any real threat to that easy familiarity was minimal, muted, so far as he was aware. Everywhere else the arbitrary, rampant loss of familiar things, the erasing of the patina of history, the dismantling of urban landscapes, roads, railways, railway stations, pubs, schools, hospitals, factories, warehouses. Struggling to contain the effect of such loss, the ongoing threat of further loss, the resultant anguish. Drink helped, softening, distracting, allaying, but only to a certain degree - and any relief was, as he well knew, temporary and illusory.

Ross McKenzie, mid-thirties, medium height, strongly built. Khaki combat jacket, jeans. Long, untidy hair. Distinct blue eyes, intense and intent when he wasn't in drink. Lately a beard, not overlong but unkempt. He looked a 'wild man', and had been something wild as a youth. A child of post-industrial Glasgow - the Glasgow of early Taggart - rough and ready, visceral, grubby, run-down. Of course, much damage had been done by then, long before he had any memories of it. The Gorbals just down the road from Govanhill had been lost in the Fifties. When he left school at sixteen, he'd become a labourer on construction sites. Often they'd be building on land cleared by demolition gangs, and sometimes he'd witness work in progress, the creation of a bomb-site where tenements, factories, warehouses, commercial buildings had lately been, sometimes odd vestiges of walls or shop fronts remaining, signs advertising goods and services to displaced, vanished customers, or the name of some business which had once flourished on what had been a busy, thriving street. All now rubble. History, texture, completely unravelled.

Born and brought up in Drumchapel, a bleak, hopeless place to outsiders, home enough to those who'd known nothing else. One of the big post-war overspill estates together with Castlemilk, Easterhouse and Pollok, away on the western fringe of the city. Still some of the feral, hunting instincts tainted him - he felt they tainted him, and he made a conscious effort to combat these wilder instincts. He'd been part of a gang that had roamed aimlessly, annoying, intimidating, fighting, vandalising. Defending territory against other rival gangs pointlessly loyal to their own little piece of urban wasteland. Till he was ten or eleven he'd thought the estate was all the world, and was content enough with it. Then, with a pound or two in his pocket, and without his parents' knowledge, he began to take the bus into the city proper.

To explore at length and by himself was a revelation. Great stone public buildings, forbidding warehouses, sometimes side by side. Commercial buildings all around the centre and along the river. Lifting his gaze he took in the height and scale of the structures around him, the lines of perspective, repeating patterns of windows, doors, chimneys. Feeling a deep, magical pleasure in these surroundings, an almost mystical experience. Wondering also what this Glasgow had to do with his own familiar territory, the contrast with the bleakness, the hard, unforgiving lines of the concrete Fifties tenements of Drumchapel.

He fell in love with the warmth and texture of stone, and the more or less elaborate detailing, sometimes plain, sometimes wildly exuberant, endless variation adding interest and movement to repeating patterns. He explored wastelands, places left in stasis where destruction had taken place. He found a secret, abandoned foot tunnel under the Clyde, littered, dark and sinister. He came across Paddy's Market, spending an hour or more wandering the stalls cramped in among the viaduct arches, entranced by the bustle, variety and colour, stallholders eyeing the unkempt youth with wary displeasure. He found areas of the city where Victorian tenements had somehow escaped the great erasing and still predominated. The satisfying buzz of activity around shops beneath flats above.

He became fascinated by the history of these places. And as he got older began to spend time in public libraries, poring through reference books on architecture and local history. He learned of architraves, porticos and pediments, cornices and balustrades, pilasters and stringcourses. The sheer variety of all the devices employed. And as he looked around the city he began to recognise examples everywhere. He read of Glasgow from earliest times through to the present. Clydeside. Photos of Hutchesontown in the Forties. The great steelworks and manufactories of Parkhead. Dennistoun. Maryhill. Sometimes so incensed and agitated by the images of destruction he'd rush out and start charging at a furious pace through crowded streets and hidden courts and down narrow alleyways, wearing himself out, calming himself. Later, he'd take himself off to the nearest bar to blunt the edge of his impotent anguish. So much lost, and the rate of change and loss, if not accelerating, relentlessly continuing.

Grant was off to school, a dedicated, studious youth of fifteen who kept himself to himself. Fiona was at work - she said she'd be home around half five. To escape the baking heat he'd gone up into the park, enjoying the calming greenness, the shade of the trees. He climbed the steps to a favourite vantage point by the flagpole, then turned and surveyed the city. A view over reaching spires and pink and blonde tenements away across to the Campsie Hills beyond. A Victorian city still, largely - at least so it appeared from here, though his eyes were drawn with bitter loathing to the sight of the riverside and city centre developments - easily, obtrusively visible. Horrible shiny monsters. A city since the war and lately and continuingly diminished in so many ways and places, as all cities had been by the indiscriminate sweeping away of the old. Overdevelopment, cold, suffocating modernism. The orgy of destruction. Loss of character, loss of texture. The human dimension of scale, materials, detailing. The means through which we relate to our environment. Evidence of past use, the sense of history. Maintaining a connection with the past; pasts. A gnawing, crowding anxiety. Nobody but he could see this or was aware of it. People tended not to see beyond the rough exterior.

He went on to the glasshouses around the far side of the park. A favourite retreat, a separate, compact world within the Victorian structure of wood, iron and glass. Within it another enclosed world, a small channel of water under a footbridge along one aisle in which a number of surprisingly large fish (he'd read somewhere they were carp) patrolled actively and purposefully. A tiny splash of water to hold an entire existence. Better than a prison cell. He'd been on a number of occasions to look at the stark, desolate form of Barlinnie, and had often wondered what meaning would be possible behind the high perimeter wall. Locked in a tiny cell with some lunatic.

After spending some time peering down at the fish in their cool domain (his favourite a large orange one that in occasionally surfacing seemed to look straight at him with benign expression), he continued through the corridor of lush greenery in the humid heat. Smaller cells within the reptile house. The only creatures in those glass boxes that betrayed any sense of urgency were the tortoises. The rest - lizards, snakes, geckos, an iguana, a tarantula, a bearded dragon - infinitely sad-looking creatures in their tiny enclosures - frozen, as if they'd had enough and thrown in the towel.

His phone bleeped. A text from Jimmy Mccluskey, his best mate. Though so unpredictable and unreliable you could almost guarantee him not being there for you when it really mattered.

Hi Ross u busy

No whats up

Can we meet up

Aye what time

Ten minutes Mullins

Aye see you there

Jimmy Mccluskey was either highly intelligent, and doing a fine job of hiding it, or else he really was as colourless and shallow as he seemed, but with the facility to occasionally simulate the appearance of someone interesting and even worthwhile. It was impossible to tell, and Ross tended to alternate in his opinion. He was a scrawny little guy, with ugly sculpted red hair, long, bony face and teeth all over the place. It was surprising how many teeth he managed to fit into his mouth - it looked over-stocked, and might well have accounted for his somewhat indistinct speech.

Ross thought privately that Jimmy was an ugly wee fucker, inexplicably popular with women - at least until they realised what a cold, selfish little cunt he really was. Yet despite all this he couldn't help liking him and enjoying the cheerfully obscene banality of his company, interspersed with occasional attempts at deep and serious conversation. He had a certain perverted charm. Ross found him in a dark corner of Mullins Bar, alone, barely acknowledging his greeting. Shifty and twitchy in the normal course, this time he seemed worse than usual - in fact he was shaking, his face drawn, eyes distracted.

'Get ye a drink?'

He nodded.

The bar was busy. Small, gloomy, cramped, jukebox at full blast and a game of pool in progress. Aye, ae'll hae ten poon on Doctor Finlay. Ten poon? Why ye wastin yir money? Ross waited for the barman to deal with orders ahead of him. Come on, a can see the fuckin shot from here. Conversation with Jimmy was generally fairly non-existent unless it was drink-fuelled. Only then would the slightly garbled and difficult-to-follow stories come out, punctuated by frequent high-pitched giggles. He claimed to have been a successful amateur boxer before taking up drinking and screwing around as his main hobbies, increasingly neglecting his training, preferring to spend the afternoon in a bar rather than at the gym or doing roadwork. Ah, that's shite. A'll hae ye another game. Ross had never seen any evidence of this sporting prowess, but took his word for it, even though he was a skinny guy and it was difficult to credit him with the punching power he claimed. Maybe just a bit of macho posturing, himself being an older man with a predictably violent past in the Drum. Och aye, the noo. Laughter.

The usual topic was women, preferably girls, Jimmy sometimes apparently sailing close to the wind age-wise. They once met up with Jimmy panic-stricken, claiming after some encounter in a dark alley outside a nightclub that he'd had no idea how young the girl was. It's fair to say the less worldly-wise the women were the better he got on with them - best of all a blank canvas onto which he could project any level of unrealistic perfection he chose, and which didn't threaten his own blankness. And none was more blank than his current girlfriend Clare, who Ross thought might possibly be the most stunningly dull woman ever to have existed. Regarded by Jimmy as The One, the epitome of female grace. And it's true she smiled prettily, sat, ate, watched TV, and responded in a perfunctory fashion when someone spoke to her. And it's true her eyes were open and her lips moved the while. In fact she did everything you might reasonably expect, and yet there was seemingly nothing there.

Still, at some other time and riding high, 'Aren't they just the best fuckin invention ever! A just love all their secret places and secret girly bits! They're jus' fuckin great - just so long as they dinnae talk, which they do all the fuckin time wi'out pausin for breath.' A high giggle and flash of yellow, lupine teeth. 'Trouble is they cannae get enough o' the sound of their own voices. All a want fae a woman,' suddenly serious, 'apart from bein willin and eager to take it up the bum, is five minutes conversation, ten minutes feelin her up, then a hand job. Or sex if a can be bothered. Any more than that's a pain in the fuckin arse.' Another giggle while he drowned his glass, almost choking himself.

He had a mumbling, indistinct style of speech, quietly spoken, often difficult to follow, any punch line accompanied by a wide-eyed, high-pitched laugh, often relating to some obscene description of a sexual act. And if you couldn't follow and asked him to repeat it, he made no adjustment, just mumbling out another take of whatever he was saying with just the same inflexions and intonations as before, so that the listener was none the wiser and just had to end up nodding and smiling.

Ross carried over two lagers and a couple of packets of crisps, sat himself down and looked inquiringly at his friend.

'So, what's up, Jimmy? Ye look terrible.'

13

'That auld bitch,' he said at last in a whisper, not touching his drink. Ross leaned closer.

'Your mother.'

'Aye, ma mother, that fuckin psycho bitch an' her two evil mates. The three fuckin witches. Sittin there talkin aboot us as if I wisnae there. An' aw a bunch o' fuckin lies.'

They'd been out together in the city centre as a group, seven or eight of them including Maz and her buddies, plus Jimmy and Clare. Ending up well tanked in a nightclub, where Maz proceeded to flirt furiously with any young lad within reach. Apparently at one point one of them objected to her hands-on antics and gave her some lip, infuriating her.

'She came across tae us, Ross, sayin a had tae go an' teach this laddie a lesson, gie him a wee slap fae insultin her. Well, a wisnae gan tae get involved in somethin fae nae good reason. So a said, A'm nae deein that, why should a? Cos a'm yir mother, ye little bastard, ye should stan' up fur your mother. A said, A'm no' hittin someone fur no reason. So then she starts screaming at us. Ye little shit, ye worthless wee bastard, in front of everyone, then she comes and slaps us round the ear and a try to grab hold ae her arms, an' she's still screamin at us. Christ Ross...' Suddenly he looks on the verge of tears. 'A cannae stand it anymore. She's just fuckin mental.'

Ross knew their relationship was strained, edgy. Sometimes guardedly amicable, more often not, though always contained in his presence. As a friend of both, neither wanted to be seen in a bad light in front of him.

'An' then when a got up this morning, a went doonstairs, an' there's the three fuckin witches fixin us wae their evil glare. What time dae ye call this? Should ye nae be at work noo? A'm no' gan tae work. How no'? A'm just not. Ye know your trouble, ye're just feckin bone idle. Ye're lazy. Ye know that, ye're just too feckin lazy to keep a job. Aye, this fae a woman who hasnae worked in twenty years. So a told her to piss the fuck off and mind her own feckin business, an' then she jumps up, tells us to get oot an' stay oot, ye're rude, ye're ignorant, ye're lazy, ye're this, that and the other, an' the other two are joinin in, God, a don't know how ye put up wi' him, a'd throw him oot the hoose, cheeky wee laddie, talkin tae his mother like that. They just widnae stop an' shut the fuck up, an aw this in ma ain hoose, ma feckin home.'

Jimmy lapsed into haunted silence. Ross tried to think of something consoling to say. He was still shaking - from his appearance he looked on the edge of a breakdown. Though not relishing the physical contact, Ross moved round to a seat alongside and put an arm around his shoulders.

'You know, ye let her get to you too much, Jimmy.'

Jimmy turned his head and looked at Ross briefly with defeated eyes before looking down once more.

'What d'ye mean?'

'I mean ye're letting her antics affect ye by actually listening to what she says and engaging wi' it. You know it can only affect ye like this if you let it. Just dinnae react to it - to anythin - let it just slip by and wash over you just like it was background noise or somethin on the radio. You know it's turned on and voices are comin oot of it, but ye're no' takin it in. You're thinkin all the time of somethin else, or nothin.' He paused and withdrew his arm. 'Like Clare, fur example.'

Jimmy turned and smiled a small, twisted smile.

'Christ, a think ye're right. A'm lettin' her get tae us, get inside ma heid.'

'That's right, that's exactly what's happening.'

'She knows just how tae get inside an' twist ye aroond. Sae ye're sayin it's up to me. A need to tune her oot.'

'Aye, that's it. Just keep smilin inside, smilin and serene while ye think of somethin beautiful and that calms ye doon. Something remote from all the crap.'

'Like Clare.'

'That's it, like Clare.'

Jimmy smiled again, this time a wider, transforming smile, and took a deep draught of lager, wiping his mouth with the back of his hand. Still smiling and nodding. Ross took the opportunity to resume his seat. He felt another glowing tribute to Clare's qualities now inevitable.

'She's just gorgeous, Ross.'

'Aye, she is.'

'There's no' another girl like her.'

Ross smiled sadly and nodded.

'A'm that serious aboot her.'

'Are ye, Jimmy?'

'Christ, yeah. We're both deadly serious.'

'She feels the same way?'

'Aye, o' course.'

'So ye're no' going to fuck it up this time, like ye always do.'

'Nae, o' course not. A might ae messed things up before, but this is different. Clare's the woman of ma life. I love her, Ross. A'll never stop lovin' her.'

'Ah Jimmy, there's a song in there somewhere.' But then Ross looked at his friend's ardent face and smiled. 'That's great, Jimmy. She is very attractive.'

'It's nae just her looks. That's no' important. We jus' get on sae well. A jus' love bein wi' her.'

'Well, a'm really pleased for ye. A think it's great.' Even though he'd heard the same thing about half a dozen times before. The sunlit discovery of The One, followed by boredom or contempt steadily setting in, or else being found out sleeping around. Followed by tearful recriminations and, eventually, hate-filled invective and the promise that she'd never have anything to do with you, you little shit, ever again. Any prospect of setting up as a couple reduced to nothing. Nights away at her place or her parents' place over and finished. Back to living with his mother full-time once more.

Stories about her from his childhood. The constant rages. Throwing him across the room. Clipping him if he didn't do as he was told straight away. Regularly coming home to find her four sheets to the wind with some guy he'd never seen before. Coming in from school one day and finding her just about to hang herself. Snatching the rope or belt from around her neck, unhooking it, contending meanwhile with the screams and wails of anguish, she wants oot, cannae take any more, leave me be will ye, subsiding into wracking sobs. Other times trying to defend her against rough handling from various boyfriends. Always the rages, the venomous lash of her tongue.

Ross suddenly felt he could understand the twitches and tics, the cold, depressive moods and the fecklessness, the inability to hold down a job (unable, however, to see that Fiona regarded him in much the same light - he'd have been truly shocked if told). How could anyone, a child especially, cope with all that and come out unscathed - which he hadn't, of course, but still it was remarkable that Jimmy was outwardly as relatively normal as he was.

He got in a bit the worse for wear. Grant would be home before long so he resisted doing what he'd prefer to do which was lie down and close his eyes. Instead he wandered through the empty flat. The living room had a bay which afforded a wide, panoramic view. He looked out, always surprised by the greenery visible from a top-floor flat in such a densely-packed area of the city, the harmony of pink and honey-coloured stone with green of trees in full profusion, the solid, seemingly permanent sculptural presence of surrounding buildings. Directly opposite a series of one-storey factory units dating from the Twenties, a constant coming and going of people and vans.

He was feeling a kind of caring towards his friend after the late display of naked vulnerability. Of course he knew what an unreliable and at times obnoxious prick the guy could be, even towards his supposed best friend - the occasional flash of ice-cold antagonism through the facade of friendliness. Knowing Jimmy's mother Maz as he did (thought he did), he wondered where the truth lay.

The room, cold in winter, wind rattling through gaps around the windows, so caked in paint at the bottom they wouldn't open, today enjoyed the sun slanting through the wavy panes. Ross stood in the path of its rays, swaying slightly, absorbing the warmth. From here you'd think the world had remained reassuringly stable over the past hundred years or so.

2

He loved the view over the city at night from the M8 - all the lights, the separate intermingled lives in all their spangled dots of white and colour. Even the tower blocks had a strange fascination at night. Sighthill. The Red Road flats. Bleak and brutally insistent by day. He remembered once looking down on the city centre from the motorway, seeing a soap factory like something from Victorian times (probably was), stone buildings, chimney. Not having a car he hadn't been that way for a while, so didn't know what had become of it. Swept away by now, probably. Warehouses in the centre demolished, the land left as waste ground or replaced by some car showroom. Like the careless erasing of complex formulations from a blackboard. He sometimes felt he could cry or scream.

Calm, calming. He thought of the view from Queen's Park. The breathless, humid air of the hothouse. The smell of the streets in the unaccustomed heat. The cooling cover of the trees, shading, dappling. The view down Victoria Road straight towards the city centre. The flat had a small third bedroom, used mainly as a study, overlooking the back courts. He picked up a booklet about the Western Isles from the desk and examined the photos of cottages and lonely roads and mountainous views. He remembered the Uists appearing from the ocean, starting as a faint grey line as the ferry chugged through a flat sea. A week's holiday years ago when Grant was still quite small. He'd imagined them living there, or maybe up in the Highlands, somewhere half-remote, detached from immediate neighbours yet easy walking to a cosy little town, bustling in summer, tiny harbour, sparkling sea. Working their own croft together, digging, planting, harvesting. On a day like today a heady mix of heat and scent of vegetation heightening the senses, inflaming their physical desire so that, still hot and sweaty, they'd tumble into bed together. Later sitting outside with a cooling drink, a fragrant breeze coming off the sea, the hills all around, a heady profusion of cottage garden flowers, the afterglow of sexual satisfaction.

She wasn't - somehow, some way - the woman he used to know and envisage beside him sharing this idyllic life. Or maybe it was he that had changed - or alternatively failed to change, develop, gain depth, maturity. That was more likely. And if maturity was another term for settling then he wasn't about to do that. If anything he saw the trajectory of his life as being true and consistent to his core beliefs and feelings. Or was it just how he saw her, their relationship. Or maybe she had in fact changed. Her career so important to her now. But he still fancied her, still wanted to touch her, feel her body. And she still responded, usually. Maybe he was still something to her - something, where once he'd felt he was her hero, and maybe taken that too much for granted. Yet he knew she'd never look elsewhere. Still, he was certain she'd changed in some way he couldn't quite determine - he could see it, or thought he could see it, in the look in her eye and the line of her mouth and the way she carried her chin. But if she was now somebody else, who was she?

The single-track roads in the Highlands, carefully, tentatively laid across the glory of the landscape. He'd heard of imminent plans to 'improve' a section of road on the east coast. A road he knew from some other holiday, Fiona driving the hire car, his window wound down, taking in with deep pleasure the walls, fencing, bridges, roadside furniture, the way the road insinuated itself, blending seamlessly and with unthinking artistry into the landscape.

He rubbed his forehead. That people could be so wilfully, senselessly destructive. Yet was it really worth getting involved in another conflict, potentially, probably, almost certainly as fruitless and frustrating as any of the others. A veteran of protests, campaigns and marches across Glasgow and beyond over many years. Against cuts and loss of services and amenities and the destruction of buildings and the loss of green spaces, and bankers and big business and any policies of the Right. Writer of countless indignant, impassioned letters to newspapers, prepared to stand up at public meetings and put his point of view in halting, imperfect cadences. Attending numerous committee meetings of obscure left-wing/anarchist political parties and activist groups, cramped in back rooms of pubs or above shops.

Yet lately he'd withdrawn from all that. Nobody shared his vision. An harmonious, preserved built environment, texture, permanence, stability. Nobody had any developed aesthetic sensibility. Pointless, all pointless. A sense of history. Continuity in a precarious, finite existence where there is, given the brevity of that existence, so little time to understand anything. Anything. To him social issues and aesthetics went hand in hand.

So now just himself, alone. A hatred of high-rise buildings such that he would have loved to dynamite all the skyscrapers of London, starting with the hated Shard. To see that unholy, loathsome thing reduced to dust, a million tiny fragments bobbing on the murky waters of the Thames. Over two hundred new skyscrapers were planned or already under construction within London, changing forever the face of the city, making it something it should never have been. And to think how beautiful London was, had been - the London of Canaletto, achingly beautiful. As late as the Thirties an organic, infinitely varied texture - wool warehouses, street markets, formal gardens, soot-encrusted public buildings, spacious parks, factories, crowding backstreets, the seething docks, the sprawling warren of the East End. Though even then the tearing down had been in full swing, a well-established metropolitan pastime.

The inhuman scale. Yet the tower blocks of Glasgow were part of him, like it or not. The orgy of destruction. Lack of continuity, scale, proportion, texture. Paddy's Market, shut down and gated. Shitheads, morons. Anything that isn't shiny and sanitised is a threat. Anything that has the beat and pulse of human life and of genuine human interaction.

He never knew the road along Loch Lomond before it had been ruined back in the Eighties, aside from photos. Constructed as a motor road in the 1920s, winding with sensuous flow and minimum impact around the banks of the loch. To be scythed through without compunction, earthmoving equipment scouring the hillsides. But then wouldn't you want to get past Loch Lomond just as quickly as you could? Of course you would, why wouldn't you. Nothing was valued. Nothing.

He saw Grant walking with a friend, coming down the street together, dressed in identical dark school blazers. They parted on the street, Grant disappearing into the close below. Ross went into the hall, where he soon heard footsteps. He quietly opened the door and peered over the railing, catching glimpses of his son's head bobbing up the spiral stairwell. He went back inside before Grant reached the last flight, wary of provoking irritation by an overt greeting on the landing.

Grant at fifteen was at just the age to see his father's faults most clearly, and to recognise not too many redeeming features or mitigating factors for the deficits.

Whenever Ross moderated his accent, which he sometimes tried to do around Grant (though it required a conscious effort), viewing a pronounced accent as unnecessarily tribal and a bad influence, Grant would regard the attempt with ill-concealed contempt, and deliberately thicken his own in response. He kept his hair short and neat. Ambitious, well-organised, a dedicated student, where once he'd idolised his father as the ideal man - tough, confident, exciting - he'd come to see him now in much the same light as did his mother, though Fiona was still denying it to herself to a degree. A dreamer, a semi-drunkard, a man going nowhere except gradually downhill. The difference being that Grant, with the certitude of youth, had no problem expressing his feelings from time to time, his judgement the more harsh for having once set his father so high, only to be disillusioned, misled. Ross saw only that his son was often surly, and that the closeness they'd once enjoyed was a thing of the past.

'Hello Grant,' smiling, 'how's it going?'

'A'm fine.' He could tell straight away his father had been drinking.

'Good day at school?'

'Aye.'

Grant threw his bag down in the hallway and headed for his bedroom.

'A'm gettin' changed, an' then a'm gan oot.'

The door closed behind him.

'Do you want anythin tae eat before ye go out?'

'Nah, a'm fine,' from behind the closed door.

Ross went into the kitchen and sat at the breakfast table, staring out at the backs of the tenements opposite. Presently Grant came through dressed in t-shirt and tracksuit bottoms, took a glass from the cupboard and filled it at the tap. Leaning on the sink, drinking his water, looking across at his father. Ross thought that in different circumstances, different times, this could have been him - physically they were very similar, though Grant was going to be taller. Well-organised, a future mapped out - Highers, university, career. Maybe not, maybe not.

'Got much homework?'

'Aye, some. A'm gan to dae it at ma friend's hoose.'

'Who're ye going to see?'

'Usman.'

Ross nodded.

'Oh, I was thinking about our holidays this year.'

'Oh aye.'

'Aye. I was thinkin it might be good to go up to the Highlands again for a week or so, maybe two. I was thinkin of Sutherland this year, some little place on the east coast. A nice wee cottage by the sea. What do you think?'

Grant pulled a face, turned and refilled his glass, then took another long draught.

'A'm no' sure,' he said at last.

'What aren't you sure about?'

'Whether a can come.'

'Why wouldn't ye be able to come?'

'Well, a mean whether a want tae come.'

Ross thought of telling him he was only fifteen and had to come whether he liked it or not, but instead took a more conciliatory approach.

'We're no' going to have that many more holidays with you before ye're off and independent, Grant. And a know your mother would be disappointed if ye didnae go.'

Grant grimaced.

'Christ, is it that bad going on holiday with your parents?'

'No, it's not that.'

'Oh well, that's good to hear, at least.'

He must have let unintended pathos creep into his tone, as his son suddenly smiled, and for a moment Grant was the eager child of four, five, six years ago, or younger still, his face lit with a warm, open expression. Ross was strangely, deeply moved - smiles were rare - a rare connection. Associations with past years flooded his emotions. A fearful sense of imminent isolation, loss, that he couldn't explain or define.

The smile faded. It occurred to him that maybe there was a girlfriend they hadn't heard about, though he knew Grant had friends who were girls. He cleared his throat.

'Look, I dinnae want tae force ye to come. Maybe ye've got other plans?'

'Aye, mebbe.'

'Well, what if it wis just a week? It would be great if ye came.'

'Can a think about it?'

'Aye, of course ye can. A havnae booked anythin yet - it was just an idea. Though we're leaving it late anyway - I don't know what might be left that hasnae been booked already, but I'll see.'

After Grant had gone on his way Ross thought he had time before Fiona got back to slip out for a little bottle of something. Being able to step out of the flat straight into the liberating anonymity of city life. Govanhill had long been a focus for migration - Irish, Jews from Poland and Lithuania, Italians, Pakistanis, more lately Roma from Slovakia and the Czech Republic, Poles, Romanians. Halal meat and chicken shops by the dozen, European, Arabic and Asian stores, Irish pubs, Czech and Slovak food shops, money transfer shops (to relatives in Pakistan and India), ice cream parlours, Islamic bookstores, recorded speeches, DVDs, perfume. Ross, in love with the exotic surrealist mix, saw the precursor of a world he imagined possible, a global flux free from walls, curtains, borders, fear, hatred, division. Shops with Arabic signage and Eastern fare within Victorian stone tenements, broad Glaswegian from the mouths of girls in brightly coloured and embroidered shalwar kameez and dupatta. Overheard conversations in Urdu, Polish, Czech, Slovak, Romani.

Contrary to his expectations he'd found the Uists too confining, constricting. You were less yourself, separate and free, than in the city. Anyway he wasn't bound ideologically to any particular part of Scotland, or even to Scotland itself. In fact he was deeply hostile to the recent upsurge of nationalism. The overriding sense of them and us, whoever *they* might be. Zealously guarding ourselves, our identity, against them. Our singularity, our one-ness, our us, our collective identity, in the face of *them*. Those who threaten our sense of us, to be treated with suspicion, distrust, anxiety, fear. Hostility. And the others, the *them*, would begin, naturally enough, with migrants, hated and scapegoated for anything that comes to hand. Ethnic and religious minorities, forced by antagonism to aggressively assert their own one-ness, or retreat and live in fear. The usual suspects. Then anyone who looks or behaves in a way that doesn't satisfy an arbitrary notion of us-ness. And finally anyone who doesn't overtly support the crusade for our us-ness and one-ness. All dangerous stupid fucking nonsense. The same kind of meaningless tribalism he'd been a part of as a youth. No more, pal. I decide who I am. I don't need a bunch of narrow-minded nationalist cunts to tell me who I am. If I fit in I fit in on my own terms, and it won't be on the basis of solidarity with scum like that.

Aesthetics, ideas, principles - these knew no national boundaries. Tribal ties and jurisdictions and emblems of local affiliation had no place in his scheme of things, and he took no part in any form of outward display. They've fucked it all along the river, more and more around the central city. Crude, shiny, anonymous buildings. Hideous monsters. That's not what Glasgow's about. That's nothing to do with Glasgow.

29

Glasgow's a Victorian city if it's anything. Why take something that's great, that's real and vital and has the pulse of human activity, and completely screw it over.

3

Fiona McKenzie had been a brash, jolly, plump-faced, red-haired girl, happiest playing out in the streets and chasing around with a football or on bikes with the boys, and never afraid to stand up for herself or put her opinions forward in forthright terms. Quieter now, naturally, and until she'd got back into study and work and the company of intelligent, responsive adults, had especially in Grant's early years been chastened by reduced expectations, and dulled by responsibility and repetition. Her hair, worn shoulder length, was no longer red but fading, starting to grey, and which she now dyed dark brown. Into her thirties her face had grown thinner, and around Ross her expression was often strained and sombre.

Born Fiona Vannucci, daughter of George and Molly (her father bore the anglicized version of his own father's name), she'd been brought up in Maryhill, an area to the north west of the city centre. Her parents still lived in the same neat and modest three bed semi in a little suburban enclave where Fiona and her older sister Morag had grown up. When they were young, nana Carlotta, grandmother on their father's side, small, dark, frail, given to gloomy self-withdrawal, and for many years widowed and living with the family in the spare bedroom, would sometimes tell them, dramatically and with much hand wringing, of how she and Giorgio, both aged twenty and newly married, arrived to a cold, wet, dark, dirty, decaying Glasgow. A city with a brooding intensity that took both of them aback as they attempted to survive and live amicably alongside locals sometimes friendly, occasionally hostile and often unintelligible. They'd left behind their families in the Quartieri Spagnoli of Naples in an attempt to escape a ravaged, broken, poverty-stricken nation in search of a better life in Britain, at that time actively encouraging especially white able-bodied Europeans to settle and participate in the rebuilding.

She told of how they found themselves in the grim, threatening wastes of the Gorbals, rented a room for ten shillings a week, filthy, damp, and with mould across the walls and lurking in every corner, and ice in shapes like the devil on the few remaining panes of glass. Of how they'd huddle in bed, shivering and miserable, with their coats pulled over thin bed covers to try to find some warmth, and of how they'd sleep at night with the gas still burning to try to stave off the rats that swarmed all over the building. And of how when Giorgio went off during the day to make a living wherever he could - at the docks at first before they found a semi-derelict shop for rent in Maryhill and slowly put it in order and started the business selling fish and chips that still flourished - she would be left with the children, one arriving almost every year for the first few years, aunts and uncles of Morag and Fiona, now mostly dispersed or deceased. And of how she would weep going about her daily tasks, on her knees sometimes, sobbing for the pity of her wretched fate, wrenched from her beloved Napoli, impoverished and decrepit as *it* was, and from all her family, from easy familiarity and the warmth of southern Italy - missing out also as it turned out on the economic miracle that was Italy in the 50s and 60s. All for dark, freezing, crumbling, hell on earth Glasgow. And all for love? What had she been thinking, when her family had opposed the marriage in the first place? Shaking her head, rolling her eyes and clutching her thin arms, beseeching them, young as they were and largely mystified, though impressed, never to put themselves in the position of being taken away from home, family and native land by a man, no matter how seductive and charming he might be. Though when she met Ross shortly before she died, around the time Fiona and Ross were about to be married, she'd taken to her granddaughter's rugged boyfriend as he listened to her stories of the Gorbals and Naples, smiled and generally made himself agreeable.

In private later he was dismissive of an old woman's exaggeration. It was lack of maintenance over decades, it was neglect, it was not lookin after the heritage ye've been given, the heritage the Victorians bequeathed tae us which for decades has been pissed on, trampled in the dirt, scorned an' destroyed by a bunch of ignorant philistine wankers. Look at the photos - aw that stuff aboot bein pu' up quickly and wi'out care is aw wilful nonsense. Look at the photos - the stonework's as good as anythin aroond here - it's aw just propaganda tae justify the destruction. Anythin, anywhere's a slum if ye dinnae look after it, if ye let it go tae wrack an' ruin, if ye let the windaes fal oot an' put cardboard in them, an' let the guttering fal off an' dinnae replace slates an' let the rubbish pile up. Rats? Aye, a'll bet they had rats in Naples, an' overcrowding an' dinnae update the buildin's wi' bathrooms an' new windaes an' plumbin' and plasterin', but there it's a feckin heritage site noo wi' guided tours. Here - here we jus' scorn them an' yank 'em doon. Meks me sae angry, the fecking ignorant bastards. Just because it's no' centuries old, disnae have history - it's only Victorian - we'll hae it doon, ye ignorant fuckers, and so on and on he'd go. Look at the photos, will ye, just take a look, ah, so beautiful, so beautiful, almost crying over black and white photos of Glasgow slums that her nana Carlotta had hated with a deep loathing. Sae sculptural, dinnae ye see it, all the shapes, the lines of the walls, the windaes at all the different levels, chimneys everywhere like some piece ae artwork, the stonework - just think if the stone had been cleaned like this place an' ye could see the colour in it, an' the windaes replaced an' generally treated wi' love an' respect. It just needed a wee bit of love, an' imagination, an' respect, an' valuin' somethin that's so feckin great, but that was always askin too much of stupid, ignorant people. The fecking ignorant shitheads.

Fiona sometimes thought of Ross as the young man she'd met as a teenager and fallen hopelessly in love with. True he'd been often feckless, sometimes thoughtless and irresponsible, though he'd outgrown the worst excesses. But laughing often too, the careless light of merriment in his eyes, fiery, impassioned, exciting. Now the laughs were rarer, and the eyes seemed often haunted, and the excitement was long gone. Her father had said to her, Are you sure you're doing the right thing, Fiona? I like Ross, of course, but he seems a wee bit wild, a bit of a wild laddie, and you're so young, and you've just started university. Why don't you wait a bit? What's the hurry? His voice soft, calm, as full of concerned caring for her wellbeing as ever. Well there was no hurry, except that at nineteen Fiona was crazily in love with her wild and passionate boyfriend - and also she was pregnant. But Ross had promised with emotional expressions of devotion to do everything in the world to make sure they had a roof over their heads, to take care of her and the baby, and for her to continue at university if she wanted to.

So they'd come to live in Govanhill a few months after Grant was born, lucky to find a big, run-down three bed flat on the top floor of a newly cleaned honey-coloured tenement, renovating it themselves, filling in gaping holes in ceilings, plastering, painting, wallpapering, putting down carpets and fitting new bathroom and kitchen when money allowed. They were friendly, on levels from the purely superficial upwards, with a number of people in the area, mainly through the local schools which Grant had attended since he was five. Fiona had decided not to continue with her degree, instead to spend the next few years as a stay-at-home mum, providing what she saw as necessary stability for Grant, though once he was at school, she found time to begin studying again. And by the time he turned nine, and capable of a measure of independence, her thoughts began to turn outwards once more.

There was always the option of some role in the family firm - in fact firms - there were now two Vannucci businesses in Maryhill. Her father, who'd begun helping in the fish and chip parlour in his teens, by his early twenties had started his own business with his parents' help - a small cafe, now established over forty years. Later he bought out his siblings' share in the original business and brought in a manager. At various times Ross was offered openings in both of the Vannucci businesses, which he refused. Fiona, gratefully and regretfully, rejected similar offers, despite knowing the pleasure her father would have taken from having both his daughters working alongside him, though Morag had stayed, and now practically ran the cafe.

For one thing, Fiona had no great desire to work alongside Morag, but also she had bigger things in mind. Once Grant had started school she gradually regained something of the ambition and sense of identity she'd lost. Self-driven and determined, she began to study both through the OU and on her own initiative computing, software development, web design, cloud systems. After gaining her degree, to her surprise, and despite little experience in the workplace, she quickly found a job with a small but dynamic software company, becoming highly regarded, her abilities valued. She progressed swiftly in responsibilities and scope of influence, to lead a nascent marketing and PR department. Wishing to extend her knowledge base (especially, as outlined in her degree application, of communication styles and technologies for different target audiences), she applied for and was accepted on a part-time doctorate at Glasgow Caledonian, part-financed by the company she worked for. Now a year into it, she was loving it, stimulated by the challenge and excited at discovering fresh areas of knowledge and expertise, with all the possibilities they might unlock.

And yet, despite all these pluses - her now flourishing career, the fact that she and Ross had made a decent life together, and that Grant was progressing well, growing up to be a pleasant young man, and excelling academically - despite all this, still there was something missing, a residual regret, a sense of emptiness and feeling of unfulfillment. Something more, she was sure, than just an occasional irritation that they'd spent their whole married life in a top floor tenement flat, with all that implied of inconvenience and limited privacy. Fiona had never wanted to live in a tenement in the first place. Ross had carried the day, and given that at first they were living with her parents with a tiny baby, and that she was desperate for independence - and also Ross was doing his best, working long hours, though in fact it was her parents who'd lent them the deposit - she felt obliged to go along with the purchase without protest. When what she'd really wanted was a neat, convenient, modern house, a suburban semi something along the lines of where she grew up, with a garden of their own for privacy where Grant could play, safe and secure, and where she could keep an eye on him while she did her jobs. The kind of quiet suburbia she liked so much and that she secretly found exciting, even now, when she went back to Maryhill to see her parents or visit one or two old friends who still lived in the area. Especially at dusk when the street and house lights started to come on, and all the mysterious lives behind glowing curtains were played out, and where as a child she'd walked and cycled and played even after dark with absolute freedom, safer and more civilized than tenement living with swarming streets filled with strangers. She'd been cautious of letting Grant play outside unsupervised, not that there was anywhere much to play, till he was almost in his teens, by which time of course it was far too late.

Ross had taken it for granted that it was what they both wanted, and she knew that Victorian Glasgow was at the forefront of his many obsessions, and felt, young and dependent as she then was, that he was entitled to make the decisions - and, anyway, she knew they were lucky to get anything. So she'd accepted it and they'd moved into an old tenement hemmed in by countless others, with back courts rough and littered with junk, having to pass by all the doors within the close every time she went up or down, past apartments of people she rarely or never saw or spoke to, and were always moving in or out, with all the smells and rubbish and litter in the close and out on the streets. And even when she did see someone from time to time they kept to themselves, often barely able to speak English, responding at best with a small smile and quickly turned face. And for all those years she'd had to negotiate Grant and a pushchair and shopping every time she went out to the shops, and then again coming back (aye, you noticed it more coming back). There were sixty one steps to climb - she knew because she'd counted them - with everything having to be carried, so that it had strained her arms, and she'd developed at times a painfully sore neck that refused to heal, and which hurt when she turned over in bed.

Something more than all this, which sounded petty even to her own ears. What then? Wondering whether he still had any feelings of love for her. Whether he'd really loved her back then at all. Or whether it had been merely youthful intoxication. He was still generally amiable - there'd never been any animosity - but she, they as a couple, certainly didn't seem to move him to any particular emotion now. Only the time-worn obsessions could do that - and she'd begun to find his crusading increasingly difficult to put up with, and anyway she knew the script off by heart. Lately even that fire seemed to have gone out of Ross. The political activism, which had never led anywhere, but which had at least given him the means to let off steam, and to which she'd given her verbal support, had seemingly died out, to be replaced by steady drinking - or rather, an increased level of drinking. She resented especially the time he spent with Jimmy, or Jimmy's blowsy mother. Anyway, none of it had ever meant anything to her, and no other common ground, apart from Grant, had appeared with the passage of the years. Her career was gathering momentum, and outside of work she just wanted a normal fulfilled family life, whatever that might consist of. The feeling of freedom her career gave her was counterbalanced by the constraint of her marriage. At least so she felt it, rightly or wrongly. Lately feelings less of loss, sadness or regret, than of impatience. Of time going to waste.

4

Watching him through the security peep-hole in the front door of the flat as he took a long draught of presumably some liquor from a small bottle, replaced the cap, then secreted the bottle in his coat. She tutted inwardly, both at his would-be secret drinking, but also her own subterfuge in spying on him. Moments passed as he hesitated, looking straight towards her, unaware of her looking back. She watched as he gathered himself, approached the door and rapped heavily. She stood back a bit and waited, then stepped forward and deliberately rattled the security chain and opened the door, looking out at him looking back at her as he leant for support on the handrail of the stairwell.

'Did you not take your key with you?'

Her voice pleasant, softly spoken and with an understated lilt.

'No, a didn't. How are ye deein, Fiona?'

His own voice rasping a little with the drink, but still a steadily-held smile. Unshaven, his hair shoulder-length, looking unwashed.

'Why not?'

'Well,' feeling in his pockets, 'maybe a did. Oh no, a think maybe a didn't.' He gave a light laugh. 'Anyway ye had the chain up, did ye no'?'

'You've been drinking.'

'Just a couple or two. Or maybe the three. A met Jimmy before.'

'Oh?'

'Ye know who a'm talkin aboot, Jimmy Mccluskey.'

'Aye, I know who you mean.'

Her tone failed to hide her dislike. She closed and locked the door, then pointed from the hall where they now stood into the living room.

'Will you get that bike out of there, Ross.'

He had a nominal business repairing and renovating bicycles. By word of mouth rather than through advertisement, via friends, and friends of friends, a trickle of bikes found their way up to the flat, where Ross would, depending on the owner's requirements, make any necessary repairs, or else give the bike a complete service, involving removing the wheels, giving everything a thorough clean, checking the crank bolts, pedals, stem bolts, seat bolts, replacing worn parts - chain, derailleurs, brakes, tyres - then put it all back together again, adjusting, realigning, lubricating, pumping up the tyres, checking everything worked. At any given time there might be three or four bikes chained to the iron balustrade at the top of the stairs, and maybe one or two in the hall itself. Once he'd made the effort to engage with a job, Ross did good, conscientious work. Making a start was often the problem, and also finishing the job when he had started. He never troubled to keep a record of accounts, of bills paid, bills pending or costs. It was all completely haphazard. As he told Fiona if she questioned the ramshackle nature of the business, he had other, more important things on his mind. Bits of bikes were often left strewn around for days on end with Ross claiming he knew exactly where everything was, and what went where.

'A've got naewhere to put it. A'm workin on it.'

'There's room for it in the hall.'

'Aye, I know but...'

She didn't want all his paraphernalia in the hall either, but it was better than the living room as a permanent workshop.

'It's no' very social workin in the hall.'

'Social, aye.' She turned towards the kitchen, then paused. 'Do you want a cup of tea - or coffee - I'm thinking maybe you could do with a coffee?'

'Aye, that would be grand.'

He followed her through to the kitchen. She switched on the kettle, put two cups by it and reached for the coffee jar. Ross, overcome with a sudden surge of drink-fuelled lust, stepped forwards and grasped his wife around the waist, pressing himself into her from behind, caressing her, gradually moving his hands down to her thighs and bum. She didn't try to move out of his reach, but neither did she respond. She finished pouring the drinks, adding the milk and sugar, then half turning, 'Here's your coffee.'

Ross relaxed his hold and stepped reluctantly back, chastened at the lack of response.

'Aye, thanks,' taking the mug.

'Where's Grant?'

'Gan oot.'

'Where's he gone?'

'To see Usman, a think. He said they're doin homework together.'

'He's never here these days. I'm gone before he's up, and he's always out somewhere in the evenings.'

'The laddie's fifteen. When a wis years younger than him a wis oot on ma own all over the city.'

'Well, he's not you.' The hint of an accusing tone - as if to say, thank God he's *not* you.

'Aye, I know that. What's wrong? What're ye sore aboot?'

'A'm no' sore. Just tired. And I'd like to have seen Grant, that's all. But it's fine, I'll see him later, mebbe.'

She turned, went across the hall to the study and firmly closed the door. Doors everywhere seemed to be slamming in his face.

The knock had come around nine in the evening. Fiona was in the kitchen washing up, with the door into the hall open so that she could hear a knock or ring, hoping and expecting that Grant would be home any time. She grabbed a towel and went quickly to the door, drying her hands as she went. Instead of Grant, standing there looking downcast was Jimmy Mccluskey, a carrier bag in each hand. He reminded Fiona of a hyena - the head large in proportion to the body, thin legs and loping gait. There was truly something animalistic about him - that long, grinning face, mouth filled with teeth. You could almost imagine the tongue lolling out, and a hideous panting. But then sometimes a gentle, ingratiating smile with lifted eyebrows intended to convey openness and sincerity, but which failed entirely to convince her. Altogether Fiona preferred that Ross meet him outside the flat, if he had to meet him at all. Yet tonight he looked forlorn. Like a small, whipped dog, ready to cringe at the slightest movement.

'Hi Fiona. How ye deein?'

'Hello Jimmy. You'll be wanting Ross, I suppose?'

'Aye, if he's aboot.'

'Come in. He's in the living room.'

She stood aside and shut the door after him with a suspicious expression, wondering about the contents of the bags. She never troubled to any great extent to hide her feelings about Jimmy, yet he never seemed to notice, or at least show any sign that he'd noticed.

Ross had postponed removing the bike to the hallway on the pretext that as he worked on it he could watch a documentary about roads as they were in the Thirties when everything was beautiful, the roads themselves sinuous and seductive, curling and curving through unspoiled landscapes, when even major arterial routes such as the Great North Road were lined with trees, hedges, golden cornfields, wayside houses, lodges, inns, churches, farmhouses, barns, telegraph poles with multiple horizontal crossarms, when traffic was sparse, slow-moving, the cars almost uniformly black. And the roads wound through towns and villages of an endlessly variegated, endlessly harmonious blending of brick, stone, wood, slate, tile, pantile, as highly integrated and satisfying as the most intricately and ingeniously wrought work of art. Fiona had looked down at the bike still upside down, rear wheel off, parts spread here and there on the floor, tins of grease and lubricating oil set down on old newspapers. Ross, seeing her looking, had said that the bike was supposed to be finished for tomorrow - someone's comin to pick it up. A'll move it out when the programme's finished, Fiona, dinnae worry. Aye, fine, and she'd gone through to the kitchen to wash up.

Ross looked up, surprised, when Jimmy came into the room, not expecting to see him again for a day or two. Dishevelled, obviously agitated. Ross took a last, reluctant look at the TV, then clicked it off.

'Jimmy, what's up? Ye been shoppin?' indicating the bags. Jimmy was looking limp and defeated, with an expression suggesting deep tragedy. 'Put your bags down, come an' sit doon. What's happened?'

'She's chucked us oot,' he said at last, slumping into an armchair.

'Who, your maw?'

'Aye.' Appearing shell-shocked. 'A had naewhere else tae go.'

'Jesus Christ. So what's happened?'

It took some time, bit by bit, haltingly, for the story to trickle out, Jimmy's shoulders hunched, barely looking up.

'After we'd met at Mullins, a went back home. An' she started up straight away. Where have ye been? Have ye phoned them at work to let them know whit ye're deein? What *have* ye bin deein? Anyway, a wis thinkin aboot what ye said, sae a just...sae a said, calm an' quiet, Nothin, a've jus' been fur a drink wi' Ross. An' a started tae make a sandwich. A'd just got somethin oot the fridge, an' she goes berserk. She jus' goes fuckin stir crazy. Ye think ye can jus' come back here, ye feckin disloyal little shit, wi' yir feckin nose i' the air as if nothin's happened, after whit ye did tae me! An' she just swept everythin a wis gettin ready ontae the floor, bread, butter, slices of ham, jar o' pickle, knife, glass a wis jus' fillin wi' lager, aw on the floor, the glass smashed an' lager everywhere. It was aw fuckin crazy, an' then the wean was cryin her eyes oot, she didnae have a clue what wis gan on or what tae do or who to go tae, and the twins were jus' lookin wi'out sayin oot as they dae. So a jus' turned aroond an' went back intae ma room wi'out sayin a word tae her. Nothin. A wis sittin on ma bed, no' thinkin of anythin much, jus' sittin there, when she comes in like this fuckin mad screamin thing, an' starts tae grab ma clothes fae the wardrobe an' chuck 'em through the door - shirts, suits, trousers aw oot, then intae ma chest of drawers, aw ma stuff an' papers, still screamin at the top of her voice, If ye like yir pal Ross sae much, ye can go an' feckin stay wi' him, but ye're no' stayin here another hour! Ye can get oot! Now! D'ye hear me! An' Pixie wis standin there cryin her eyes oot. There wis nothin a could dae - a jus' had nae choice but tae get oot an' come here.' He paused for a moment. 'A need tae stay wi' ye just till a get sorted, Ross. A've got naewhere else tae go.'

He was now perched on the edge of his seat. Appearing to Ross, as he had to Fiona, like some poor defeated wee creature, looking up imploringly, pathetically, with big fear-filled eyes. Ross meanwhile thinking that he needed to learn to keep his mouth shut, then maybe none of this would have happened. Also thinking, what's wrong with Clare's place. But there was no chance he'd be allowed to stay there. She still lived with her parents, and they weren't that keen on Jimmy, in fact were probably hoping that she'd grow out of the attachment sooner rather than later. Both professionals of some kind or another, he couldn't remember what - Jimmy might have said - anyway wealthy, living in a large, imposing villa in its own grounds in Bearsden, the semi-autonomous dormitory for Glasgow's wealthiest. Jimmy felt like a movie star on location when he was there, so unreal did it all seem. He became a different person, relaxed, polite, affable, charming, witty even, or maybe that was just the image he tried desperately to project and believe in among these successful, sophisticated people. And Clare's personality, such as it was, resided in the wooded grounds, the tennis court, the elegant furniture, the expensively fitted bathrooms, and the thick carpeting.

Ross was about to reply when the flat door banged shut, and a few moments later Grant came into the room. Seeing Jimmy, he nodded at Jimmy's greeting, then said he thought his mother might have been in here. Fiona appeared, having heard the door shut, pleased and relieved as ever that Grant was home safe and sound.

'Hello, my darling, you're back. Have you had a good day?'

She reached up to ruffle his hair affectionately, which Grant - normally accommodating to his mother's occasional caresses, but just not now, not in company - evaded with an irritated, embarrassed twitch of his head.

'Aye fine. Anyway, a've got some work tae finish,' and strutted off to his room without further comment or eye contact.

'I'll pop in and see you shortly, sweetheart,' called Fiona after him, which received no reply other than his bedroom door being slammed shut, and almost immediately a loud blast of music. She turned back to Ross and Jimmy.

'Do you want a cup of coffee, either of you?'

Ross looked at his friend. 'There's some lager in the fridge if ye'd prefer that, Jimmy?'

'Aye, that'd be fine.'

Ross makes to get up, but Fiona says, No, don't stir yourself, I'll get it, and there's a certain something in her tone that prompts Ross and Jimmy to exchange a look. She comes back, hands a four-pack of lager to Ross, then says she's going through to the study to do some work. A further blast of noise from Grant's room just across the hallway after she goes out.

'A don't know how he works wi aw that racket,' said Ross. 'Not that a ever studied that much,' he added. 'A

49

wis never intae pop music in a big way, even when a wis his age.'

'Sounded like Nineties stuff,' said Jimmy.

'Aye, that's what he's intae. Britpop an all that stuff - Oasis, Blur, Pulp.'

'A remember - well, a dinnae remember, but a know it was just an English thing - Oasis versus Blur, north versus south - aw that shite.'

'A dinnae think he's bothered aboot that. He just likes the music.'

'He's a really bright laddie is Grant. A dinnae think he thinks much o' me, though,' smiling a sort of injured, plaintive smile.

Ross laughed. 'Dinnae be daft. Anyway, he disnae know ye that well.'

'Mebbe just as well,' said Jimmy, smiling. 'He's on tae bigger an' better things. He's aimin' fur uni, is he no'?'

'Aye, he's already got his eyes set on some prestigious place down south somewhere. He disnae want tae stay in Glesgae, anyway.'

'Ye'll miss him when he goes.'

'Aye. Still, it's not fur a few years yet.'

The idea of Grant not being around on a daily basis was so strange a thought that Ross could barely imagine it, or imagine how he would feel. Just an indefinable emptiness at the thought. Strange and uncomfortable even to contemplate.

'Clare's waitin fur her results. They'll be oot in a couple o' months. Her first choice is Newcastle - well, Northumbria at Newcastle. A dinnae know why. But anyway, if she gets the grades, that's where she'll be gan. An' a'm thinkin now of mebbe gan wi' her.'

'Ye're movin' tae Newcastle?' Ross couldn't hide his surprise.

'Aye, mebbe, if she's gets in. A havnae discussed it wi' her yet, so it isnae certain. But there's nothin fur us here, especially now a've been chucked oot.'

Ross felt this as a double dig at himself in the way Jimmy referred to it. He clearly saw Ross in some way responsible for his mother throwing him out. And their friendship clearly counted for little when Jimmy was contemplating leaving Glasgow at the drop of a hat. A double whammy. Nice one, Jimmy, you wee cunt.

'A'm sorry if anythin a said to ye had anythin to dae wi' what's happened,' said Ross, trying to keep his voice friendly.

'What d'ye mean?'

'About your mother, an' me advising ye not to pay too much attention tae what she says to you.'

'Christ no, dinnae worry about that, it was comin anyway. The woman's just crazy, unbalanced, totally fuckin insane. It would have happened sooner or later anyway.'

So that effectively dismissed the value of his advice into the bargain, while failing to reassure Ross that he wasn't to some degree responsible for the whole fiasco, such that he felt morally obliged to let Jimmy stay, for a while at least.

'Why don't I speak to her,' suddenly sensing a possible solution, 'an' see if a can straighten things out between you.'

Jimmy gave a look of tired, amused scepticism and shook his head.

'It widnae make any difference. A know when her mind's set.'

'A could gie it a shot? See if she'll listen tae reason?'

Jimmy shook his head again. 'Nah. Well, ye can if ye want, but it'll do nae good. A know her too well.' A pause, and then he looked up again with those big, sad eyes. 'So Ross, can a stay here fur now, then? A've got naewhere else tae stay.'

And he looks so pathetic and forlorn that Ross can only say yes, while having a fair idea of what Fiona's reaction will be. So he says yes, of course, he'll just go and check it out with Fiona, but he's sure it'll be fine.'

'A dinnae think she's too keen on me, Ross.'

'Whit ye talkin' aboot - of course she is. Look, a'll just go and have a quick word.'

Fiona becomes stony-faced as Ross tells her that Jimmy has had a problem at home with his mother, and needs to stay with them for a while. She asks, how long? Ross says he's not sure. Not long.

'And where's he going to sleep?'

'Well a was thinkin in here, I suppose. It's got the bed, and it is really a third bedroom - we just use it as a study.'

'*I* use the room as a study, to do the work for the PhD and for my job. It's set up as a study - ' indicating the desk, computer, printer, reference books, files, box-files - 'and I need the room as a study.' There was a silence as Ross looked at the various items indicated, as if he'd never really seen them before. Fiona said, more quietly, 'So you're saying I've got to move out of here so that Jimmy can move in.'

'It'll only be temporary. I'll go and see Maz tomorrow and see if a can straighten things out. It'll jus' be for a few days, a week at most, probably.'

She made an expression of disgust.

'I don't know how you can have anything to do with that woman.'

'She's Jimmy's mother. That's the only reason a know her. She's fine once ye get to know her.'

'I don't want to get to know her.'

'Now ye're just being snobbish.'

'That's a stupid word. Of course I'm not. I just can't stand her, that's all.'

'Ye've only met her a couple of times.'

'Aye, that was enough. And another thing. The bathroom's right next door.'

'So? What's that got tae do wae anythin?'

'There'll be no privacy. I won't have any privacy knowing he's just the other side of the wall. How do you think I'll feel taking my clothes off and havin a shower knowing he's just there?'

'The door'll be locked, for Christ sake. He's no' going to just appear through a solid wall or break through the door. Ye're being ridiculous.'

'Aye fine, well have it your own way. But a tell ye this, an' a'm no' jokin, Ross - either you get him out of here - in two or three days max - or I'll be getting out myself. And if I do a'll no' be coming back in a hurry.'

'I don't understand your problem.' An involuntary hushed tone. 'What have you got against Jimmy?'

'I don't like him - it's that simple.' Her expression tense but determined. 'I dinnae like him, and I dinnae want him in the flat. And a should be able to decide who lives in this flat and who doesn't.'

'I live here too.'

'Aye, and so dae I.'

'A never said ye didn't. Ah, this conversation's feckin ridiculous.'

'Aye, everything's ridiculous to you.'

'What's the hell's that supposed to mean?'

Fiona sighed wearily. 'Oh, nothing, nothing.'

'He's ma best friend. Are ye forgettin that? And you seem to forget it's my flat too. Dinnae I have a say?'

She looked gloomily towards him.

'Look, I didn't mean...oh, I can't discuss this anymore tonight, Ross. I'm tired and I've got to be up early tomorrow. There's a staff meeting before work. I need to be up at seven or earlier.'

Aye, feckin staff meeting. Ross felt a certain jealousy towards Fiona's work colleagues, and of the time she spent with them, and of her stories of sharing moments of humour, of problem solving together. All smooth wee bastards. His resentment was a vague, indeterminate thing, but gnawing for all that. He didn't for a moment imagine that Fiona - hardly able to acknowledge it to herself - was fighting a battle between her loyalty to him, and attraction to a colleague, in fact the company's founder and joint-director, who had pushed and promoted her within the firm. Entirely unbeknown to Ross - who had no suspicions at all beyond the formless jealousy - the degree of this attraction was on a knife-edge, in danger of slipping irrevocably beyond the point of no return.

Fiona felt increasingly resentful of his failure to bring money into the house, bar odd coppers for repairing the occasional push-bike, which would in any case go immediately on drink. She'd thought she was a modern woman, and that it didn't matter who brought what money into the marriage, or if one brought in none at all. But, when she could face the fact, she realised there was this constant low-level resentment lurking. Truth was that the intensity of his obsessions - and the drinking - and the lack of any sense of progression in their life together - had worn her down. The impatience once more. The repeated patterns that led nowhere.

5

Screams of Ross, baby, come sit ye doon ma love, hae a drink! Come and sit on ma lap, darlin! Raucous laughter. What ye up tae? Whenever Ross called at Maz's flat for Jimmy, six or seven times out of ten the convention would be in full swing in a haze of smoke and alcoholic fumes. This was a Saturday morning, but still there was Doreen, a small, rodent-like creature with a reputation for shagging or sucking off anything within grabbing distance. A sharp, inquisitive nose, puffy cheeks, short, greasy hair and indeterminate body shape. None of which were a hindrance to sexual predation, where availability and determination count for everything. And Lizzie, an attractive youngish woman with two small children, currently in the middle of a conspicuous affair with a local publican, to her husband's stinging humiliation. The surprising thing was that Maz had no problem having these women as friends, despite her self-proclaimed moral strictures concerning sleeping around.

Marion 'Maz' Mccluskey was just shy of forty. Big, buxom, gypsy-like, a plethora of jewellery and make-up. Mesmeric dark eyes. Julie Driscoll grown out, older and with longer hair. A big, extrovert personality concealing a destructive coldness, evasiveness and self-destructive perverseness. Given to manipulation of male friends and admirers - easy enough as men were drawn to her like flies to overripe fruit. A woman of extremes who destroyed all she touched. Living in her own world where she is principal actor and shining light. Reading nothing bar celebrity chat mags and TV guides - no fiction - disdaining all novels - they weren't about her and therefore of zero interest. Her stock-in-trade was sincerity. That isn't to say she was sincere. But the appearance and apparent affirmation of sincerity were of first importance, provided these didn't conflict in any way with her desires. She believed fully in her own integrity - was taken in by the idea just as surely as others were. Rumours spread by Maz included a slave imprisoned in a hidden Roma caravan park, and a killer clown on the loose. Whether any of this was any closer to the truth than the warm, sincere - always of primary importance, that appearance of sincerity - put-upon, oppressed and misused persona she presented, Ross could never be completely sure. In her company he felt only a strong, warm attraction - a sexual attraction, though he never had and never would cheat on Fiona. But the feeling was there, strong and steady.

Pixie was sitting on a cushion watching The Lion King on a huge flat screen TV that dominated the room, oblivious to the chat, laughter and cigarette smoke swirling around her. Eight years old, tiny for her age, chubby and with features entirely lacking the startling harmoniousness of her mother, having more in common with the large-chinned coarseness of her father. Only the eyes, dark, remote, impenetrable, gave the unmistakeable clue to her lineage. Ross struggled to understand the dynamic of the relationship between Maz and Brian. Nominally still partners, she displayed towards him in company a coolness bordering on complete detachment, barely so much as glancing his way if they had to engage in conversation - in contrast to her intimate chats with Ross, when she would stand close, cigarette in one hand, drink in the other, her eyes fixed on his, holding him in the spell of her physicality, her bawdy humour and her scurrilous and highly amusing insults directed at almost every member of her family and most of her circle of friends - Brian the favourite subject and target - his ugliness, stupidity, disloyalty amounting to outright treachery, selfishness, emotional coldness, self-absorption, long absences (he was a long-distance lorry driver) - while she was marooned at home with four children (though that included Jimmy and the twins, all now technically adults). Sometimes reaching out to touch Ross's arm or hand - or thigh if they were seated next to each other - to emphasise a point, her voice with that characteristic rising inflection at the end of a sentence.

'Come on through tae the kitchen - a'm gettin a wee snack fur Pixie.' Maz, still in her pyjamas and without make-up, her hair untidy, detached herself from her mates, and Ross followed. 'A cannae get rid o' them,' she said in a stage whisper, indicating with her head her friends Lizzie and Doreen.

58

'A thought they were your pals?'

She pulled a face. 'Nah. A cannae stop them fae comin around.' She opened a tin of spaghetti, put it in a bowl, into the microwave, then dropped a couple of slices of bread in the toaster, lit a cigarette, inhaled deeply and blew the smoke to one side. 'So, what's up?' A careless tone. 'Ye said ye wanted tae have a quick word.'

Ross took a deep breath.

'It's about Jimmy.'

'Ugh!' She pulled a face as if she'd swallowed vinegar. 'Dinnae talk to me about that little twat. A havnae had ma breakfast.' She laughed, her eyes glittering, wary, defensive, almost taunting. 'A'll no be able to keep anythin doon if ye sae much as mention the name of that laddie.' And she laughed again that dangerous, mirthless laugh. 'If a told ye aw the things he's done tae me over the years, ye widnae believe it.'

She took the bowl from the microwave, put some spread on the toast, filled a glass with Coke, all with the cigarette clamped in her mouth, narrowing her eyes as the smoke drifted back towards her face, her head tilted back a little to avoid the worst of it, then carried everything through to Pixie. Ross, peering through into the living room, saw Maz put Pixie's breakfast (or whatever it was) down beside her with a There y'are, darlin, as the cackle of voices swelled to include Maz. Pixie didn't turn her head from the screen, but reached out for the glass of Coke.

Maz came back into the kitchen, shut the door to the living room, and went to the fridge.

'Stella?'

'Aye, cheers.'

She handed a can to Ross, and opened one for herself. The lager was immediately relaxing, creating a deceptive bond of shared intimacy through the first seductive taste. Such a sexy, earthy, luscious woman, even in shapeless pyjamas and with her hair a mess. Ross struggled to expel from his mind visions of her naked.

'How's Fiona?'

'Oh, she's good. Busy as usual.'

'An' Grant? He's sae tall now, your laddie - a saw him in the street the other day, an' a couldnae believe it.'

'Aye, he's mebbe taller than me now. He's fine - busy wae his school work. A dinnae know where he gets that dedication from - not fae me, anyway.'

'From his mother, then, mebbe.'

'Aye, Fiona's got the work ethic, awrite. She's yir typical modern career wummin. An' a wish her aw the best wi' it.'

'She couldnae ha' done it wi'out you Ross, tae look after the wean when he was younger.'

'He wisnae really that small when she went back tae work - eight a think, or nine - aye, that's aboot right.'

'Still, ye were there tae see him tae school, and look after him after school, an' during the holidays. Not many men wid be willin tae dae that. For sure not that fat twat a'm stuck wi'. Pixie hardly sees the fat cunt -

not that she's missin much. He disnae do anythin wi' her when he is around. An' a'm no' missin much either.'

Ross had met Brian a number of times over the three years or so he'd known Jimmy. A dull, heavyset man, a self-proclaimed man's man, whose topics of conversation tended to revolve around ingenious short-cuts on his delivery routes that nobody else knew about and that saved huge amounts of time and diesel, and obscure trade outlets where he could pick up high-quality tools at bargain prices. Ross had always found him fairly pleasant and not unfriendly, though he sometimes wondered what went through Brian's mind when he came back to the flat after a two or three day stint of driving and found Ross, or one of her other male friends, drinking with Maz. Or when he phoned Maz on one of his deliveries, as he did frequently to make contact and tell her where he was and what he was doing, and Maz, rolling her eyes at Ross and miming extreme boredom and disinterest, ostentatiously informed Brian that Ross was there with her, before closing the conversation as quickly as she could, after showing zero interest, sometimes even feigning a poor connection and abruptly turning her phone off. 'All the fat twat does is talk about what he's deein, what road he's on, whether he's ahead or behind schedule, what the road conditions are like. The boring cunt. As if a could gie a shit.'

Ross wondered how Brian felt about this cold unresponsiveness, or whether he even noticed - he never gave any sign that he did. Yet it was his long hours of work that sustained the whole Mccluskey clan, of which only Pixie was actually his child, though for some reason she didn't bear his surname. The twins, Kylie and Chelsea, and Jimmy - children to a different, long-departed father - as well as Pixie and Maz, relied to a large extent on his financial input to provide them with a warm, comfortable home, food on the table, drink in the fridge, and all bills paid. Maz's scorn and contempt, while amusing Ross, still struck him as calculated ingratitude, whatever failings Brian might have.

'How did ye and Brian meet?' said Ross. 'A was lookin at all those nice photos of ye both in the living room the other day.'

'Ha!' She laughed, tipped back her head and blew out a plume of smoke. 'Ye talkin aboot those we had taken last Christmas? What a feckin joke that was. We'd arranged to take Pixie tae see a film in town, an' after tae meet Santa Claus. Next thing I know, that daft bugger has booked us intae a photographer's studio, tae be there an hour or so before the film starts. So a had tae get aw dressed up, spend a fuckin fortune gettin ma hair done an' all the kind of crap a couldnae be bothered tae do, an' then make myself dae aw these ridiculous happy family poses, wi' ma teeth clenched an' ma smile stretched sae wide a thought ma feckin face wis gan tae freeze like that.'

Ross laughed.

'What a bloody charade, the stupid fat bastard. Whit the hell did he think he wis deein playin at happy families. Ye must hae thought we were some kind of ideal feckin family.' She laughed uproariously. 'Meet The Mccluskey's. The Fockin Mccluskey's!' They laughed. 'You want another one, darlin?'

'Aye, that'd be great, cheers Maz.' Then, more quietly, 'What about your friends through there, though?'

'Ah, fuck them.'

Ross laughed. 'Aye, fair enough. Cheers. You never married Brian though, did you?'

'Nah.' She looked shocked, as if repulsed at the thought. 'A'm still married tae that other cunt.'

'You're still married to Rob? A never knew that.'

'Aye, we're still married, technically. A cannae get rid of the bastard. Hangs on like a feckin barnacle.'

'He's not still hoping to get together wae you again, is he?'

'Psssh! Nah. He's got nae chance. A just havnae got aroond tae all the shit ye have tae do to get a divorce. He wis a complete bastard. Knocked us aroon from pillar tae post.'

'Ye still have him over every Christmas though, don't you?'

'Aye, well, he's still the father, if ye can call him that, of Jimmy and the twins. He's a nasty piece of work. Horrible man.' She shuddered convincingly. 'Always violent to me. He's aw smiles when he comes round - mister feckin charming - and the twins an' Jimmy treat him like he's feckin royalty, even though they know full well what he wis like an' what he's done tae me. A had tae try an' protect them from him when he came back full of drink an' bouncin me off the walls. A took it aw tae protect them.'

'How did ye get together wae him?'

'A never wanted tae get together wae him in the first place. A for sure never wanted tae marry the cunt. A never even liked him. A met him in some night club in town when a wis only fifteen - a'd got in somehow. An' because a'd too much tae drink we must have had sex somewhere - a dinnae even know where - an' that wis it - ma whole life, ma future, set out, decided fur me then an' there. The rest of ma feckin life fucked. One mistake, an' that wis it.'

She was trying to smile, to take it casually, but looked suddenly stricken.

'So a had Jimmy at sixteen, an' we got married. He didnae want it any more than I did. He'd go on aboot it as if a'd trapped him intae it, even though a didnae remember anything aboot it - thank God. We applied fur a council hoose an' in a few months we got a flat in Easterhoose - feckin' shithole that it is. Ah, ye're from the Drum, sae ye know whit a mean.'

'A never minded it - a suppose a never knew any different.'

'Well, try lookin after a baby when ye're stuck in some dump wi' nae shops, nae life, wi' damp an' mould an' noise comin through the ceiling an' walls day an' night, an' gangs of wild laddies roamin the streets so ye dare not go out.'

Ross thought of his own feral youth in Drumchapel.

'An ye cannae even take the wean out fur some fresh air. Christ, my life has been hell. Unbearable.' And she started suddenly to sob, collapsing onto a chair, crying and sobbing. Ross took the chair alongside and put his arm around her, and she leaned into him, putting her head on his shoulder.

After a while, through her tears, 'An' people shovin stuff through the door tryin tae set fire tae the flat. An' that bastard comin back an knockin us aboot. An' then, when Jimmy was four, an' a could hope at last for a bit of peace when he starts school, a discover a'm four months pregnant wi' twins. Jesus fuckin Christ. An' then it aw starts again times two. Times three, as Jimmy wis always a difficult child, kickin and screamin whatever ye wanted him tae do, never happy, an' aw that never stopped when a' was suddenly stuck wi' two new-born weans tae look after.'

Kylie and Chelsea, now nineteen, were identical twins who'd shared a bedroom their entire lives, and still spent most of their time there together. In the rare times he encountered them Ross couldn't tell them apart. So alike were they, and so little did they communicate with outsiders, even including other members of their family, that they could easily have pretended to be each other without anyone knowing or noticing. Maybe they did - the non-communication with anyone but themselves made picking up on individual nuances of character near impossible. They were like two halves of the same unit, communicating often by facial expression alone - or when they did speak, speaking sometimes simultaneously, or completing each other's sentences, or sometimes using a shorthand of verbal expression amounting almost to a separate language that nobody else could understand, and in any case speaking almost exclusively to each other with barely any communication bar a nod or gesture to their mother or siblings. There was some evidence over the years that one felt pain experienced by the other, but whether this apparent synchronicity extended to actual telepathy, no-one but themselves knew.

Tall, striking young women, with long pale faces framed by long straight hair. Both were on the dole, practically unemployable due to their inability or extreme discomfort in interacting with others. They spent their days as they'd always done, immured within their room, eating together, watching films and TV together, grooming each other, taking it in turns to brush each other's long straight hair with long slow strokes. Sitting together in front of the dressing table mirror, slowly, carefully applying elaborate make-up, surveying the results in the other's reflection, before helping each other to dress in fashionable, striking clothes they'd ordered online. Glammed up to the nth. degree, yet going out nowhere, displaying themselves to no-one but themselves.

'A've been so lonely and miserable ma whole life, Ross.' A heartrending emotional appeal from the desolate, tear-stained face. 'They aw hate me, an' a've cried blood fur them. An' aw a get in return is hatred and contempt. Ye know the twins never communicate - it's like livin wi' a pair of ghosts. Pixie - a love her tae death an' a'd cry tears of blood fur her, but God's truth is she's just like her father. Selfish an' whingy an' self-obsessed. An' then there's Jimmy, who hates ma guts. A've got nobody who cares about me, who wants tae be wi' me. It's so lonely battling on your own wi' people who dinnae like you. That's why a like tae have ma friends aroon me sometimes, somebody tae talk to - somebody tae have a laugh wi'. An' aw a ever wanted wis the chance fur a career, like your wifey. But a never had the chance.'

Tears streaming down her face. He hugged her more tightly, caressing her face, head, hair, while at the same time trying to avoid getting the tears on his hand, the touch of which for some reason he found repellent. Feeling himself nevertheless becoming aroused, which struck him as inappropriate from every point of view. Although never the smartest or quickest at picking up on things, Ross realised that, notwithstanding the possible truth of anything she'd been saying (he knew there were always at least two sides to everything), and that he felt genuinely sorry for her, Maz had nevertheless taken the initiative and outflanked him on the matter of Jimmy, setting herself up once more as hapless victim, thus effectively disarming any argument he might raise on Jimmy's behalf.

Still, he felt he had to press on, for Fiona's sake if nothing else. So when she'd calmed down sufficiently, he told Maz that Jimmy had arrived at their flat last night under the impression he'd been permanently thrown out and barred from his home. And he, Ross, was sure this couldn't be the case. Surely it wasn't too late to patch things up between herself and Jimmy. He was sure she knew, without him telling her, that there was the risk of a permanent breach if both of them didn't make up, concede some ground and patch things up, and so on with more arguments along these lines. He could sense the change in atmosphere as he outlined this well-intentioned though not entirely selfless case, and could feel the chill wind of hostility begin to whistle around him.

She pulled away from him, grabbed a couple of tissues and dried her eyes, which were now hard and cold, then stood up facing him like a boxer before the bell. Ross also stood up, wondering how far over the line he'd stepped.

'Whit's he been telling you?'

Her tone now harsh, uncompromising. He felt she was holding in her anger only by a supreme effort of will, and her face, aside from the stabbing eyes, was twisted with an ironic half-smile of ferocious intensity.

'Well, he was telling me you'd all been out for the evening at a nightclub in town, and you'd been getting friendly wae some young lad, but then ye'd fallen out wi' him, and then tried to get Jimmy tae intervene and gie this lad a bit of a smack. And when he widnae dae it ye became mad at him. Isn't that how this all came about? You know, Jimmy hasn't really done anything wrong, Maz. Come on, you dinnae want tae run the risk of fallin out wi' him permanently, do you?'

Even Ross could hardly fail to be aware, as he tried to come across as reasonable, friendly, yet persuasive, of the caustic forces bubbling just below the surface a few feet away. At that moment Pixie came through demanding something else to eat. She looked at Ross and greeted him with, Hi Ross. With the door open came cries of, Ross, darlin, whit ye deein? Come on through. A want tae talk to ye. Whit ye two up tae through there? Cackles of laughter.

'Ye've just had breakfast, Pixie - ye cannae still be hungry.'

'A am, maw - can a have a packet of crisps?'

Maz went to the cupboard.

'Aye, here ye are, now go through an' settle doon an' watch the rest of your film.'

'It's finished.'

'Fur God's sake, watch something else, then.'

And she shooed and hustled Pixie back into the living room, closed the door behind her, and went on the attack.

'Ye don't know the half ae it wi' him. Ye think he's so feckin wonderful, such a great mate, tellin ye how awfu' his mother is. The lyin wee bastard. Everything he says is just a bunch o' feckin lies. A wis not pickin up some lad, like that lying little shit says, this laddie wis hangin aroon me, tryin tae chat us up. What wid a be deein wi' a teenage lad? Sae when a asked Jimmy just tae hae a quick word wi' him tae warn off this laddie, he starts givin me a mouthful of abuse in front of everyone, callin me aw the names under the sun. A'm not even gan tae repeat some of the things he said, it was that horrible and vicious. You think he's sae feckin wonderful,' her voice filled with bileful scorn, 'a'm tellin ye he's vicious an' horrible, wi' a vicious temper an' a vicious tongue, an' he always was from being wee. Even when he wis small he wis hittin and kickin us an' refusing tae dae anything a tell him. Of course a know he got it aw from his father - he's seen us knocked aboot by that bastard, sae he thought that wis normal tae behave like that. He's always had this evil temper. An' lazy - ye cannae get the little shit out of bed fur love nae money. Ye could bang a drum outside his door an' still the lazy wee bastard widnae come oot. Expects everything tae be done fur him - meals, washing up, cleaning, washing his horrible, stinking clothes - the little shit never lifts a finger. Has he told ye the suicide fairy story? Aye, a thought he wid dae, the lyin wee shit. He came back fae school once, the twins hadnae been tae school an' had been in their room aw day wi'out a word tae me, an' at that moment ma life wis just so feckin awfu' an' terrible a was sittin there wi' a drink an' wis' cryin an' that. Aye, a admit it. An' so that horrible, vindictive little twat invents all this bollocks aboot me tryin tae dee maself in, an' him saving us. As if he'd dae anythin tae save me - he'd just laugh in ma face if he thought a wis dying.'

In her current state of anger and extreme agitation, Ross didn't have any idea of the truth of anything she was saying - in fact almost anything to do with this woman and her family seemed possible.

'If ye have any doubts about what that laddie's capable of, a'm tellin ye that's just what he did tae us - laughed in ma face while this wifey a'd never seen before in ma life gie us a right beating in the street. Aye, ye can well look surprised and shocked. A wis feckin surprised an' shocked, a can tell ye. Came up tae us in the street when a wis out fur a drink wi' some friends, mindin ma own business, an' starts hittin us an' knockin us doon sae a'm lyin in the street, aw bruised an' covered in blood. An' then across the street a suddenly see Jimmy, lookin on wi' a sly smile on his face.'

'Jimmy? You really think Jimmy arranged it?'

'Whit dae ye think? Of course he did, the evil little swine. Sae that's yir wonderful mate fur ye. As far as a'm concerned, he's gone, oot of my life, and good riddance. Aye, and ye can tell him so fae me he's no' coming back. Ever.'

It was just past midday when Ross turned into the close, feeling shell-shocked, and began the slow trudge up the spiral staircase, wondering if his relationship with Maz was as conclusively stone dead as apparently was Jimmy's. The image of her face, contorted with hostility, was still as vivid in his mind as the accusations she'd strewn around.

Fiona was waiting for Ross as soon as he stepped in the flat.

'Where have you been?'

'A've just been oot.'

'I know you've been out. What I'm asking is, where you've been.'

She motioned him through to their bedroom, and closed the door.

'I've been on my own in this place for over an hour, Ross, with your friend Jimmy.'

Ross didn't point out the anomaly in this statement - he'd had enough for the time being of inviting hostile responses from wide-eyed women.

'So, what's the problem?'

'You've been out all morning, Grant went out about eleven - '

'Where did he go?'

She rolled her eyes in irritation.

'He went into town to meet some friends and go to the cinema. That's not the point, Ross - the point is, with you having gone out, and then Grant, that left me alone in the flat with Jimmy.'

'Where is he? A havnae seen him.'

'I don't know - still in his room, presumably. I don't fecking care.'

'So what's the problem, Fiona? A dinnae understand what ye're on aboot.'

'A'll tell ye what the problem is. I don't want tae be alone with him - alone in the flat with him. Can you not understand? Can ye not get that through your head?'

'Ah, you're making too much out of nothing. Jimmy's totally harmless.' Thinking, meanwhile, even as he said it, of the accusations he'd just heard.

'So it doesn't matter to you what my feelings are about him - that him being in this flat makes me uncomfortable - never mind being here alone with him. I've lost the use of the study so I have to work at the table in the kitchen - or in the living room - an' all the while I cannae concentrate on what I'm supposed to be doing for never knowing whether he'll be coming into the room at any moment. I don't feel comfortable in my own home anymore.'

Ross sat down on the bed, closed his eyes briefly and rubbed his forehead.

'Look, a don't know what to say, Fiona. A'm really sorry ye feel this way about Jimmy, truly. A think ye're wrong - a know ye dinnae like the guy, but in my experience, as a say, he's completely harmless - a widnae have let him into the flat in the first place if a'd thought anything different. Anyway, it'll no' be for long, I promise.'

'How long, Ross?'

'I don't know. Christ, I'll speak to him. I'll see if there's anywhere else he can go.'

'Can he not go back to his mother's? Maybe all that business has blown over now.'

Ross looked at her.

'A dinnae think so.' He paused. 'That's where a've just been, tae see if a could smooth things over.'

'Ye've been to speak to his mother?'

'Aye.'

'I was wondering why you were up and about so early this morning.' Fiona's face had become an expressionless mask. 'So what did she have to say for herself?'

'Oh, this and that. But the top and bottom of it is that she won't have Jimmy back there.'

'That's great. So we're stuck with this situation now, are we? What a ridiculous mess this is. The people you get yourself in with, Ross.'

Ross glared at her. 'Hey, dinnae be sae feckin stuck up. A dinnae criticise your friends.'

'A dinnae have friends who are fecking lunatics and deadbeats like you do.'

Something twitched in Ross's cheek. No, he thought, ye don't, do ye - but maybe that's because all your friends are smooth wee bastards, wi' faces ye cannae trust.

A couple of days later, Ross and Jimmy were out for an afternoon pool and drinking session at some local bar, when out of the blue Jimmy told him he'd been talking to a couple of mates, and one of them had said he could put him up for a month or two, no problem. Ross, caught off-balance by this sudden and unexpected solution to the Jimmy problem, regrouped sufficiently quickly to come out with the obligatory expressions of regret at Jimmy leaving so soon, and that he really didn't have to leave, he could stay as long as he wanted.

In truth it was a big relief, though he felt bad in terms of his friendship with Jimmy for the emotion, and straight away began anticipating the moment of giving Fiona the good news. Things had been fraught between them of late, but this would set everything to rights. And he had a surprise in store for her. He'd secretly booked a week in a cottage up in the Highlands for the last week of the school holidays, hoping all the while that Grant would come. A chance for the three of them to spend time together away from everyone else, away from all the hurly-burly and stresses of city life and all the craziness. The cottage was set away on its own at the end of a track off the main road, with nothing around it but hills and woodland and a nestling stream. Somewhere to unwind, take in the peace and tranquility, go for walks in the hills, get a good blaze going in the evenings. Maybe even play some board games. It would be like old times. And he and Fiona would share a bottle of wine last thing when Grant had gone to bed, and they'd cuddle up in front of the fire. Followed by the strange excitement of an unfamiliar bed. This vision was highly-developed in his mind, and he'd sometimes dwell on the details in anticipation.

The Road

6

Mid-August, the last week of the school holidays, and Ross, Fiona and Grant were settled into their holiday cottage in the Highlands, away off the main road a quarter of a mile or so up a track that climbed slightly, so that from the garden or either of the bedrooms you could see the sea - sombre grey, white/silver sheen, blue/green, indeterminate dark, graphite, black - just the far side of the main road.

The surprise holiday that Ross had sprung on Fiona hadn't received the warmest reception at first - that he hadn't consulted her, that he'd assumed she'd automatically be able to take leave for that particular week. The recriminations had rumbled on for a while, but in the end she'd been able to take the week off, and Grant had finally agreed to go, so there they were, a couple of days into a week's holiday. A reconnecting, a remaking of their relationship, that was the general idea (that was Ross's idea, at any rate). And for the first few days all seemed promising. They went for walks together, exploring the stream in the woods behind the cottage where the hills rose and became a palpable presence as dusk fell, and along the seashore, deserted and unworldly, where the renovating wind off the sea seemed to disperse the tensions and grievances which had begun to gather around their marriage. At such moments all the accumulated clutter appeared to fall away, and she became almost the Fiona of old, lively and affectionate, much as he'd first known her, pleased apparently once more to be with him. Even Grant was happy to go along with things for the most part, even if he was doing something with his phone most of the time.

The cottage was pleasant, if basic and old-fashioned, with a sizable plot of land surrounding it - not a garden as such, just an area of grass sufficient to have a game of frisbee or kick a football around. But the cottage did at least have the internet, a requirement which both Fiona and Grant had made clear was non-negotiable. Ross had been obliged to check and reassure them, before inquiring whether such things were really necessary when they were going to be surrounded by all that natural beauty, such pristine sands and empty moors and pure blue lochs, and they'd looked at him as if he'd somehow stumbled into their time from the Dark Ages. Yet for the first few days they'd all enjoyed the change from Glasgow, as great a change as you could imagine with such wide vistas, stark beauty of landscape and sweetness of air.

Then inevitably the novelty began to pall slightly as the views became familiar and the local walks routine. And Ross himself appeared increasingly preoccupied, reluctant to venture far, uncommunicative. Almost imperceptibly they began to withdraw into themselves, and each had their private reasons for welcoming time to spend in their own personal mental space.

Grant had recently found himself in the grip of the first and, so far as he was concerned, one and only love affair of his life, intense and uncompromising, with a tall girl in the year ahead of him whose personality was so pure and had such depth that he hardly thought at all about her physicality. At least he tried not to, and in fact there had been practically no physical contact between them as yet. By now they'd been to each other's houses a time or two, and been introduced to each other's parents, but they preferred when out of school to escape everyone else and go for walks together, often into Queen's Park, or sometimes taking the train into the city centre where they might visit the Necropolis and the cathedral, or Glasgow Green, or further west wander along the river in Kelvingrove. Old-fashioned, decorous dates, both of them afraid to make the first move. And the longer it went on like this the more difficult it became in every sense, and the exquisite tension of non-contact became normalised, and in fact became a heady drug of sexual longing sustained through mutual self-denial.

In his bedroom in the cottage, with his parents out for a walk after he'd made some excuse not to go with them, he'd sit on the bed with the laptop on his knees, or lie full length on his front with the screen in front of him and via Skype gaze into Sabiha's face, and imagine everything possible. A world of endless promise and of unexpressed emotions could be read into that perfectly oval, olive-skinned, dark-eyed face that stared back at him with absolute self-possession, thick, straight curtains of black hair sometimes flicked back from the face with a swift, almost haughty gesture that half intimidated and half made him sick with desire. He would describe the tedium of his family's holiday activities, then each would talk of their parents in patronising tones, indulging in gleeful character assassination that exposed weaknesses mercilessly, portraying at length absurd limitations and embarrassing idiosyncrasies, each competing with the other to present the most stupid and/or unbelievable behaviour that might shock or amuse. It was a game that gave endless pleasure.

And all the while Grant was aware of the pure white shirt she was wearing, with the occasional glimpse, as she sometimes leaned back, of the slight suggestion of her breasts, and when she got up to answer a knock on her bedroom door, saw vividly, try as he might to deliberately avert his gaze, the form-fitting contours of her jeans. And tried with conscious effort not to think of the wonders that lay beneath each garment, pure and perfect as those wonders might be.

Fiona meanwhile was in daily contact with Mark, her boss, work colleague and close friend, either texting or emailing, especially late in the evenings when Grant had gone to his bedroom, and Ross, who had taken to finishing the day off with a bottle of wine, dozed in an armchair. The exchange of messages was becoming more frequent, and the tone and content increasingly intimate and personal, each confiding to the other in progressively more explicit terms the shortcomings of their respective spouses. Older than Fiona, in his early forties, balding, with a much younger wife and two small children. The love had evaporated from his marriage with the arrival of the children. He felt, rightly or wrongly, nobody's fault, of course, that she'd failed to keep pace with him intellectually as his career had gathered momentum. In fact in spending her time almost exclusively in looking after the children, as babies, toddlers, and now small children, she seemed to have regressed, so that they had drawn apart as all her attention became focused on the needs of the little ones. She appeared completely uninterested in the demands, struggles and small triumphs of his work. There was no longer any connection of any kind or on any level. Fiona could only empathise and relate to this, feeling his loneliness, aware of a certain glow within that she was able to provide a sounding board, an intellectual and emotional connection that Janet was unable to do.

It was all so hard, so very hard. They had so much common ground in this respect. But what could you do apart from make the best of it and carry on as best as possible. There was just no connection any more. God knows he/she had tried, repeatedly and at length, but there was simply no response, none whatsoever. The silences, the intangible divide, the disappointed hopes. Oh it was so hard, such that neither of them knew what to do any more. What *could* you do in this situation? And with each conversation they edged closer to a possible solution as yet hardly dreamed, much less spoken of, awaiting only a catalyst to reach the tipping point from which there would be no return.

Of all this Ross knew nothing. After only a few days of increasingly clouded relaxation, his mind was in a state of disarray, such that he could think of little else but the section of road to the north soon to be altered beyond recognition. Not knowing what he would find when at last he nerved himself to go and see. A road he remembered well for its sensuous beauty and perfect harmonisation with the landscape. The signs warning of 'improvement' had been prominently displayed even before they'd reached the turn-off to the cottage, advertising the new sections and alignments through which, reflected Ross bitterly, would occur the usual senseless extinction of character and individuality, loss of identity, and permanent scarring of the landscape.

What was the point of going except to torment himself. Why not just not go? Hadn't he detached himself from all that nonsense at last. He couldn't change anything or make any difference, he knew that now, so just close your eyes to it. Don't go and invite the inevitable pain, that would just be fucking stupid. Pretend it isn't happening, live in a bubble like everyone else. Deny everything. Just enjoy yourself, have a nice time. Have a nice life. It's not indifference, just self-preservation. What's the point of inflicting pain on yourself. Stupid, stupid wee man. And so, drawn by the inevitable pull of such desires as cannot be resisted, he determined to face the horror and visit the scene of desecration.

The road north wound its way past tall pines to one side, and thick gorse overflowing grassy banks to the other, the surface worn and shiny, curving and dipping, a view of the sea suddenly directly ahead, light grey dissolving in the distance into mist. Now climbing and turning inland, past a line of broken wooden fence paling bordering gorse and rough pasture, now twisting back through a corridor of overhanging trees before emerging past a white-painted cottage nestling alongside the road with pretty garden, cultivated plot, and, partly hidden by growth, a blue Reliant Rialto without wheels forming part of a hedge. The road was worn and patched, and now ahead on a section fairly straight and lined by stone walls set back beyond wide grass verges rose the great bulk of a hillside filling the horizon with its mass, dull russet in colour, pocked by rock outcroppings and marked by the faint lines of tracks. Now past extensive pasture land, willow green with flecks of yellow, dipping to the sea, contrasting with the darker shades of gorse and full-leafed trees, now climbing and curving around a headland, the ground falling away steeply to a hidden cove. Under the wide sky, past lonely cottages, the road wended its way, an intrinsic part of the landscape, embedded in total harmony with the topography of the hills, valleys and pasture lands through which it passed. It was a living, organic entity. It was a beautiful thing.

Such were Ross's thoughts as they made their way along this road, Fiona at the wheel of the rental car, Ross peering around, looking this way and that at ominous signs of the new alignments - effectively a new road - that would overlay and largely obliterate the existing road. Excavations and earth moving had begun. The course of new sections were already marked out with wooden posts and red and white streamers. Alongside the road they passed a large area of open land that had become a depot for the construction team, with portakabins and various pieces of heavy equipment.

After a dozen or so miles they turned off, parked and made their way into the hills. They had a picnic in a sunlit glade they happened upon. There was little conversation. Ross was silent and preoccupied. His anguish and anger at what was happening had been building since he saw the first signs, and now there was a savage, reckless edge to that anger. On the way back, he got Fiona to pull in repeatedly, on the grassy verge or any handy lay-by, and he would jump from the car and wander along the road, dodging the occasional traffic, taking photos, awake to all the details of line, camber, surface, hedge, wall, fencing, roadside vegetation, wild flowers in exquisite careless effusions here and there, feeling a love for the totality of the experience of this entity of earth, stones and tarmacadam as visceral and powerful as if it was some exquisite piece of music - symphony, concerto, tone poem - and he was faced with the threat of the very last copy of the sheet music being ripped up and burnt. Wondering at the senselessness of it all, feeling his hatred growing.

Fiona made some tea when they got back, then settled down on her laptop, while Grant disappeared to his room. Ross prowled uneasily around the living room until Fiona gave him a look, and a sharp, Why don't you sit down? At which he went out into the garden, and walked round and round the house as the light faded and a delicious, fragrant coolness descended. He stopped, his mind jangling, and looked across to where the sea still shimmered beyond the road, and came to a sudden decision.

Fiona was still sitting in the gloom as Ross came in, her face glowing from the screen. She looked up.

'A'm gan oot,' he said.

'Where are you going? I thought you were out just now.'

'Aye, a was. A'm gan fur a walk.' At which he abruptly left the room. She heard the door close behind him.

It was late and now completely dark outside. Fiona, wondering vaguely where Ross had got to, was in the kitchen tidying up, replaying in her mind that evening's email exchanges with Mark. Feeling an illicit thrill at the clandestine game they were playing, the frisson of virtual flirting injecting a long-missed heady excitement into her life. Each now waiting only for the other to make that critical first step that would make it much more than a game. Rinsing the dishes, daydreaming guiltily of seemingly untenable possibilities, instead of her own reflection caught dully in the window above the sink, beams of light swept the trees, their multiform shapes suddenly revealed in a shifting tangle of tracery, and she heard the sound of a car and then the crunch of gravel, and for some reason felt a stab of fear. She turned, facing the door, standing still and silent, her hands dripping, heart beating fast. She jumped as the knock came, loud and urgent. Taking some breaths, she made a conscious effort to remain calm, even as the thought flashed into her mind that Ross knew or suspected or had somehow sensed or found out what was going on (but nothing was, really) and had done something stupid. Controlling her swirling thoughts as best she could, she dried her hands, then answered the door with at least the appearance of tranquility. As if to confirm her apprehension, and giving her another jolt of fear, two police officers stood looking back at her with cool, neutral expressions.

'Mrs McKenzie?'

'Yes,' she managed to reply.

'Sorry to trouble you this late. May we come in for a moment?'

'What's happened? Is it my husband? Is he okay?'

'Don't worry yourself,' said marginally the larger of the officers, gazing at her keenly and holding up an enormous hand, as if about to direct traffic. 'Nobody's been hurt. We just need to come in and speak to you for a few minutes.'

She stepped aside and motioned them into the living room, almost faint with shock and relief. They sat down, and Fiona took a few deep breaths.

'What's happened? What's...'

At this moment Grant, who also had heard the crunching of the car on the gravel, came through from his bedroom and took in the officers, and his father's absence, and experienced the same sudden shock of undefined fear as his mother.

'Where's Dad?' His voice high, uncertain.

'Everything's alright, lad. We just need to speak to your mother on her own for a few minutes.'

'I want to know what's happened.'

Before she could check herself Fiona glared and told him impatiently to go back to his room and she'd come and see him in a few minutes. He wavered for a moment, taking in the two large, heavily-built police officers with their surprisingly similar pasty slab-like faces and dead expressions, seemingly occupying a disproportionate part of the room, then turned and went back to his bedroom, sat on his bed and engaged in various lines of anxious imagining.

'What's your husband's name, Mrs McKenzie?'

'Ross. Ross McKenzie. What's happened to him?'

The officer who'd taken the lead, and who was now surveying her with bright, steady blue eyes, leaned forward slightly as he spoke.

'We're trying to confirm the identity of a man arrested this evening. He's refused to cooperate so far or respond to any questions put to him. He wouldn't tell us who he was or where he's from. We searched his pockets but found no ID on him. All we found apart from odds and ends and loose change were a bunch of keys and a leaflet for this cottage.'

Fiona looked down at the coffee table. For some reason Ross had left his mobile behind when he went out for his walk.

'So we asked Annie at the farm and she pointed us in your direction.'

'What's he done - if it is my husband?'

'I'm afraid I'm not permitted to go into details,' he replied, though having established this fact he then proceeded to do so. 'Suffice to say, the man we arrested was caught smashing up portakabins and contractors plant at the depot just north of here on the main road where they've started the road improvements.'

From that moment she knew beyond a doubt it was Ross. Yet another of his crazy, pointless obsessions.

'The security person on site called the police, and locked himself in his cabin for his own safety. When we got there it took a while to subdue the man causing the damage.' Fiona shook her head but said nothing. 'So, just to say, he's been arrested, and charged with a number of offences. He's been taken to the police station in Dornoch, and he'll be kept there in a cell overnight.'

'Dornoch? Why Dornoch?'

'It was the nearest station. He'll be held there overnight in a custody cell. The usual procedure would be that a report of the incident will be faxed over to the

Procurator Fiscal's office in Inverness, and then, depending on their decision, in the morning he'll likely be taken to court in Tain and charged. I can't speculate on what might happen to him beyond that. That's all in the hands of higher authorities.' He puffed out his chest at this, as if to convey that they, whoever they might be, might technically be a higher authority, but were he to be given that authority - not that he was claiming any entitlement, you understand - but still, nevertheless, if given that authority, he'd be more than capable of dealing with the matter in his own way and to his own entire satisfaction. He reached into a pocket and drew out a set of keys on a ring. 'Do you recognise these keys, Mrs McKenzie?'

One quick look was enough.

'Aye, they're my husband's.'

The officer nodded sagely, as though he'd at last solved the final part of an abstruse puzzle, then dropped the keys back into his pocket.

'Your husband hasn't wanted to speak to anyone, as yet. That's why we had to come out and call on you, to establish his identity.'

'Is he allowed to phone me from the police station?'

'No, I'm sorry, that's a common misconception. But if you want to phone Dornoch police station tomorrow morning they'll be able to inform you what time your husband will be brought before the court.'

'Okay, thank you.'

He rose, followed by his colleague.

'Well, thanks Mrs McKenzie. And goodnight to you.'

She showed them out, then sat down heavily on the sofa, closed her eyes and took some deep breaths to try to calm herself and steady her emotions. Why would he do such a thing? But then why had he done any of the things he'd done over the years that had achieved nothing but provoke conflict with the authorities in various forms? Putting his family at risk. Never once caring about the possible consequences. Never valuing her achievements. A certain bitterness tainting her thoughts. Thinking of her work brought Mark immediately to mind, and she realised how much she wanted to hear his voice, quiet, gentle, thoughtful, consoling. Considered and responsive, appreciative and supportive of her and of her talents.

She glanced at the time, and was about to text him, when Grant came through from his bedroom. To Fiona he looked like a small child, anxious and bewildered, gone for the moment the swagger and assurance of youth.

'I heard them go,' he said, sitting down. 'What's happened to Dad?'

She told him the little she knew, feeling it was something you should never have to tell a child. He didn't react to what she said, but listened intently.

'So what happens next?'

'I don't know yet, Grant. He'll have to go to court tomorrow, so we'll know more after that. But anyway, I think it's fair to say the holiday's over. We'll just pack the stuff up in the morning, and I'll phone the police station, and we'll find out what's going on. Then hopefully we can pick your dad up from Tain, wherever that is.'

When Fiona had been told that nobody had been hurt, that wasn't strictly accurate. Left alone in his cell (or custody suite, to give its correct, misleadingly urbane title, a bare room with a shiny steel toilet and sink just across from his bunk), Ross lay back and stared at the ceiling, from time to time tentatively feeling the various parts of his body that were aching or tender to the touch. His face had various abrasions, one eye felt puffy and sore, as did his upper lip, his legs were bruised, and there was a constant dull pain in his side. When he'd peed earlier there'd been a discolouration from blood in his stream. Apart from that, he thought with a bitter, wry twist of his damaged mouth that hurt even as he attempted the smile, he felt fine. He'd had worse, certainly shed more blood from cuts and abrasions during some of the territorial battles of his youth, and he wasn't about to make an issue of it. Okay, it hadn't exactly been a fair fight, four against one, but he'd enjoyed it while it lasted, and it had released some of the frustration and anger at what was happening with the road, and given him a sense of purpose - empty and meaningless as it might be - as if his actions might actually have some effect. In the drama of the moment, he'd genuinely half-believed that it might make a difference - the crusader for a code of aesthetic principles all his own, making an heroic lone stand against the destroyers of beauty, and suffering in the attempt. And to be fair, the cops he'd thumped - well, they'd be hurting a bit too. And still he tried to sustain that level of self-delusion, though all he could really think about, apart from the various points of pain in his body, was that with or without his tiny gesture that beautiful road would inevitably be destroyed, for no good reason whatsoever. Also that Fiona would be angry, and he knew the recriminations would be emphatic and prolonged.

They'd found out his name, but he'd continued to refuse to say anything. He'd been charged with various offences, and a solicitor on call had appeared without warning sometime late in the evening and attempted dialogue with Ross. But Ross couldn't summon up the energy even to be offensive, and had simply waited it out until she'd given up and left, then tried to catch some sleep. A disturbed night of noise, discomfort, and troubled half-waking dreams before he was roused, and after various preliminaries bundled into a van. While being marched to the vehicle he'd seen it was a G4S van, and therefore not even a proper prison vehicle run by trained staff. He'd always regarded private contractors like G4S who'd taken over government jobs as a bunch of cowboys, in this instance cowboys in matching white shirts. He couldn't keep it out of his mind that such people had his life in their hands. Locked in his tiny, claustrophobic cell within the van he was convinced that it would collide with something en route, or just run off the road and end up on its side and then catch fire, and he'd be trapped, entombed, incinerated, and none of those feckless fat fucks would be sufficiently competent to rescue him.

Despite his fears, which made the relatively short journey a long and anxious affair, they made it without incident to Tain, and after a couple of hours wait in a cell, again attended by the solicitor, he was brought into the courtroom. He remained in a resolutely uncooperative mood, still determined to show his disdain for the entire process, thereby hanging onto some sense of meaning for the episode. Again the duty solicitor tried to get through to Ross, earnestly advising him to plead guilty and show remorse, while she would explain that it was out of character, an aberration of which Ross was ashamed, no doubt brought on by the usual go-to excuse of family tensions. He'd get off, maybe, with a deferred sentence and a fine, possibly with the requirement to undergo anger management counselling or community service or some such. That, she'd said, was the likely outcome if Ross could just bring himself to cooperate in a sensible and reasonable fashion. But Ross, hurting in his limbs and various other parts of his body, and obstinately clinging to the righteousness of his cause, was in no mood to cooperate. In the absence of any response from Ross, a not guilty plea was entered on his behalf, after which followed a few moments murmured consultation between the Sheriff, the prosecuting lawyer and his solicitor. A trial date was set for October. Quite abruptly, after a few seconds more consultation between the legal parties, Ross was released on bail, with the proviso that he report weekly to the police station closest to his home address.

He stepped out of the courtroom onto the narrow street outside with an initial exuberance of emotion at his sudden freedom. To be out in the sweet air and the sunshine, unshackled and at liberty to walk the streets just like anybody else. Just to breathe in that perfumed Highland air after the closeness of police and court cells. And he'd made his point - he'd done what he could, admittedly with no real planning or preparation. But at least he'd expressed his contempt for the mindless vandalism. Of course as a gesture he knew it was a mere pinprick in the face of the seething welter of destruction taking place everywhere and in all directions. But though of no real effect whatsoever - even if it was picked up by the local papers it would be presented as nothing more than vandalism on his part, the ignorant fucking bastards - it would at least serve as a fitting coda to his career as campaigner. A last stand, for which he'd paid a price in being knocked about a bit and stuck in a cell overnight. Yet still he loved that road so much, in all its special, distinctive character. Such a beautiful thing.

He tried to put it out of mind - to compartmentalise - and for now to simply enjoy wandering the high street of Tain as though he was just another carefree tourist, as he had nominally been the day before. Carefree. Why were these things done that tormented him so much. Did nobody else care at all? Blindness. Complete lack of aesthetic sensibility. He knew it was so, that's why he'd abandoned the campaigning at last. Nobody shared his vision. And if nobody else cared, why should he. Why bother. Ah, but you just had to drive along it. Is it not blindingly obvious that such a thing is a perfect work of art. Then why destroy it. What is the point of anything if you destroy things that are beautiful. It eliminates all meaning. To destroy beauty is to render everything meaningless.

He needed a drink. He had the few pounds on him that had been returned to him. There wasn't too much to Tain, truth be told, and Ross felt that give it a couple of days and he'd find it as claustrophobic as the little settlements they'd encountered on the Uists. But he found a bar where there was a pay phone, and by tensely concentrating for a few moments was able to dredge up Fiona's mobile number. Fiona had decided to wait to hear from Ross when she found out that his was the first case scheduled for that morning. It was a short conversation. She'd pick him up in an hour or so. No, they'd be going straight back to Glasgow. He took his lager to a seat in the window and spent the time looking out at passers-by and occasional traffic. He expected, and received, an icy welcome from Fiona, while Grant, after a diffident greeting, taken aback by his dad's battered appearance, sat in the back apparently absorbed in his iPhone. And then the long, silent drive back to Glasgow.

7

On his mother's prompting Grant had gone ahead with his stuff, leaving Ross and Fiona sitting in the car on the street outside the flat. It had been a warm and tiring drive. Fiona sat back with her eyes closed. A midweek afternoon, the school holidays, kids playing in the street. Younger ones being taken for walks, maybe a picnic up in the park where there was coolness and shade, and where the lively chatter of birds created the illusion of some tropical paradise. People out shopping, enjoying the warmth. Cars parked nose to tail on both sides - by chance Fiona had found a place almost outside the close entrance. Across the road the MOT/servicing garage was busy, cars strewn around the forecourt. The glazing centre, from where first thing every morning came (somewhat inexplicably) the crashing of broken glass, was in full swing. A van was backing up to the furniture factory. All the usual satisfying, chaotic, harmonious blending of activities. Yet as Ross took it in, everything seemed at once less familiar, less intimately warm and reassuring, discordant even, somehow distant, as if it was some street scene on YouTube. A dislocation the more profound for its apparent normalcy. The prospect, the reality of his trial in the near future, with the real possibility of prison, was finally having its effect, as all the adrenaline and sense of drama of his Highland adventure subsided. And if the solicitor had been right, everything could have been over and done with by now.

Fiona had opened her eyes, and now she turned to him, regarding him with an expression, not of hostility, but of contained, tense enquiry, sombre bemusement, perplexity.

'What on earth were you thinking of, Ross?'

Where to start. How to explain what had been in his mind, both then and in all the years past, that had driven him through all his campaigning, of which Fiona in any case had shown little interest. To begin now with explanations and expositions of his inner obsessions, of the aesthetic imperative that drove him and of which she would never think to credit him - of his secret inner core - seemed beyond futile.

'You know Grant's in a state of shock. To hear that his own father's been arrested. The police told me something of what you'd done. My God, Ross, what were you thinking?'

Ross tried once more to find a starting point for some kind of reply, but found it impossible, so said nothing. Fiona's eyes remained fixed on him for several seconds before she turned and looked out of her side window for a moment at the factory units, before turning to him again.

'So is that the end of it? Or are you still going to be charged, or what?'

He forced his mind to contemplate what he would have preferred to forget.

'A was charged. Now there's going to be a trial in a couple of months. A don't know what'll happen.'

'So what happened in court? Why does it have to go to trial?'

He related the bare facts of that morning's proceedings, and something of the events that led up to them.

'Why didn't you just plead guilty as your solicitor advised you to? There obviously wasn't any doubt about what you'd done. Why prolong all this, when from what you say everything could have been resolved by now?'

'Because a didnae feel guilty of anythin but tryin to stop what they were up tae.'

She turned her head away from Ross for a moment.

'And so you have to go back to Tain?'

'Aye.'

'So you might end up going to prison?'

'Aye, mebbe.'

'Aye, is that it?' She flared up angrily. 'Is that all you've got to say? Did you give no thought to the consequences? What it might mean for your family? What on earth were you thinking?' She couldn't help repeating the question. 'I just don't understand any of this, Ross, I really don't.' Shaking her head.

So many questions, too many to begin to formulate a coherent answer, so instead he just made a small gesture with his hands and remained silent. Thinking how strange it was, the two of them who'd shared so much, even of the greatest intimacy, and over so many years, now sitting together in a rental car (Ross had always opposed the idea of owning a car, for reasons Fiona never understood, making her journey to and from work more laborious than it need have been) outside the flat in strained silence. It was ridiculous. In fact he had to consciously restrain an impulse to laugh out loud in semi-hysterical release from the absurdity of it all, a reaction to certain situations that had got him into trouble in the past. The absurdity especially of a situation where a person could be faced with the rigour of the law for trying to prevent senseless destruction. Could anyone tell him where the sense was in that? It was just too ridiculous for words. More than that, it was insane. A mad, destructive world that tears apart what is best worth preserving. He thought again of trying to explain all this to Fiona, but at that moment they happened to meet each other's gaze, each perhaps searching for something in the other they could recognize and hold onto. Fiona took in the injuries to his face, again with a slight shake of the head.

'Look at the state you're in, Ross,' she said, more composed now.

'Aye, thanks for the sympathy.' He tried a half-smile, though his mouth still hurt. 'A didn't exactly do this tae maself.'

'Have you told anyone you got beaten up?'

'Is it no' obvious? Anyway, like who? The polis?'

'Your solicitor.'

He didn't reply.

'Well, what did they say?'

'They've seen it all before. Anyway, a'm fine. It disnae hurt that much.'

It was just the kind of fatuous macho posturing she disliked. Involuntarily she thought of Mark, of how soft-spoken and undemonstrative he was. Quiet, civilized, yet with an occasionally sharp sense of humour that she appreciated and responded to. She made an effort to shift her thoughts; thinking of Mark when Ross was present seemed more overtly disloyal than at other times. She looked across at Ross, this time a long, steady look, as if to gauge once and for all, after all this time and after all the layers of wishful thinking and youthful misreadings had eroded away at last, what manner of man she had married. And as she looked she saw not a bad or unpleasant man, but just one with whom she now felt little or no connection, bar the years they'd spent under the same roof and the child they'd raised together. Ross, seeing her intent look, and mistaking it for an expression of affection, possibly even forgiveness, turned in his seat and leant towards her, placing his hand on her thigh, as he would often do when they were driving somewhere, massaging gently with increasing ardour and intent. But as he moved to kiss her, instead of responding, inviting the kiss, as she would once have done, she turned her face slightly - it was the smallest movement - but enough for Ross, chastened, to sit back in his seat, and after half a minute or so, unable any longer to remain in the confines of the car, get out, slam the door, grab as many of their bags as he could manage, and make his way into the close. Fiona closed her eyes once more and tried to think beyond the gnawing confusion of divided loyalties. Her world seemed to have closed in, and she could see no clear way ahead.

After a few minutes she brought up the last of their stuff, put it down in the hall and called to Grant, without response. She heard the shower running, and after shouting through the door several times received an impatient reply to the effect that he was having a shower and then going out. She found Ross in the living room. He turned an empty look to her as she came in.

'Do you want a cup of tea, Ross?'

'Aye, I'll get it, though. You've been driving.'

So she went through to their bedroom and started putting the clean clothes away that hadn't been needed on their aborted holiday, until Ross called her through. She found him by the window looking down at the street.

'Are you not having one?'

'What?'

He came and sat down opposite her.

'Are you not having a cup of tea?'

He shook his head, his eyes seemingly glazed, unfocused. Fiona wet her lips, then spoke quietly.

'What are we going to do, Ross? We can't go on like this.'

He looked up.

'What do you mean?'

'Well, us. We can't - '

'Us? What's us? What're ye talkin aboot?'

'Oh, I don't know. Things seem a bit...'

'Is this all to do wi' the bother a'm in? You know, you're making it into something bigger than it is. It's really no big deal unless you make it intae one.'

'Going to prison's no big deal?'

Ross jumped up. What he saw as her negativity, together with the thought of being stuck in the flat for the next however many hours, days and weeks with it all hanging over him, made everything suddenly oppressive beyond bearing.

'I'm gan oot.'

Fiona looked at him.

'We've only just got here.'

'Aye, I know. I just need some space.'

'Right, fine. Just - for God's sake, Ross, don't get into any more trouble.'

Ross almost ran down the close stairs, ignoring some neighbourly greeting on the first floor landing in his haste.

When Grant had left, presumably to meet up with Sabiha, and with Ross still not back, Fiona texted Mark. It was now late afternoon. Mark replied that he could finish early and meet her in the city centre. Though Ross had paid no particular attention at the time, he'd met Mark Leavis a couple of years before at some company function that Fiona had persuaded him to attend. It had been the occasion of the launch of their latest product, a mobile app which Mark himself had developed and which the company was now promoting. Ross, with zero interest in or understanding of software, or any of the company's products, or even to any great extent what the company was actually about, found himself standing in a corner slowly sipping a glass of wine, feeling pretty much a spare part, disregarded by everyone around him as they laughed and chattered excitedly about, as he saw it, fuck knows what. He found all this digital business inexplicable and unintelligible, and was at a loss to understand how anyone could take any interest in it. None of this so-called software, digital products, or whatever the fuck it was, made anything tangible, that's what he couldn't fathom. Take some traditional industrial enterprise like, say, a coal mine, iron foundry, chemical works, shipyard, steel works, machine tools manufactory, brickworks, car factory - these were real places making real, three dimensional artefacts and/or the raw materials necessary to produce them, obtained and processed with the greatest difficulty by the strength of human hand and arm and the skill and steady judgment of eye and brain, often amid conditions of smoke and fumes and heat and dust. It was real. Real things were made that people used - for fuel, transport, construction, household goods - a thousand things for practical uses. What did these digital devices actually produce? Nothing. Nothing at all, so far as he could see.

As Mark delivered his speech, informal in tone, articulate and engaging, introducing and demonstrating the app, Ross from the sidelines took in the slightly chubby physique, large, smooth, egg-shaped head, wide mouth, long, arrow-like nose, and close-cropped hair receding to reveal a shiny pink dome. He thought he'd detected the hint of a patronising tone when they'd been introduced, Mark pleasant and smiling, a warm, flabby handshake, but paid no great heed, dismissing him as just one of the soft, smooth wee bastards that Fiona inexplicably enjoyed working with. It was of course good that she brought in a decent income, he couldn't deny that, but still he couldn't understand how she could enjoy spending time with these people.

Caledon Technology was based in offices within a large new shiny building on a business park just north of the city centre. It took Mark about the same time to finish what he was doing, drive down and find somewhere to park as it took Fiona to get ready and take the train up to Central Station, and from there to walk to the cafe/restaurant where from time to time they'd meet for coffee and cakes and discussion of company and other matters. A light embrace and quick peck on the cheek was exchanged, nothing more than a mere token of friendship. They took a glass of wine in advance of a panini and salad, seated in a quiet corner of the pleasantly dark and intimate interior. A sip or two of the wine, relaxing somewhat the air of nervous expectancy between them.

'It's surprisingly quiet in here at the moment,' said Fiona, breaking the charged silence.

'It is, yes,' said Mark, thinking how tense she looked, yet how unbearably alluring, dark hair attractively styled, such pale skin, yet with a distinct glow to her cheeks. That full, strong, typically Glaswegian shape of face, broad, fine forehead, something about the high cheekbones, the symmetry, the friendly, open smile and clear blue eyes. 'Early yet, I suppose. It'll get busy in the evening.' His voice, which Fiona found so seductive, had nothing of Glasgow in it. Raised in Surrey, he'd come to Glasgow in the early Nineties to do a degree in Computing Science, loved the city and the easy access to the wilds of Scotland, started his company, met Janet and never returned.

She asked after his wife, and was told that Janet was fine, looking forward to Jessica starting school in a week's time. Of course, they were both naturally nervous, their first child starting full-time schooling, although Jessica had been at nursery the past couple of years, and many of her little friends at nursery would be starting at the same time, so there was some continuity. It would all be fine - a couple of weeks to settle in, and then Jessica would be quite happy, no doubt, and glad to be at school. A difficult transition for Janet, though. Worse for the mother than the child, in many ways. How had she found it with Grant? Well, and here Fiona laughed, a somewhat forced release of nervous tension, that's a long time ago now. But yes, it had been strange for her, Grant all at once no longer a constant presence in the flat. You quickly got used to it, of course, and anyway for the first few years she used to go and pick him up each day at midday and bring him home for dinner, so that made things easier. And she was studying then as well, so the extra free time came in useful. Of course, you were on with your degree. Yes, I began with the OU after he started school. And I only had Grant. There was never a second child. At least Janet will still have Toby at home. Yes, that's true.

The paninis arrived, followed by a period of silence, apart from the murmur of voices and occasional clinking of knives and forks from other tables. The conversation had been rather constrained, in direct contrast with their late email exchanges. Perhaps it was their very warmth which resulted now in a certain awkwardness. Also the arrest drama of Ross, which Fiona had alluded to obliquely in their recent texting as explanation for her early return from holiday, and tacit pretext for this meeting, hovering like a third party presence at the table. Mark felt it was Fiona's prerogative to raise the matter if she wished, which she did at last (feeling the benefit of the glass of wine, and promptly ordering another), though not without experiencing a further twinge of feeling she was being disloyal to Ross.

'I'd better tell you what's happened, I suppose,' she began. Mark looked up expectantly. 'Well, Ross was arrested when we were on holiday and he's been charged with various things - vandalism, resisting arrest, assault - he had a tussle with the police officers trying to arrest him, and - well, that's all the charges against him, I think. I'm not even sure.' She seemed embarrassed even to be talking about it.

'My God, I'm sorry, Fiona. So what happened?'

She looked down for a moment.

'Well, it was Ross off on one of his crusades. Saving the world, trying to prevent catastrophic damage to the built environment. All the usual stuff. He has his own agenda and unique aesthetic standards that nobody else can live up to.' Ross would have been surprised, shocked had he heard both Fiona's dismissive tone, but also her precise analysis of the motivation for his campaigning. 'They're improving a road up there, and Ross took exception to the changes and started to smash up some of the contractors plant - smashing the windows of JCBs and the like, that kind of thing. To what end or to what purpose I've no idea, except to make some kind of point. Ross takes exception to all forms of change, and he's done things like this before, though nothing quite this daft. But it's the possible effect on Grant of all this that I'm really worried about. If Ross ends up going to prison...'

'Is that likely?'

'I don't know. Yes, I think it's possible. And it could all have been over and done with if he'd just been able to bring himself to show a bit of contrition and plead guilty, but as far as he's concerned he isn't guilty of anything. So he ignored everything the solicitor was telling him, trying to persuade him to just plead guilty and say how sorry he was, and get it over with. And so we end up in the mess we're in now.'

'Ross told you all this?'

'Well, most of it, and I can fill in the blanks easily enough knowing what he's like.'

'I'm really sorry, Fiona. I don't know what else to say.'

Sensing her anguish, and feeling the need to console in some way, he reached out and put his hand on hers, which had been distractedly tracing shapes on the table top. He had no other conscious motive at that moment. She looked up into his eyes. They held each other's gaze for some moments. Mark kept his hand upon hers, and she made no move to remove it.

'I'm sorry,' he repeated, though in her confusion Fiona wasn't sure whether this was just a repeated attempt at consolation, or an apology for, as it seemed to her, the portentous act of placing his hand on hers. And still he made no move to remove his hand, nor she to remove hers.

'It's the effect on the children,' said Fiona, in almost a whisper.

He nodded.

'I know.'

'Not knowing what to do for the best.'

Suddenly he began to move his hand, very gently, stroking. The restaurant and all the world outside had disappeared. There was just the two of them, their eyes locked, their senses heightened to near breaking point, as every slight move, movement, word or gesture seemed charged with enormous import. And then her hand opened, and clasped his in a warm, tight hold.

'I wouldn't want to...' she began. 'It's the effect on the children of things like...'

'I know. I feel the same way. But maybe sometimes there's no way around it.'

8

Ross wandered around, wrapped in his thoughts, until he found himself outside Mullins. Quieter today, just a few regulars up at the bar. He took his beer to a table with his back to the window and drank most of it straight off in an attempt to calm his agitation, then sat back in his chair. He'd had no choice, that was the thing. It was too easy just to see it as the biggest fuck-up of his life, but that was way too simplistic. Anyway, where *do* you draw the line in sticking to your principles? Surely at the point where it begins to impact on your family. And it would seem he'd overshot that by some distance. Those parts of the world that aren't too fussy about human rights begin the whole process of clamping down by spreading fear, counting on the basic human instinct to protect your family above all else, keeping your head down and your mouth shut. What about, though, when looking out for your family has to give way to the best interests of the community, local or national? That's the question. But that won't wash where the moral issue is to do with aesthetics, that's for sure - that's if such things can be said to be a moral issue, and he couldn't decide at that moment if they were or not. Probably not when it's to do with changing the alignment of a road, or pulling a few buildings down. Who gives a shit about things like that. Ah, ye daft wee beggar.

He got a second pint in, together with a couple of whiskies, sat down again and began to wonder what his parents would have made of his situation. Predicted it, probably. He'd often been in trouble as a youth and sometimes the police had been involved, to his father's disgust and anger. Twenty, twenty-five years later, thought Ross, nothing much had changed. An image of his mother came to mind. More a vague impression. He couldn't really see her face. He hadn't looked at a photo of either of them in years. Thinking of his mother and father conjured up a composite, compressed image, as if his entire childhood could be crystallised in a single, frozen moment in time, his mother sitting in an armchair with her hand over her face in front of rows of remorseless grey tenement blocks in a rubbish-strewn wasteland, while from his bedroom window he looked out as dusk fell on glowing windows of tenements and tower blocks and the lonely orange halos of streetlamps below and into the distance, a group of mates shouting up at him to come out, while somewhere in a corner, tight and silent, sat his father.

Fiona had always dreaded the occasional weekend visits, involving a change of bus in town, to see Ross's parents. She could never uncover much human warmth in either of them, finding them a hard-bitten pair, often dour, though to be fair his mother was often unwell. The trail into town with Grant and Ross, and then a longer trail down the Western Road to Drumchapel, a place she found hideous and intimidating. Inside the well-kept second floor flat her hands were full trying to keep Grant quiet and occupied. Meanwhile, Ross's father would expound indignantly from his well-worn armchair in a gravelly voice on the evils of Thatcher, the stupidity of Scargill, the betrayal of socialism by New Labour, as Jimmy Reid, his great hero, looked down from a framed, signed photo showing him addressing a mass meeting at the time of the work-in. He always reminded Fiona of the Jane Bown portrait of Samuel Beckett, grim and implacable.

From his teen years Alex McKenzie had worked at Fairfield's in Govan. He'd been there when Reid had made his famous speech. He'd met Anne Barr through the sister of a friend, and they'd married within a few months, he nineteen, she two years younger. They applied for and in due course were allocated a flat in Drumchapel, and they remained there for almost the next fifty years. By bus, motorbike or lift in a mate's car Alex had made his way to Govan each day, managing to survive through all the regroupings and rebrandings of Fairfield's - Upper Clyde Shipbuilders, British Shipbuilders, Kvaerner Govan, BAE Systems Marine, BAE Systems Surface Ships - through until retirement in 2005. And this despite following the lead of his hero Jimmy Reid in joining the Communist Party, even emulating his hero by later leaving the communists and joining the Labour Party, though he drew the line at joining the nationalists, Reid's next political realignment.

112

Fiona knew that Ross had arrived from nowhere after twenty years of childless marriage. Unexpected clearly didn't cover it. And she gathered that rather than the expected outpouring of joy, his parents seemed instead at a loss to know how to deal with the situation. His mother had had to give up her job, a secretarial position at the nearby Goodyear factory (which in any event closed down that year) to look after Ross, who from a young age proved resistant to discipline. Acute loneliness and depression followed. And then came the darkest days of Drumchapel, when the planners' dreams of a clean, functional, utilitarian, hygienic, bright tomorrow became instead a nightmare, ill-conceived and banal, and to live there was to be constantly under siege. Through the Seventies and Eighties there was hardly a bleaker or more barren place in the whole of Scotland. Though to Ross as a child it was home, and exciting enough before he discovered another world.

Fiona only knew Ross's mother for three or four years, and remembered her as frail and often bedbound with various ailments. When she died the visits became more infrequent but more of a trial. Ross's father became taciturn, uncommunicative, seemingly diminished by the loss of his wife, turned in upon himself and often irritable with Grant, whose inquisitive hands were into everything, making the visits a tense affair, especially for Fiona, who had the task of looking after Grant and keeping him out of trouble.

Though Ross's father managed to see through the last couple of years before retirement, he died a year or so afterwards, and Fiona couldn't hide a certain relief from herself. And if Ross himself was much affected by the loss of his parents he didn't show it, and he never talked of them. Fiona privately thought that Ross must have inherited his wild-eyed crusading fervour from his father, even though they'd seemingly always been at odds. She sometimes wondered whether Ross had been in fear of his dad, and whether he'd received the kind of beatings for his frequent misdemeanours that were a not unusual punishment from fathers of that generation.

Ross looked up as two young men in shirt sleeves came in, abrasive voices cocky and assertive. He discovered that his tolerance level to annoyance was very low. He had to overcome the temptation to go up to the bar, deliberately jostle one of them and start something up for the sheer hell of it, just to release some of the pent up angst and frustration and utter boredom at his situation. The scuffle with the police had reawakened his taste for violence, something he thought he'd sufficiently tamed or subsumed within the framework of his life as married man and responsible father, and it took some effort to control his instincts now, just managing to think clearly enough to see how much worse it would look in court if he started a brawl for no reason whatsoever. So he finished his beer, went up to the bar, keeping his distance from the two young guys, who were not really doing anything much at all, and tried to close his mind to their voices as he waited to be served. A third pint, then back in his seat he took out his mobile and texted Jimmy.

Hey Jimmy whats up. You around? Want tae meet up for a drink?

He waited an hour or so for a reply, drinking all the while. Then, irritated though not surprised at Jimmy's failure to reply, debated whether to return home or stay in the pub drinking until he either fell over or they wouldn't serve him any more - or do something else. Then he thought of Maz. He needed a sympathetic ear, and although their relationship had been strained by the Jimmy episode, they'd exchanged texts since, and he thought he'd at least go round and give it a shot. Jimmy. What an unreliable and ungrateful little twat he was. He'd stayed a week or so in the flat, an uncomfortable time for all concerned. Conversation between them had been forced, Jimmy sitting stiffly, lager in hand, trying to make small talk, but with none of the usual flow of obscene reminiscences. A few desultory exchanges on his latest job of supervisor at a local supermarket (Ross continually surprised and mystified at Jimmy's capacity to land quite responsible jobs with apparent ease, though they never lasted long), or the referendum, the Scottish League, the relative merits of the current Rangers and Celtic teams (Jimmy was, surprisingly, non-partisan), Alex Ferguson's time at Aberdeen, Jimmy Johnstone, an upcoming middleweight bout on TV. Both of them feeling self-conscious out of their habitual environment of pub bar or pool hall, and each topic begun with an initial wave of enthusiasm soon trailed off into strained silence. Or a couple of times Clare would sit there with Jimmy while they ate a takeaway, maybe watched a little TV, before with small smiles they got up, shuffled to the door and retired to the spare bedroom/study, not to be seen or heard from again until they might be spotted slipping quietly out of the flat next morning. And all the while Fiona would conspicuously avoid the living room, spending her time either at the kitchen table or in the bedroom with her laptop perched on her knees and papers scattered on the bed.

And then came the unexpected release, a relief all round, as Jimmy went to stay for several weeks with his new best mate Andy. Ridiculous though he knew it was, Ross was surprised and dismayed by the speed and ease with which he'd been dropped by Jimmy. No more texts suggesting they meet up, and the couple of times they'd met subsequently, Jimmy's mate Andy had been there, a tall, angular, loud, untidy youth with acne and a jocular, matey manner that grated on Ross, such that a couple of times he felt he'd just like to clip him one on the chin and lay him out flat on his back, just to put his lights out and put a stop to his banter for a few minutes. He'd heard nothing from Jimmy the last couple of weeks, and figured he must be preparing to move to Newcastle with Clare by now - if not already gone.

He left the bar fairly steadily, stepped outside and blinked in the bright, warm sunlight that greeted him, breathing in the familiar fragrance of the street. From Mullins to Maz's flat took about five minutes. Ross immediately put Jimmy firmly out of mind, and in his favourite place and on the streets he loved best found himself feeling pleasantly detached, benevolent and full of goodwill. Catching the eye of passers-by he would smile, and meeting elderly couples or mothers with pushchairs he would ceremoniously step off the pavement allowing them right of way. If he'd had a hat he'd have tipped it. Gone and forgotten was the urge to start a fight and get himself into trouble. The drink had effectively blanked out most of the fine detail of the present, and pretty much all of the future.

9

Ross knocked on Maz's door with a warm and rather fatuous smile on his face. Maz opened the door, looked at Ross, drew back slightly and frowned theatrically.

'Whit the fuck's up wi' ye?'

'What do ye mean?'

She narrowed her eyes and smiled.

'Ye just look like ye've had a few!'

Then she laughed, and gestured with her head for him to come in.

'A dinnae blame ye - a've bin sittin watchin the box an' goin out of ma feckin mind, waitin fur some excuse tae get pissed. Not that a need one.'

They passed the living room from where came the noise of the TV - some game show or daytime chat show - and went into the kitchen. Kylie and Chelsea were standing together at the cooker, their heads bent over, examining the contents of several saucepans. They didn't turn around or acknowledge Ross.

'Do ye want a coffee, darlin? Or do ye fancy something stronger?'

'What have you got?'

'A've got a bottle of Lambrini - a've just been waiting for an excuse to open it.'

'Aye, that'd be grand.'

'Are you sure ye can take any more? A dinnae want ye passin oot on us.'

A bright, brittle, mischievous laugh and flash of her eyes as she made her way to the fridge. The twins turned around and went across to the cupboards for some ingredients or seasoning. A brief, darted sideways glance at Ross. Trying not to stare, Ross nevertheless found it difficult to look away. They were dressed identically, as ever, but it was the manner of their dress which was so extraordinary (and, thought Ross, particularly unsuited for a cooking session), reminding him of wood nymphs from a book of myths and legends he'd once taken out of the library. They were wearing Twenties-style knee-length slimline dresses of a dark yet glittering and scintillating green, sequinned and decorated with red, brown and white flower motifs, thin shoulder straps, cut to follow closely the slim contours of their bodies, the hem flaring out just a little in dark, lacy additions at the knee. Their hair, usually brown, long and straight, falling below the shoulders, was now a golden halo around their heads (whether from being tied up, cut shorter or manipulated by some other means Ross wasn't sure), and speckled with flowers of various shapes and colours, mainly whites and reds. Their eyes were heavily made-up with red eye shadow, matching the reds of the flowers in their dresses and hair, and all kinds of bangles and bracelets on their arms and wrists.

It was an extraordinary, strange yet wonderful and even moving effect - a certain pathos in the representation of a vanished age, or the ephemeral nature of female youth and beauty, or woodland spirits cast adrift in urban Glasgow, or mainly perhaps, in the fact that nobody but themselves, their family and occasional visitors like Ross would ever see them. Remaining, like rare orchids in the wild, hidden and unheralded. That their life seemed to consist entirely of celebrating their own beauty, and that they appeared to contribute nothing more substantive or tangible to society beyond the aesthetic form of their own bodies, which they chose to share with nobody, struck Ross as infinitely poignant, yet curiously audacious - the celebration of beauty for its own sake, seeking neither publicity nor acclaim. Such unworldly, iridescent creatures to be found cooking their tea in the kitchen of a flat in Glasgow.

He followed Maz, who was clutching a large bottle of Lambrini and a couple of glasses, through into the living room. It was a room dominated by a pair of big, not quite matching, well-worn and stained dark leather sofas, lumpy and uncomfortable, with the TV in one corner (Maz edged the sound down as she sat), coffee tables littered with dirty glasses and overflowing ashtrays (the only tangible sign that day of Maz's friends), while scattered on the ground next to the wall adjoining the hallway was a collection of Pixie's toys, mostly pink, with several boxes overflowing with more toys and DVDs. Facing them as Ross sat down next to Maz as she opened the bottle and filled their glasses, was a painting by Thomas Kinkade employing some of his characteristic motifs - a lonely stone and wood cottage in sylvan setting with bright, warm, glowing yellow light pouring from every window, a frothy tinkling stream cascading down a mountainside over rocks, underneath a wooden bridge and into a pool reflecting the lights from the cottage and the reds and browns of trees nestling by, sunlight dappling the foreground, a moored boat, wading birds, birds in flight, a gypsy camp fire, bright purple heather, more bright autumnal shades from overhanging trees, a stag standing proud and erect on a rocky outcrop in the middle distance, while beyond arose tree-covered mountains with mist-shrouded hollows, the whole crowned by a lurid orange sunset between bright pink clouds. High above, in lonely splendour against the backdrop of the sunset, an eagle circled.

Christ, thought Ross, taking in the picture as he sampled the Lambrini, that guy disnae leave anythin tae chance. He wondered how Maz had managed to afford it - he'd read somewhere that those things cost thousands of dollars. More likely a counterfeit from China or Thailand.

'Cheers, Maz.'

They clinked glasses.

'Cheers, darlin.'

'Were ye on your way out? A havnae stopped ye gan oot, have a?'

She turned in her seat and pulled a confused face.

'Nah. Why?'

'Ye look aw dressed up.'

121

Maz was at her most stunning and alluring in tight black jeans encasing her long legs, white lacy top, and immaculate hair and make-up.

'Aye, aw dressed up wi' nae feckin place tae go,' laughing, taking a drink and lighting up a cigarette. 'Ah, thank God fur a drink,' finishing her glass with a flourish before pouring herself another and topping up Ross. 'This is feckin great. A'd forgotten how good this stuff is. Ye cannae beat Lambrini!'

'Aye, ye're right - fur the price.'

'Aye, fur the price, mister feckin moneybags! Mebbe a should go down on ma hands and knees to ye fur no' havin yir favourite vintage on ice.'

Ross laughed. 'Aye, ye dee that, Maz. A'd like tae see that.'

'Aye, a'll bet ye wid, wi' your dirty mind.' She giggled wildly in a way that reminded Ross vividly of Jimmy. 'Well, what do ye think of ma new picture?'

Ross looked up at the lonely mountain cottage, glanced at Maz, then back at the painting.

'Not that one, ye daft bugger. Behind you.'

Ross twisted round, and saw Elvis looking down at him. He couldn't understand how he could possibly have missed it when he came into the room. He got up - he wasn't sure how, suddenly he found himself standing and making his way around the sofa - 'Ye didn't have tae get up, Ross - mind how ye go, darlin,' laughing - and, glass in hand, surveyed the picture. It was a big 3D portrait of Elvis from his Aloha concert in Hawaii, jumpsuit shining a brilliant white, all his bling and finery present and correct, hair jet black, legs spread, one arm outstretched, hand imploring, the other tightly clutching the microphone. As Ross looked up he thought Elvis moved slightly. He peered closer, and Elvis curled one side of his upper lip with the hint of a sneer.

'Wow, great picture,' said Ross. 'Is it new? A havnae seen it before.'

'Aye, a just got it from the Barras. Just tae fill a space on the wall.'

Ross couldn't take his eyes away, fascinated by the suggestion of movement, and the sneering lip.

'Are ye no' a fan, then?'

'Oh aye, o' course - The Wonder of You, Can't Help Falling in Love, Angel, Don't Be Cruel,' singing the first couple of lines of each song as she thought of the title, head thrown back, glass in hand, relaxed, happy. Ross had resumed his seat, almost falling back onto the sofa, touching shoulders with Maz in the process. She laughed as he wiped off a few splashes of wine from his t-shirt with his hand. The contact between them, sitting so close, his light-headedness, combined to make Ross all too aware of her physicality, making it difficult to dispel various erotic speculations. 'An' a like tae watch some of the old films, like Blue Hawaii, Paradise Hawaiian Style - what's that other one? Oh, Fun in Acapulco. He was sae feckin gorgeous in that film.'

'Aye, it was great,' said Ross, though in fact he couldn't distinguish between one Elvis film and another, and would never choose to watch one.

'That wis the one wi' Ursula Andress. Ye know a wis told a looked like her when a wis young.'

'Ah, ye're far better looking than she ever was.'

'Ah, dinnae be sae daft!' Laughing and giving Ross a mischievous flash of those dark eyes. 'Ye're full o' shit!'

'A'm just tellin ye what a see,' said Ross, smiling.

'Acapulco,' said Maz, relaxing back into the sofa, glass of wine held high, her thigh now brushing against Ross. 'A could just see maself livin there. Or Rio de Janeiro. Milan. Venice. Paris. Hawaii. Ye know, a should just get on a plane tomorrow and fly off somewhere an' never come back.' She gave Ross another warm, flirtatious look, and laid a hand on his arm. 'We should move to Hawaii together, darlin, just you and me. Leave everything and every other fucker behind.' She began to sing, in a deep and sexy voice, *Dreams come true, In blue Hawaii, And mine could all come true, This magic night of nights with you*. Holding the *you* before dissolving into laughter. 'Oh, a'm sorry darlin, a shouldnae be tempting ye tae run away fae home!'

Ross laughed. 'A'm tempted, dinnae ye worry.'

'Ah, but what about yir wifey?'

Ross had hardly given a thought to Fiona all the time he'd been out.

'Aye, aye, good point.'

'Anyway a can dream about aw those kind of places, but somewhere like that wee hoose is where I'd really like tae live,' indicating the idyllic vision of bucolic isolation on the wall before them. 'Somewhere completely away from everybody. Away fae aw the twats and feckin family a have tae put wi'. A'd like tae shut oot the world, an' become a hermit. A'd become the old wummin living aw alone in her cottage, never seein anybody, wi' just ma cat an' a tumbler or two of whisky tae keep out the cold. That'd suit me fine.'

Ross tried to imagine Maz all alone in that unblemished Eden. Living, by default, a perfect, blameless, empty life. It was difficult to imagine her without her circle of friends, without people to hate, and without ready access to supermarket, off-licence and pub.

'Ye'd go out of your mind wi' boredom living there,' said Ross.

'Wid a fuck.' She refilled their glasses. 'I'm flying to Milan, darling,' putting on a cut-glass Joan Collins voice, 'but I have to simply adjust my hair and make-up before Venice, such a bore, meeting Liz and Larry there, simply darlings, you know, and then of course it's Paris, oh wait a moment darling, I simply must check my - '

But that was as far as she got before both of them were overcome with laughter.

'Oh my God,' wailed Maz, still half-laughing, 'ma feckin awfu' life. Christ, Ross, ye've nae idea the half of it. Ye really haven't.'

Ross unsure if this was still part of the performance.

'What do ye mean?'

'Have a not told ye the latest? A'm not gan tae any of those places - a'm gan tae feckin Birmingham if that fat twat has his way.'

125

'Brian? Birmingham?'

'Aye, feckin Brian fae Birmingham.'

'What ye gan tae Birmingham for?'

'Did ye not hear aboot it? He's gan tae have a fleet of trucks, according to him. He's gan tae run his own haulage business. Oh aye, an' join the Haulage Exchange. It's the Haulage Exchange this, the Haulage Exchange that. Ye'd think the fat twat had shares in it. Aye, take a look at the Haulage Exchange - over 50% of all journeys are around the Midlands - the hub of national distribution. A've heard his spiel sae often a know it aw off by feckin heart. An' aw his great distribution empire will ever consist of is one feckin second-hand Transit.' She laughed with scornful bile. 'Why wid a want tae live in feckin Birmingham or Leicester or Nottingham or any of those shitholes anyway. With ready access to England's motorway network' (again simulating a posh English accent) 'we'll accommodate all of your logistical requirements. Aye, according tae him he'll have specialist vehicles tae cater fur aw requirements - chilled or frozen goods deliveries, flatbeds, aw the way tae worldwide freight services. Brian Maston Logistics - the daft fat cunt. Noo a go tae sleep at night wi' aw this crap running through ma mind - flatbed trucks, a fast, secure way of getting your goods to their destination - for all your urgent international consignments - just take a look at available loads on the Haulage Exchange with an easy to use app, no more empty return runs. A'm tellin' ye, that fat bastard's got me brainwashed. At least when a'm havin tae lie next to the fat twat in bed, a can think of aw his haulage schemes instead of thinkin how feckin awfu' ma life is havin tae share a bed wi' some fat cunt a feckin hate.'

Her voice filled with bitterness and hatred, though Ross felt only a guilty, jealous pleasure and amusement in her diatribes against Brian.

'And he wants his own feckin website an' everything - a said ye can dae it aw on Facebook. Ye dinnae need a website. Oh, I must have a website. It's got to look professional. The daft cunt.'

'Ye're no' really gan tae move down there, are you?'

'Christ, no. Why wid a want tae move there.'

'But what if Brian goes ahead wi' his haulage scheme?'

'He'll never dae it, the useless fat twat. An' even if he did a widnae go. Nae chance.'

'Ye'd stay here if he went?'

'Why wid a want tae move tae the feckin Midlands, an' leave aw ma friends behind. He must think a'm just some feckin appendage. Christ, if a'd just never had kids, ma life wid have been completely different. A'd just walk away from the fat bastard.'

'Ah, ye dinnae mean that aboot your kids.'

'A'm not sayin' a dinnae love them. A'm no' sayin that. A mother has tae love her kids. But it disnae mean a have tae like them. An' it disnae mean a cannae wonder what ma life wid hae been like if a hadnae had them.'

'But ye chose tae keep them aw. Ye didn't think of - well, you know - abortion?'

Maz looked shocked. 'A could never hae done that. No way.' A pause. 'Have a ever told ye aboot ma maw?'

'Aye, ye might hae mentioned her. A never met her, though.'

'She wis a feckin nutcase. She believed in the Devil. Aye, literally. She'd scare us aw tae death wi' what he'd dee tae us if we didnae behave. Mad as a bloody hatter. She was a Jehovah's Witness. Devout. We were aw brought up tae believe the Bible wis gospel truth. A could quote ye a thousand things oot the Bible. An' she did the whole Jehovah's Witness thing while she could still walk. She'd go tae the meeting hall every Sunday, go round the streets wi' leaflets, handing them oot, knockin on doors, aw that stuff. Later she could hardly walk, an' hardly ever went out. She had aw kinds of health problems - diabetes, heart attacks, problems wi' her kidneys, arthritis, swollen ankles. She could still eat, though. Oh aye, she still liked her food. She didnae like me much, though. After ma dad died, she couldnae be bothered wi' us. So a spent as little time at home as a could an' a hardly ever went tae school. A'd just roam aroon, deein this an' that, gettin intae trouble. A never went tae school at all fur two years, an' then a met Rob, an' a had Jimmy, an' that was that. But a could never have got rid of him. Even though he's been a horrible wee bastard tae me, a still have tae love him. Ma maw wid always say the Bible tells you that life begins at conception, that aw life is sacred tae God, an' if ye kill un unborn child you'll incur God's wrath, and receive His just punishment. Aye, an' ma maw believed in spirits - she said she could see them aw around her - people she knew, people she didn't know - members of the family that had died - she'd talk tae them as if they were there. An' she said if ye got rid of the child, its spirit wid haunt ye for the rest of your life. Ye'd never have a moment's peace wi'out this wee spirit cryin an' bawlin an' accusin ye of murdering it.'

Ross was looking at her, trying to gauge the level of her conviction.

'Ye dinnae believe aw that, do you?'

'Well, a wisnae gan tae take the bloody chance of findin oot! So I end up wi' this lot that disnae gie a shit aboot me, an' that a never wanted in the first place.'

The bottle of Lambrini now stood empty on the coffee table.

'What time is it, darlin?'

Ross held out his arm and focused on his watch.

'Quarter to six.'

Maz yawned widely.

'Pixie should be back soon. How did your holiday go, darlin? Did ye have a good time?'

The abrupt change of subject took Ross by surprise. He had to marshal his thoughts even to remember that he'd been on holiday. In the end he managed to tell her the tale, though at this moment he was supremely unconcerned about the prospect of jail. It was as if the whole thing was just a dream, floating and cushioned as he was in a haze - the Lambrini had been the finishing touch.

'Bloody Hell! So when's the trial?'

'A'm no sure - October, mebbe.'

'Have ye heard from yir pal? Have ye told him aboot it?'

A glint in her eye.

'Jimmy? No.'

'Ye'll not hear anythin else from him now, now ye're no longer any use tae him. Ye never wanted tae believe me, but a'm tellin ye, he's a horrible, horrible laddie. Ye've nae idea. Aw his lies. He lives in a fantasy world. He wis gan tae sign fur Rangers at one point, according tae him. He wis gan tae race cars, he wis gan tae be a snooker champion, he wis gan tae be a boxing champion. A've lost count of aw the things he wis gan tae be a champion of. An' aw he wis ever really good at was lyin in bed till all hours, doin feck all, never lifting a finger tae help around the hoose, an giving cheek tae his mother while he sits around wi' his mates drinking till all hours.'

There'd been a knocking on the flat door, and Maz had been on her way out of the room as she finished this speech. Ross heard voices, then Pixie came in, red-faced, and threw herself back onto the sofa where her mother had been sitting. She lay back, arms outstretched, theatrically gasping for breath.

'Hi Ross. God, I'm pooped.'

Ross smiled.

'Hi Pixie. What's up?'

'Oh, a'm just feckin exhausted.'

Ross couldn't help laughing. Maz came back into the room, sat down next to Pixie and began asking what she'd being doing. Ross, taking his cue to depart, made his farewells, then walked home, slowly and laboriously.

He found Fiona in the study working at the computer, sitting with her back to him. Despite the appearance of industry, her mind was largely occupied with Mark and what had taken place at the restaurant. Still she wasn't sure - couldn't, within the churning turmoil of her mind, bring herself to commit irrevocably. She thought she could always put it down to the wine, and it could all be brushed under the carpet and forgotten. Okay, hardly forgotten, but seen as just an aberration under pressure.

Ross, his mind in a haze, stood looking down at the crown of her head, before starting to rub her neck and shoulders for several seconds, then reaching under her arms and cupping her breasts. Fiona turned abruptly, freed herself from his grasp, pushed back her chair and stood up facing him.

'What are you doing, Ross?'

She looked genuinely disturbed and upset. Ross couldn't make any sense of any of this. He was suddenly, dimly aware, through the alcoholic fog, of standing on the edge of something - he didn't know what - and struggling to keep his balance. Everything seemed to be turning inside out for reasons he didn't understand.

'Nothing,' he said. 'What's wrong?'

'I'm trying to do some work.'

'A wasn't stopping you fae working.'

She continued to regard him in a way that unsettled him.

'Where's Grant?' he said at last.

'He's out.'

He nodded, tried to think of something else to say, then turned away from the unwelcoming gaze and stumbled through to the bedroom, where he kicked off his shoes, threw himself down on the bed and half-submerged his face in the pillow, before swiftly losing track of everything.

Sabiha. The name itself had mythical properties, and carried in its three syllables a wealth of heady associations and magical potentialities. The absence so far of physical contact meant that kissing open-mouthed was the most that Grant would allow himself to contemplate, and even the prospect of that was sufficiently intoxicating, in conjunction with her proximity and the lingering scent of her perfume, as to leave him with an aching long after they'd parted which he nevertheless refused to appease, believing that it would somehow taint the purity of their relationship.

They met on Victoria Road and headed for a small cafe they'd been to several times before, whose interior had great charm for them, mainly because it had literally not changed in any respect in decades. Little cubicle seats, the hiss of the shiny chromed tea-making machine. Random pictures hanging lop-sided on the walls. Worn and sticky formica table tops. There ye are, Johnny, a tall, middle-aged, still youthful-looking woman with big, black-framed magnifying lens glasses and dark hair cut short and brushed up in a semi-pompadour, placing a fry-up on his table. Aye, they're puttin' him in a home now. Andy bin in this week? He wis in on Monday. A high ceiling with remnants of coving and ancient disused light fittings. A ceiling rose over which had been placed a cold strip light. Glass cabinets taped up here and there, and inside the most basic white mugs, biscuits, shortcakes, KitKats, and Tunnock's caramel wafers and tea cakes.

Grant and Sabiha, who'd ordered at the counter as they came in - a cup of tea and two Tunnock's tea cakes each - the sweetest, gooiest confection imaginable, precisely to their taste - sat down in a free cubicle at the far end of the cafe, just next to a doorway that led to the kitchen. It was busy, and most seats were occupied, and as the cafe was small and the seats were set fairly close together, conversation from every table was clearly audible. Aye, a'll hae a cut, shampoo and set. A noo they're screwin me. Dinnae worry, a'm used tae coverin vast distances on foot. Ye want tae Google it. Aye, it's shut now fae good. Bin gan there fae thirty years. They would take great pleasure in listening in, grinning and sniggering to each other, sometimes contributing sotto voce to the dialogue, to their great self-satisfaction and amusement. Elderly women with shopping bags. A grim-looking old man with white beard and walking stick enjoying his daily fry-up. A pair of rough-looking guys, one helping the other fill out a housing application form. Just put social care, that'll

133

dae. Yes, aye, that's right. The woman cooking behind you never saw, though sometimes you heard her voice as she conducted a conversation with a customer, both so familiar to each other that face to face contact wasn't necessary.

Their cups of tea delivered to their table, the woman's eyes huge through her glasses, a smile at the young folk, then the tea cakes, keeping a straight face till she'd gone, then a whispered exchange about the size of her eyes, delight on their faces. Trying to find a place on the table that wasn't sticky each time they lifted up the cup, more merriment at this, then laughing again in recollection of the sight they'd witnessed on the way to the cafe of some woman bending over a rubbish container down a side street outside a pub and baring her arse. They saw her later in the street shouting the odds at somebody. Washing facilities. Just tick that. Aye, put that doon. That'll dae. Put Govanhill as your local neighbourhood. It's gan tae take him that long tae walk up there. It wis November. November the first.

After they'd consumed the tea cakes with an almost sensuous pleasure, Grant bought them a second cup of tea, then told Sabiha about his dad's antics. Her mood changed as she saw the expression on Grant's face, and her own became grave and concerned. She'd been to Grant's flat a couple of times and had met his dad, finding him kind and pleasant, even charming in his own way. Despite the rough appearance and manner of speech, she found it difficult to believe that he'd get himself mixed up in violence. And she couldn't understand the reason for it all in the first place.

'But why did he do it?'

'God knows. He's a bloody lunatic sometimes. Always has been. He used to be into loads of environmental and political stuff - going on marches, going to meetings, campaigning for all kinds of things, or against things. It was something like that, I suppose. And now the silly sod might be going to prison. You know, he really can be just too fucking annoying and stupid sometimes.'

Quite abruptly Grant had lost the feeling of exhilaration that he always felt in Sabiha's company - that they'd both been feeling - and in fact looked on the verge of tears, something Sabiha had never seen before.

'He was looking terrible. Just awfu'. He was all bashed up around his face. His mouth was cut, and he had bruises. And he looked like he had a black eye - although, I don't know, maybe that was just lack of sleep.'

He stared down at the table top. All he could think of at this moment was his dad in prison, and what might happen to him. And of all the times he'd picked him up from school from when he was little, and the times he'd taken him to the park, and played games with him, and taken him for all kinds of exploring adventures, and been there with him through the school holidays, and looked after him when he was ill. And smiled at him. And of all the times he, Grant, had failed to return the smile. It was all he could do to stop himself from crying in front of Sabiha.

They'd finished their cups of tea, but the form-filling was still in progress. Put anything on the Southside - Daisy Street, Langside Road, Annette Street. A've recently experienced a downturn in ma mental health resulting in - Aye, put that. An' she wis behaving strangely. She'd come in wearin a big coat, an' she widnae take it off, so ye didnae have a clue if she wis losin weight or not. Aye, the social gives us so much. A think ye get fifty poond when ye die? Aye, that's whit a'm sayin. She says, who's yir daughter? A says, this is her sittin beside me. She says, she lives wi' ye? A says, nah, she lives in Cumberland Street. Grant and Sabiha got up and made their way out, saying thanks to the woman now sitting behind the counter reading a paper as they went. He wis sittin there watchin the telly an' the telephone wis ringin an' he just sat there an' widnae answer it. A think it's terrible. A mean, he's seventeen.

They made their way into the park, and after climbing up the steps and following a path for some distance, found a secluded corner where, surrounded only by trees and the chatter of birds, and brought suddenly closer by the revealing of unwonted emotions, they held hands at last, and later exchanged the kiss that Grant had long dreamed of.

10

The date of the trial had been set for the second week of October. As the day approached Ross met with a solicitor a couple of times, but made little effort either to tidy up his appearance or engage with what was being discussed. Fiona had insisted, against strong resistance from Ross, that he engage someone, who in turn would arrange for his case to be presented in court by a barrister. Ross had said he didn't need anyone to speak for him; he was quite capable of telling his own story and putting his own case. Fiona had then become angry. What was he trying to do? Was he quite intent on destroying himself? Had he completely lost his mind? He needed a professional barrister to present his case properly, and ensure that he got the lightest possible sentence. Behind her anger was a growing unease at the downturn in Ross. Never one to bother overmuch about his appearance (a trait Fiona had once found endearing), he'd become more unkempt, less engaged with family life, and was now drinking excessively. She felt a disquiet at his frequent surliness; sometimes he seemed to stop just short of snarling at her. And with this apparent disengagement of Ross, she also increasingly withdrew.

One evening a week before the trial Ross was busy fitting new tyres and brake pads to a customer's bike, plus some basic maintenance. The prospect of the trial together with uncertainty over the outcome meant he'd stopped taking on new work. The collection of bikes in the hall and chained to the railing on the landing had gradually dwindled, so that it was likely this current job would be his last, for the time being at least. He'd been thinking for a while that he should stop and clean up and get started on something for tea, but the occasional tot from the half-bottle of whisky he kept handy while he worked, plus all the warring thoughts swirling around his head, had left him feeling difficult and morose.

And at the root of this difficult mood was the fact that Fiona had taken to sleeping in the study so regularly that in a short space of time it had become established that they were no longer sleeping together. It had taken a while for Ross to take this in, and to realise that it wasn't just an occasional occurrence that could be put down (at a stretch) to courtesy in not wishing to disturb him after she'd been working late, but was instead quite clearly a permanent arrangement. And with this realisation came a resentment combined with bewilderment, the resentment at least partly fuelled by, and fuelling, the drinking - bitter that in his time of need she had withdrawn her affection and consolation - resulting in a near-constant mutinous feeling of having nothing much left to lose.

He heard the key in the lock, then the door opening and closing, the light clunk of a briefcase being put down next to the hall table, a knock on Grant's door, voices, various words exchanged. Then a hand on the living room door and the slight creak of the door opening. He concentrated on carefully checking the alignment of the chain. Fiona stood in the doorway, neither fully in nor fully out of the room. At last Ross stood up and turned to her.

'Are ye coming in, or are ye just on your way oot?'

She stared at him for a few moments as he coolly returned her gaze, then turned and left the room. Ross stood there, eyes closed, massaging his forehead, inadvertently leaving a few streaks of lubricating oil behind. Before he had an opportunity to work out his next move, the door opened again and Fiona came into the room.

'Have you had something to eat?'

'No.'

'Do you want something? I'm just going to make something quick.'

Ross shook his head.

'Fine. I'll just make something for Grant and myself then.'

She turned to leave.

'Wait,' said Ross. 'Have you got a minute?'

'Sure,' in a bright, unconcerned tone. 'What is it?'

'Let's sit down,' said Ross.

As they seated themselves, Ross in the armchair that faced the TV, Fiona on the sofa, Ross took in how

Fiona was dressed. Dark jacket and mid-length skirt suit with white shirt, restrained make-up, earrings, and a bracelet he hadn't seen before. She looked to his eyes even more attractive now than when they'd married fifteen years before. She'd never bothered particularly with what she'd worn in those early years at home looking after Grant - t-shirts, jumpers and jeans or tracksuit bottoms her usual get-up. To see her now, mature, business-like, elegant and poised, was disconcerting to Ross, who had never paid much attention to his own appearance, and felt unusually aware of the disparity.

He took a few deep breaths, then breathed out audibly in a sort of sigh. When it came to it he was reluctant to broach the subject that was principally occupying his mind, fearful of what her response might be. Also, he was finding it difficult to collect his thoughts. But after a few seconds more of indecision, he thought he might as well jump straight in, there being no way around it.

'So, what's going on, Fiona?'

Fiona was startled, and her mind began to race, trying to think of what Ross might have found out, and how - if indeed he knew anything and wasn't just shooting in the dark - and if he did know, for how long he'd known. She thought then of what there was to know. In the weeks since the first physical contact, the charged connection of hand pressed on hand, an intimacy had swiftly developed that stopped just short of sexual relations. They met outside work as often as they could and enjoyed coffee and dinners and drinks together, and walks through the city and visits to art galleries and historic monuments. And occasional trips further afield, to Stirling, or Edinburgh, or once across to Ayr and a walk on the sands hand in hand with the romantic outline of Arran as backdrop. A few hours snatched here and there from the working day, but often enough to excite comment and speculation among colleagues. A reciprocal emotional need had been established, an interconnectedness, such that there was no going back.

'I don't know what you mean,' she said at last, not knowing what else to say.

'Aye, a think ye dee.'

'Well...you'd better tell me what's on your mind, so that we both know.'

'Something's gan on. A know it.'

She remained silent, wondering how, when Ross came to the point, she would deal with it.

'Is there somebody else?' said Ross abruptly, speaking the words slowly and carefully.

'What do you mean?'

She felt suddenly outside her body, as if looking down, observing a scene in a play.

'Whit dae ye think a mean? Have ye met somebody else?' Again with slow, heavy emphasis.

'No.'

The word came out before she had a chance to contemplate the implications of denial.

'No?'

'No, there's nobody else.'

'Aye, is that right? Ye didnae seem surprised at the question.' He paused, looking closely into her face. 'So why dae ye no' sleep in the bedroom anymore?'

Relief, immediately tempered by the question itself, which brought its own difficulties. But at least it seemed clear that Ross knew nothing about her and Mark, and the calamitous moment of discovery, or necessary disclosure, had at least been postponed.

'I've just been really busy recently, so I've been working late in the study.'

'So why dee ye no' come through when ye're finished?'

'Well, the bed's just there in the room, and sometimes it's easier to just sleep in there sometimes as I'm already there.'

'That's bullshit. That's total fuckin bullshit, an' ye know it. An' it's no' sometimes noo, it's every night.'

Fiona appeared infuriatingly calm to Ross, though in fact she was feeling anything but.

'Okay, I…sometimes I just need my own space, Ross. I need my own space for a while, just to work some things out.'

'Your own space? Aye, an' what things are ye working oot? We're supposed to be husband and wife. Dis that no' mean sharin' the same bed? Isnae that the whole idea of it? Whit's the point in it otherwise?'

'There's a bit more to it than that, Ross, I hope.'

'What more to it is there fur us? Ye have yir own life workin at that place, Caledon fuckin Technology. An' a hardly ever see ye. Ye come in an' ye're in that spare bedroom fur the rest of the evening, an' now ye're sleepin in there. Whit the fuck's gan on?'

'Ross, stop shouting. Just calm down.'

'A'll no' calm doon. Dinnae tell *me* tae calm doon, ye cheeky wee bitch. Caledon Technology. What kind of a fuckin daft name is that? Caledonia, that's a historical name. Caledon means fuck all. It's just some stupid thing invented by one o' those smooth wee bastards ye work wi'.' The line of her mouth tightened. 'Is that whit's happening? Aye, a'll bet it's one o' those smooth wee bastards.'

'What is?'

'A'll bet it's one o' them ye're gan on wi'.'

'Don't be so stupid. I keep telling you I'm not having an affair. There's nobody else.'

'Dinnae try tae kid me. A know something's gan on.'

She got up. 'I'm going to make something to eat.'

'Sit ye doon. A havnae finished wi' this.'

'Well, I've finished with it.' And she made to walk out of the room. Ross jumped up and grabbed hold of her.

'What are you doing? For God's sake, Ross, you've been drinking again. You're drinking all the time now.'

'Aw the time now, is it? Is that whit it is? An' what difference dis it make to you one way or the other?'

'I said get off.'

He pushed her up against a wall, then tried to kiss her and at the same time made a grab for her breasts. Fiona, genuinely angry and upset at the impersonal crudeness of his advances, gave him a violent shove

143

which served to detach him, and he stumbled back a few paces, almost losing his balance against the sofa.

'Keep your hands to yourself, or I'm walking out right now.'

She left the room, and Ross, shocked by both her expression and the strength of her repulse, not knowing particularly what he was doing, snatched up his jacket and left the flat. He spent the next couple of hours wandering aimlessly. It was now quite dark, and the gates to the park were locked, so he spent the time tracing and re-tracing the familiar streets. He got back to the flat around nine, having thought of nothing and solved nothing. Everything seemed strangely, deceptively normal. The elegant hall table - a rare instance of Fiona's taste in the flat - complete with vase and cut flowers, familiar pictures on the wall, music coming from Grant's room. Ross looked up at the decorative coving he and Fiona had once spent several evenings painting together many years ago, and he could almost imagine that things were just as they had been. There was something eerie and mocking in the unchangingness. In the living room the bike was still upside down, resting on its handlebars and seat as he'd left it. He couldn't bear even to see it - at that moment it seemed somehow to symbolise the futility of his life - and he bundled it out into the hall, swept up all the tools and other sundries and deposited them next to it, then came back into the room, switched on the TV, and collapsed into the armchair.

Maybe if he went through to the study now and had a proper mature conversation with Fiona. Maybe that would set things right. The walk outside in the cold had woken him up to a degree, and he felt a little less fuzzy-headed. Maybe if he just went through right now they could talk things through and resolve all their problems, whatever they might be. He'd promise to do anything she wanted to set things right. He'd change his ways - stop drinking even, if he could. He'd try to fit in with whatever she wanted. He was desperate for physical contact, yet she kept herself aloof, which just made everything intolerable. If she could just bring herself to show that she cared for him, valued him. Yet stymieing any reasonable, conciliatory thoughts were feelings of underlying resentment, that she was so unconcerned about what may be about to happen to him. She had seemed to care at first - enough, at least, to express her anger that he'd got himself into such a stupid situation. Now he couldn't rid himself of the feeling that his life and future were of no interest or importance to her, and that she'd withdrawn into herself. It was no longer us, together against the world. The us-ness of their relationship had disappeared.

But by this time he was settled in his chair and loath to move, and a documentary had begun that at first took his attention and then entranced him. A film from the late 1950s following a team of drivers in the days of British Road Services with lorries in trademark red livery, and all home-grown makes - Foden, Leyland, Bedford, ERF, Bristol, Guy, AEC, Atkinson. He watched with that familiar gutted feeling of hopeless longing and regret for all that had been lost, the sooty buildings, the stone sett approaches to works yards, the phalanx of cranes and rows of dark sheds by murky rivers, smoke and steam from locomotives and engines everywhere, shrill wail and shriek of whistles, terraces with untold chimneys clustering nearby. On across a rolling wooded landscape to obscure stone-built factories down back streets of market towns, whisky distilleries, cement works, cattle markets, engineering works, tall chimneys in all directions. Vehicles carrying everything imaginable to all four corners of Scotland and beyond. A Scotland building, making, transporting things. And not an app in sight. You didn't need apps for that. Fecking bastard apps. A'd like tae take aw their feckin' apps an' shove 'em doon the throats of aw ye smooth wee bastards an' let ye aw choke on them. A vision that for a few moments gave Ross great satisfaction.

His solicitor, in a cold, bleak, bare office up worn stone steps on Cathcart Road (Ross thought afterwards he should maybe have considered that clutter, here noticeably absent, in the form of files and papers and boxes of documents, would have meant the solicitor was doing good business), was tall, thin, desiccated looking, with threadbare grey hair, long, lined cadaverous face and worn dark business suit, peering at him from pale, watery blue eyes through heavy glasses. He was particularly concerned that Ross should understand the full implications of any answers he gave in court, should he be questioned, and therefore, in short, take what he considered to be the only viable approach, though of course they still had to consult counsel. And it was moot at this stage whether counsel would call him to give evidence. But so slow and hesitant was he, spending so long peering at documents and statements without speaking, then referring to other documents and statements in Ross's file, before outlining his advice so slowly and with so many looks off to the side as if searching for inspiration in the bare cream walls of the office, that Ross found great difficulty in concentrating on what he was saying. Besides which, despite having made it clear he was pleading not guilty, and indeed considered himself guilty of nothing apart from making a stand against state-sponsored vandalism and defending himself against police violence, so far as he attended to or understood what the solicitor was on about, nothing that was said seemed to acknowledge or be appropriate to his plea, though it's true he had at first been earnestly advised to plead guilty, before Ross had dug his heels in.

'So, remember,' at their second and last meeting, and with counsel still not appointed, turning a pencil endlessly end over end, murmuring in a soft-spoken Highland accent as he reiterated much of the advice of the duty solicitor up in Tain, 'keep your eyes on the judge at all times. Remember that it's him, or her, that you're addressing, that is if at any point you are directly questioned. Whatever questions you're asked by your own counsel or prosecuting counsel - that is if counsel does call you to give evidence - remember to address your answers to the judge. It's him you need to convince of your contrition - that it was an isolated moment, an aberration in an otherwise unblemished life as a family man, caring for your family and bringing up your son, who is now, fifteen? - fifteen, soon to be sixteen, a dedicated scholar at an important stage of his schooling, taking his Highers next year, and so on. But I must emphasise once again, I strongly advise you not to make any reference to aesthetics or the built environment or the destruction caused by the new road project. The judge won't want to hear any of that. He will be looking for you to demonstrate humility and contrition, so you just need to be respectful and polite, and keep your eyes on him at all times. And then, hopefully, we should be in with a very good chance of receiving perhaps just a warning and possibly also a fine, or community service, or at the very worst a suspended sentence. Also, I should mention that the smarter your appearance, the better the impression you'll make. And the key, as I've said - to focus entirely on the judge, and to remember to direct all your answers to him, or her, if questioned, as he is the person you have to convince that this was a one-off occurrence, an aberration under stress, and that nothing would be achieved by a custodial sentence.'

Ross had nodded and agreed, just to get it over with - Aye, okay, he'd show contrition, and direct all his answers to the judge, him or her, if questioned, and he wouldn't say a word about why he'd really done it - about the clamouring madness in his head that senseless vandalism always brought about and the rage and confusion at the arbitrary destruction of beauty. Aye, he'd keep his mouth shut, and let all the slick, well-spoken lawyers in their expensive suits decide his destiny and sort it out among themselves, and he wouldn't say a feckin word.

But as he watched the bygone lorries and their team of dedicated drivers with their old-fashioned haircuts and dirty hands from real labour, and the functional and harmonious stone factories and warehouses rolling past, and the bright, nestling fishing harbours, and the sparkling eager rivers and rainswept mountains and glens, and imagined himself in one of those lorries traversing those winding, twisting roads (not excluding the unreconstructed arterial routes), through unspoilt landscapes and unmutilated towns and cities, any idea of contrition disappeared. This was exactly what he'd been fighting for all these years. This was why he'd done what he'd done, and he'd be damned if he'd tamely apologise for it. He wasn't guilty of anything, and he'd shout it from the rooftops if necessary, and maybe, aye just maybe somebody might actually listen.

11

On the morning of the day before the trial there was a tense, anxious atmosphere in the flat. It was eight o'clock, and everyone was up and about. Grant was already in his school uniform, sitting opposite his mother at the kitchen table. Ross in t-shirt, tracksuit bottoms and bare feet was cooking himself breakfast in the form of fried sausages and bacon, to be shoved between a couple of slices of bread. Fiona was trying to contain her irritation at the smell of frying, having just showered, thinking of the smell impregnating her clothes for the rest of the day. She went over to open the window, which Ross had neglected to do, then sat down again at the table.

For the past couple of days she'd been feeling an increased sympathy and sense of caring for Ross, and had made a determined effort to be more overtly friendly, though without Ross showing much sign of responding, as he began to insulate himself within himself, to construct a protective mental shield and build himself up for the ordeal ahead. Also for the past week or so he'd been attempting to substantially reduce his booze intake (wondering how he'd manage if he did end up in prison), which did nothing to improve his mood. His reaction to Fiona's more friendly approach was, if anything, to be more surly and offhand than ever, given that they were still not sharing a bed, but Fiona resolved to continue to be friendly, to smile and be conciliatory and soft-spoken, whatever response she received. She'd decided to overlook, though she couldn't forget, Ross's behaviour of a week or so ago, and had tried to calm their relationship.

Grant was sitting silently, apparently staring at the slices of toast his mother had made for him, but which he hadn't touched. He'd heard all the horror stories of prison, and knew all the over-familiar tropes of prison life from films. He didn't know how accurate or representative they were, or whether US prisons (from where most of the more unpleasant images derived) were worse and less civilized than prisons in the UK, but could only hope so. He could hardly bear to imagine his dad in some hideous place surrounded by violent and/or predatory lunatics, even though he knew Ross could take care of himself in normal circumstances.

Ross meanwhile didn't seem outwardly concerned about anything much. He finished making his fry-up sandwiches then came and sat down at the kitchen table and started to munch them. Fiona wondered whether her son, who had sat motionless for the past ten minutes, might show some sign of life now that his dad was at the table.

'Are you not going to have anything to eat, Grant?'

A slight shake of his head. 'I'm not hungry.'

Fiona glanced at Ross, who had his eyes on his food, then back to Grant. He looked so young still, and though his face had begun to change shape, his jaw to gain strength and definition, and his looks generally to lose that youthful, round innocent look that she so loved, there were still times, especially now when he was anxious, when Fiona thought he looked all of nine or ten.

'Well,' gently cajoling, as though he really were still that age, 'are you going to get ready for school, then? It's gone eight.'

'I am ready.' Pause. 'Can I not come up with you? It wouldn't matter just taking the odd day off school. There's nothing much going on just now anyway.'

'No, Grant.' Strain and irritation caused her to harden her voice. 'We've had this discussion. You can't afford to take time off school. Besides which, they're very strict nowadays about unauthorised absences. We're only going to be gone for one night - we'll be back tomorrow evening. And Grandma will be here when you get back from school.'

'A dinnae need someone tae look after me.'

'It's your grandma, Grant.'

'Aye, I know. It's not that.'

She looked to Ross for support, but he showed no sign of getting involved.

'Well, you're going to school, and that's that, so you'd best get ready.'

At this Grant scraped back his chair and banged out of the room.

Fiona was immediately sorry she'd raised her voice to him, and had to bite her tongue from the urge to say something to Ross for doing nothing.

Five minutes later, as Ross was making a coffee for Fiona and himself, Grant came back into the kitchen, backpack over his shoulder.

'Well, I'm off, then.'

He looked uncertainly towards his dad. Ross turned towards Grant and made himself look cheerful.

'Are ye on your way, then, Grant?'

'Aye, I'd better go.'

There was a pause while they looked at each other. Then Ross smiled. He felt a surge of emotion at Grant's pensive expression, and was caught between wanting to protect himself, and the desire to protect and comfort Grant.

'Well, we'll see ye tomorrow, nae problem. So anyway have a great day. And dinnae worry about any of this nonsense. It'll aw be fine. An' a'll be back tomorrow night, an' we can get back to normal.'

Grant nodded. 'Okay. Well...I hope everything goes okay.'

'Aye, it'll be fine. Go on, on your way. Take it easy.'

Grant nodded again, then turned and went out, and a few seconds later they heard the front door shut.

Ross took a deep breath and sat down, handing Fiona her coffee. She was glad he'd been able to make the gesture of trying to normalise the situation, and hadn't just shut Grant out. They sat in silence for a while, sipping their coffees.

'Ross?'

'Aye?'

'We need to discuss a few things.'

'Aye?' he repeated. 'Like what?'

She searched his face intently, a face she knew so well.

'I'm sorry things have come to this, Ross.'

He frowned, and looked confused.

'What dae ye mean?'

She paused, then seemed to pull back from whatever she might have been going to say.

'I just mean, you know, I'm sorry you're in this situation, and that things haven't worked out better.'

'Aye, well, that's the way it goes. Anyway, it'll all be done wi' soon, one way or the other.'

'You don't seem too worried about the outcome.'

'A cannae afford tae be worried. A have tae face whatever comes, an' a have tae - you know, tae face it, face it doon.'

'Yes, I know what you mean.' She paused again. Then, 'Do you have any idea...I mean, if things don't go the way we hope, do you know where you'll be sent?'

'The solicitor said most likely Grampian.'

'Where's that?'

'It's up in Peterhead, somewhere near Aberdeen. It's some new prison.'

Actually stating outright the hateful word prison was a shock for both of them. It seemed to hang in the air, and all its associated meanings ran through both their minds with chilling clarity.

'Why Grampian?' said Fiona at last, quietly, as if in awe at the very prospect. 'That's miles away. Why not somewhere local, within Glasgow, like Barlinnie?'

'I don't know,' said Ross. 'A think mebbe it has tae be local to the Sheriff Court the trial's held in, but a'm no' sure. A just asked him, an' he said maybe Grampian, and a didnae ask any more. Ma mind wis more on the hope that a wisnae gan to prison anywhere at all.'

She nodded, then hesitated before asking, 'Are you still planning to plead not guilty?'

'Aye, probably.'

She looked at Ross for a moment. 'So are you going to, you know, get tidied up a bit, get a haircut and a shave?'

'Aye? Should a buy maself a smart suit as well? A could gie maself a makeover, an' mek maself into a smooth wee businessman tae impress the judge. Do ye think that might dae the trick?'

Fiona looked momentarily exasperated.

'I'm not saying that. I'm just saying maybe you'd want to, you know, present yourself in the best possible light, for your own sake, and for Grant.'

'Grant?'

'I'm just saying, Ross, you will be sensible at this trial, won't you? Grant needs his dad around.'

Ross thought the implication of this was clear - that Grant needed him around, but that she didn't. Then he thought he was maybe reading too much into it. It was only a form of words, after all. And he knew he'd never been the brightest or quickest at interpreting the words

155

of others, or articulating his own thoughts - or formulating them, for that matter. She just meant Grant needs his dad, just as he needs his mother. You can tie yourself in knots if you start to read too much into other people's words, when most of the time they probably don't mean what they're saying anyway, or maybe aren't even sure what they mean, or what they feel. Aye, just let it go. So he just said, trying not be offended, Yes, he'd try to be sensible, if that didn't mean compromising his beliefs. But no, he wasn't changing his appearance to impress anybody. He'd be himself. Maybe that would be enough. Anyway we'll see.

Fiona sighed. 'What sort of time do you want to set off?'

'After dinner mebbe? There's no' going to be anythin' much tae do when we get there.'

She got up and washed out her cup at the sink.

'Aye fine. Well, I'd best go and collect the car.'

Ross had read up online on what he might be allowed to take into prison. So now, in an act that seemed hideously momentous, yet had mocking overtones of going on holiday, he began to pack a bag specially bought for the purpose with clothes, mainly underwear and socks, a couple of t-shirts and trousers, plus sundries - towels, wash bag with toothbrush, razors and nail clippers, diary, pen, alarm clock, address book, a few photos. He had no definite idea of what or how much of these he'd be able to keep, and only knew from what he'd read that at first much of it might be taken off him, and that he might well have to put up with prison issue clothing to begin with.

Fiona returned with the hire car, and after a quick bite to eat they set off north out of the city towards Stirling, across to Perth, and then the long trek up the A9 to Inverness, a journey made for the most part in silence. They took the scenic route where possible, there being no time imperative, Fiona thinking she might as well get some enjoyment out of the trip, so far as she could. Ross had plenty of time to consider the possibility of being in a prison cell by the next night. He had at least experienced being in a cell, so that aspect wouldn't be too much of a shock, though the photos he'd seen of cells at Barlinnie looked considerably smaller than the one he'd been in, and had to accommodate two people. It might be different at Grampian, a newly-built jail. Who he'd end up sharing a cell with, if he had to share, was something that concentrated the mind. It wasn't being negative or pessimistic thinking in these terms; it was necessary. To harden the mind, to prepare for the worst case scenario.

He wished it had been Barlinnie if it had to be anywhere. He knew it as a brooding masterpiece of Victorian design, one of the jewels of Glasgow's Victorian heritage. At least going there would have had some aesthetic interest. He knew also of its fearsome reputation and of all the hard, perverted, lunatic bastards that it had played host to over the years. He felt fairly confident of being able to hold his own against most, one-to-one, if he clicked back into his old mindset, formed and moulded in Drumchapel. Which was what he'd being doing, had to do. The only real element of fear he allowed himself or recognised at this point was the prospect of another, possibly longer, journey in the crushing confines of a prison van. Sweat box. Clearly he wasn't the only one who felt the fear. You could catch a glimpse of Barlinnie from the M8, just where you turn off to Stepps. You could even walk around part of it, as he'd done several times, a narrow road bounded on one side by modern tenements and semis, looking up at the great stone perimeter wall topped by barbed wire, and beyond it a glimpse of the tops of the prison blocks themselves. The distinctive cornicing, tall arched windows at each end, sculpted chimneys topped by octagonal pots. Ross loved the look of those tall chimneys, a forest of stone across the roofs of the five blocks.

What a wee cunt that Jimmy was, though. He couldn't get over the response he'd received from Jimmy when he eventually managed to get through to him and told him what had happened. Not a hint of concern or commiseration, in fact the opposite. Ill-concealed malice, mockery even - at least that's how it came across to Ross. Ye daft bugger, what the hell were ye deein? Aye well, enjoy your time in jail. Ah ye'll be fine. Just remember tae keep your back tae the wall. An' make sure ye dinnae drop your soap in the showers. Ross didn't care if he never saw the little bastard ever again. Living in Newcastle now with Clare life was just perfect, honestly Ross, couldn't be better, best decision of ma life tae leave Glasgow. Didn't miss that shithole one little bit. Clare was the woman of his dreams, they were renting a one bed flat together, Newcastle was the best place he'd ever been to, best night life in the world. Oh and he'd got a job as supervisor at a DIY chain. Paid him a fuckin fortune, and the job was a piece of piss. Ross just couldn't understand how the little bugger kept getting these jobs. He wouldn't give him a job shining shoes. He'd broken off all contact with his mother. He'd never get in touch with her or speak to her again. She was just a horrible, evil woman. Clare hated her too, couldn't stand her. Ross had cut the conversation short in disgust at Jimmy's cold self-absorption. Maz had at least expressed what sounded something like sincere sympathy at his plight in recent conversations, even though she was mainly concerned that Brian's haulage scheme looked to be actually taking off - he'd just had a business loan approved, and now she didn't know what the fuck to do, everyone was unsettled, Pixie was upset, the twins had indicated that they didn't want to move and had apparently been in contact with their father. It was all a fecking mess, thanks to that stupid fat cunt and all his daft ideas.

'How are you feeling, Ross?'

Ross looked up suddenly. The hum of the car and immersion in his problems had made him lose track.

'Aye, fine. Where are we?'

'It's about ten miles to Inverness, and then maybe another thirty or forty to Tain. Do you want to stop in Inverness?'

'Not unless you do. We might as well just get there.'

Apprehension was growing in his stomach, despite his best efforts. Just the thought that they'd soon be in Tain. They'd stopped in Pitlochry for a break and taken a walk through some woods, thinking how beautiful and peaceful it was, or rather would have been under different circumstances. He wanted to keep all reminders of anything to do with pleasure at arm's-length for now, and keep his mind hard to face his ordeal.

There was still a lot of Scotland that remained untouched and undamaged, to be fair. Some of the roads they'd covered on the way up, through places he'd never heard of, had looked fundamentally unchanged from when they must have first been developed as motor roads in the Twenties. The A9 had been completely screwed, though, back in the Seventies. Bits and pieces still survived, but the immersive experience - that was all gone, destroyed forever. He needed to remember, keep in mind, why he'd done what he'd done. An attempt, foredoomed no doubt, pointless, naive, to at least draw attention to another piece of aesthetic perfection being casually torn apart by destructive swine.

12

After a half-hearted attempt at breakfast, they agreed that Ross would go ahead to meet with his counsel, and that Fiona would follow for the trial itself. They didn't say goodbye to each other, as it didn't occur to either of them that there wouldn't be another opportunity if the verdict went against him. It was a cold, fresh October morning in Tain, with a certain harsh, unpitying quality to the air, reflected in the sombre, unsmiling face of this former royal burgh. Going on alone on the short walk to the court gave Ross the opportunity, by ducking down a side alley out of sight, to consume most of a small bottle of whisky he'd kept concealed in his jacket pocket for the purpose, which left him feeling immediately light-headed and insulated from proceedings to some degree. The thought that it might be his last drink for a long while he managed successfully to deflect, but remembered to pop a mint in his mouth to mask the whisky on his breath.

Ross finally met with his counsel, a barrister based in Inverness engaged at the last moment by his solicitor (more incompetence by that useless bastard). They shook hands just inside the court - Euan Alexander, Hello - and were directed to a vacant interview room. The barrister looked no more than thirty, tall, broad-shouldered, startlingly good looking with bright, attentive blue eyes and a mop of light brown hair carelessly brushed back - a matinée idol, thought Ross, if ever he'd seen one. When he spoke, it was with just the kind of Edinburgh accent that Ross particularly disliked, that too precise, mincing, sing-song diction, soft and insidious, with those extended, sliding vowel sounds that seemed to reek of effortless, disdainful superiority. To Ross his voice epitomised that continuum of privilege (as he imagined it) from wealthy background and expensive public school to grouse shooting on the moors and an inexorable upwardly mobile path in the professions. Even the building they were in, a fine stone structure in the Scottish baronial style, all turrets and steep gables, seemed to speak of entrenched privilege and dour, judgemental conservatism. Ross suddenly knew with absolute clarity that he hadn't got a chance in this place, and had an unexpected flash of his father, working in all weathers and in dangerous conditions his whole life, and felt an abrupt, savage anger that the Socialism of the post-war period hadn't gone further and deeper.

The whisky seemed to have gone to his head, making him feel both relaxed and combative, almost belligerent. Having tried to cut down during the week before the trial, the sudden injection of alcohol seemed to be having a disproportionate effect. Now he really couldn't give a shit, and whatever this dandy wee specimen in front of him might tell him to do, he'd say exactly what he wanted in court, and to hell with the consequences, and maybe something might even get into the local press, maybe make people think a bit, though even in his present high-flown state of mind he knew it would make no difference. But there was no need for that accent - it was just a ridiculous affectation - the professional Scotsman, reeking of heather and the kilt. It was as bad as all those tourist traps on the Royal Mile selling a fatuously sanitised brand of Scotland, when the real Scotland was gritty and grubby, dark and tough, built on hard labour, sweat, blood and ingenuity. But there you go, everything was being ripped away, trodden underfoot and generally pissed on by all the smooth wee fucks in smart suits. Ross, preoccupied with his barrister's accent, and feeling scruffy and inadequate by comparison with the handsome young lawyer sitting alongside him, found it difficult at times to concentrate on what was actually being said, and therefore didn't take much in from the meeting. In fact, he couldn't take his eyes off the guy's shoes; never in his life had he seen such long, pointed, shiny shoes. They made him think of a pair of sleek liners about to glide down the slipway into the Clyde.

After introducing himself his counsel apologised for the last minute nature of the meeting, and also that he hadn't had time to familiarise himself with the case, and would Ross excuse him if he quickly read over the notes in the file. Aye, nae problem, though Ross felt that this was just fecking great, dinnae expect much oot of this. In the silence he thought of the last half inch or so of whisky in the bottle in his pocket, and wished he could have just a wee taste.

'Right. Okay. So, Mr McKenzie, I understand that you're still determined to plead not guilty to the charges against you, which are...' shuffling the papers, '...vandalism, resisting arrest, and assault. Is that correct?'

'Dae ye mean are those the charges against me, or am a still determined tae plead not guilty?'

The barrister gave him a quizzical look, as if he wasn't sure whether Ross was attempting a joke.

'I'm asking you to confirm your plea of not guilty.'

'Aye, that's right.'

'Well, I would still, even at this late stage, strongly advise you to change your mind. There would really seem to be nothing to be gained, as all the evidence appears to support the prosecution case. And there's little doubt that the Sheriff would take a more lenient approach in terms of sentencing if you did plead guilty.'

'A'm no' changing ma plea.'

'Can I ask why?'

'Because a did what a did fae good reasons. An' as fur the assault charge, a wis jus' defendin' maself fae the polis.'

Mr Alexander nodded. He was no clearer in establishing Ross's motives, but decided to press on anyway.

'Okay. So. Just to go over the main features of the case. Now, you were on holiday.'

'Aye.'

'Just for the week?'

'Aye.'

'And your holiday cottage was situated adjacent to the coast road?'

'Aye.'

'Close to it, at least. Situated at the end of its own private track. But roughly adjacent. And the coast road, as I understand it, is undergoing a programme of improvement.'

'That's one way of puttin it.'

'Then at least of realignment, straightening, and widening.'

'Aye,' said Ross, feeling a cold anger at the very thought.

'And you objected to this?'

'A dae object tae it.'

'On aesthetic grounds.'

'Aye, if ye want tae put it that way.'

'So would you say this was a gesture of protest, or of anger?'

'A bit of both.'

'Right. I see.' He was making notes as they spoke. 'So. Now, the form of protest that you employed was to cause damage to contractors' equipment on a depot situated close or adjacent to the road. Is that correct?'

Why the fuck dis he keep saying adjacent. 'Aye, that's correct.'

'So would you say this was mainly a calculated act, this attempt to sabotage equipment at the depot site, that is an act that you had premeditated, planned in advance, or was it predominantly a spur of the moment expression of anger at the, as you saw it, unwarranted destruction of something that you viewed, or view, as having aesthetic value?'

What the fuck. 'It wisnae planned in advance as such. A knew aboot the scheme, but a wis just wantin tae see what wis bein done.'

'And then events got out of hand.'

'Aye, ye could say that.'

'So we can reasonably say, that there was no premeditation of either doing damage, or instigating or being involved with the subsequent violence.'

'It wisnae me started any violence. A wis just breakin a few windaes when aw of a sudden a had four feckin great polis jumpin on top of us and kicking the shit out of us.'

'I think...yes, the police claim that when they arrived, you were engaged in causing damage to equipment on the site. And when they approached you and attempted to make an arrest, you actively and violently resisted, causing injury to two of the officers.'

'It wis them started tae push me aboot. A wisnae resisting arrest. Aye, awrite, they may have said they were arrestin' us, but then a couple of 'em started tae push us aroond. An' that's when a thought, the fuck wi' this, an' a started tae defend maself. Four cops in two patrol cars. A dinnae know where the feck they came fae in the middle o' nowhere. Anyway, it wisnae anythin much. A just mebbe pushed a couple of them aroond a wee bit.'

'It says in the report that you hit one officer on the left ear, causing considerable pain and resulting in a ringing in the ear which persisted for several hours afterwards, necessitating an out-patient visit to hospital. And in the case of the second officer, you hit them directly in the solar plexus, causing the officer to sink to the ground, where he remained for several minutes while he recovered his breath and composure.'

'It wis me who was on the ground wi' ma heid pushed intae it, an' the polis hittin an' kickin us in the ribs an' kidneys. A' wis pissin' blood fur a couple of days after. Anyway it wis four against one. An' truth tae tell a hardly touched them. It wis nothin. A've told aw this tae the solicitor already,' he added.

'Yes I know, Mr McKenzie, but I just wanted to hear your story in your own words, so that I can gain a clear picture of the situation.'

He was silent for a few moments, rustling the sheets of notes again as he glanced through them.

'In your own mind then, you were the victim of police violence when being arrested, and all you did was strike out in self-defence.'

'Aye, that's aboot it.'

'Okay. So. Did you get your injuries checked out by a doctor when you were taken into custody?'

'Nah. A wisnae given the opportunity. A wis bundled intae a cell an' that wis it till a wis brought intae the court the next morning.'

'Right. Okay. And you were treated okay at the police station?'

'Aye, fine. It wisnae exactly the height of luxury, but a wisnae knocked aboot any more, if that's whit ye mean.'

167

'Okay. Fine.' Pause. 'I'm just looking at the notes from your solicitor here. Hmm. Hmm. Yes. So.'

Ross grimaced. He didn't think this smooth wee laddie had any more idea what he was about than the other one. And that fecking accent - where has he come oot fae, some kind of time capsule? How does a young guy in the modern world get away wi' talkin like that?

'Right. So. I have to agree with your solicitor that it would be better not to refer too much to your motives for doing what you did.'

'Whit dae ye mean?'

'Well, what I mean is that it would perhaps be better to say in mitigation that this was very much a one-off incident, that you were under stress at the time - we needn't go into specifics - we could just refer to private personal matters - and that you experienced something of an inexplicable meltdown, when everything boiled over, and you were hardly even aware of what you were doing. And that as far as the assault on the police officers was concerned, you were caught by surprise, and were simply acting in self-defence. You didn't hear any words informing you that you were being placed under arrest, and the officers were on top of you before you realised what was happening. At the same time, you would like to offer a profound and sincere apology for any hurt or injuries caused, as you were not fully aware of what you were doing at the time. I think something along those lines might be the best approach - to make at least a show of contrition, even if you believe there were, in fact, very good reasons in your own mind at the time for doing what you did.'

'So ye just want us tae tell a pack o' lies then? Is that the plan?'

'I'm not suggesting that we tell any untruths. What I would suggest, however, is that we exercise a certain degree of caution. It's not necessary to go into chapter and verse about your true, inner motives. If you are questioned by the Sheriff, be reticent in your replies. Be polite, be brief, and try to demonstrate a sincere and humble contrition, at least so far as the assault on the police is concerned. I'm sure such an approach would go down well in your favour. And hopefully - '

The door opened and a small, balding man in glasses came in, whispered in the barrister's ear, then left the room again. Ross felt like some character in a play who doesn't know who half the other actors are, isn't sure of how to play his part, and has in any case forgotten all his lines.

'Okay. Now. They're ready for us, so we need to go through to the courtroom. I'll be assisted by my colleague, Mr Muir, who came in just now, and who will take notes. So, Mr McKenzie, do you feel ready?'

Ross felt thoroughly confused and isolated. He didn't feel as if he knew what he was doing, or what he would say to any questions put to him, or why he was there. The whole affair was bloody stupid. It was meaningless. This was all a pantomime, a charade. All these people were playing parts, not very well at that, yet taking it all so seriously. It was ridiculous. The long, serious faces, when anybody could see that the whole affair was fecking stupid. Somebody had been trying to destroy something that was beautiful, and he'd tried in his own small way to stop them. That's all there was to it. He got up, picked up the bag he'd packed that morning, and followed the barrister. On the way Ross felt in his pocket. The bottle was still there, tempting and inviting. Quickly he took out the bottle, unscrewed the cap and drank off the rest of the contents, wiping his mouth with the back of his hand.

Fiona had persuaded Ross to wear a jacket, so he'd worn an old black one he'd found at the back of the wardrobe, but still insisted on wearing jeans and a pair of trainers. He'd read that if you end up going to prison you'd be taken straight there in the shoes you had on, so shiny new footwear wouldn't be the best thing to go with the worn and tattered prison clothing you'd likely be given. Still, he might have given his hair and beard a trim. He felt like the wild man of the woods as he made his way into the courtroom. The first thing Ross noticed, before being shown where to go by the court officer directing him, was Fiona sitting to his left in the public seats. He caught her eye, and she gave him a small smile. She too was playing her part, that of concerned and supportive wife. He felt like laughing out loud at this mock-up courtroom and all these people playing their roles with such fatuous solemnity. Though to be fair to Fiona she had at least summoned up a smile, appropriate to her part. In fact you had to give them all credit, they were all diligently doing their best. He determined at once not to be intimidated by all the po-faced ritual, black gowns and wigs. They were just puppets on a stage, slavish tools of a system that destroyed without sense or discrimination. And it was all dead tradition, the archaic forms of address and procedure. He was struck by the irony, that this was just the kind of stability and continuity that he craved, and yet he despised formality and entrenched forms of process. The fact that he hadn't eaten much that morning, or the day before, and that he had drunk very little during the preceding week, meant that now, with half a bottle of neat whisky coursing through his system, he felt a burst of aggressive confidence, albeit through something of a haze, and refused to be overawed by the formality. After all, take away all the ritual and solemnity and you're left with a bunch of wee people reciting formulas that have been employed thousands of times before. It was all just meaningless rote.

Everybody rose as the Sheriff entered the room, followed by mutual bowing between the Sheriff and the other court officials. The case was announced and Ross called forward to take his place between two G4S security guards in the accused box - a pointless precaution, as he'd been completely free for the past two months to run hog wild if he'd wanted to, and if he was going to go crazy in the courtroom, it would take more than those two to stop him. The layout of personnel seemed pretty much as on his previous appearance, with a cop on security duty, the lawyers all huddled together, the court officer that showed him in, the clerk of the court. Fiona was the only person observing from the public area, and somebody he took to be a journalist in a seating area close to the witness box. Mr Alexander stood to announce that he appeared for Ross McKenzie, who pleaded not guilty to the charges on the indictment. The Sheriff, a short, round-faced elderly woman in a black robe that seemed to enfold her, with a wig perched on top of her head, and her own hair, white and cut short, visible beneath it, peered over the top of half-moon glasses at Ross as his plea was given in a way that, had Ross not been in a state of semi-intoxication, feeling both detached and contentious, might have sent a chill through his soul.

The procurator fiscal opened proceedings, making the case for the Crown against Ross. She was a tall, youngish woman with untidy straw blonde hair and a long, angular face that reminded Ross of a Halloween mask, with a severe, thin gash for a mouth, a soft voice and cold manner. She called the cops he'd tussled with as witnesses, as well as the security guy at the site. In examination she established Ross's wild behaviour at the time of the alleged offences, his attack on the officers and the injuries they'd received, necessitating, as she elicited, hospital treatment. On that day he was, she suggested, out of control, violent, and wholly unwilling to cooperate with them or desist in his violent behaviour, and the officers agreed that this was the case.

Cross-examined by Mr Alexander, tall, debonair and assured, a suggestion was put to the officers, gently, sorrowfully and with only a hint of reproach, that their testimony was a pack of lies, and that in fact it was his client who had been on the receiving end of a dose of police brutality, resulting in a black eye, abrasions to his face as a result of having it forcibly pushed down into the ground, numerous bruises all over his body from repeated punches and kicks, and internal trauma sufficiently severe as to result in Mr McKenzie passing blood for several days. At this point the Sheriff intervened, asking whether Mr McKenzie had been examined by a doctor following his arrest, and whether there was any medical report extant confirming these alleged injuries. Mr Alexander had to inform her in a grave tone that, regretfully, his client was not at any time afforded the opportunity of receiving medical attention. She nodded slightly, and went back to her notes.

Ross was impressed. The wee laddie was doing far better than he'd expected. But the briskness of proceedings took him by surprise, engaged as he was for much of the time in rehearsing what he would say, given the chance, putting the whole business into perspective, explaining and fully justifying his actions. He found himself focusing rather on the face of the prosecutor than anything she was saying, and especially on the way words escaped those compressed lips, which seemed hardly to move or open as she spoke. He saw himself in the witness box facing her uncanny look. Yes, he'd always lived in Glasgow. Yes, he was self-employed. Repairing and servicing bikes. Yes, they'd gone up to the Highlands in August for a week's holiday. Why did you go to the contractor's site, Mr McKenzie? What purpose did you have in mind? Would he at this point have followed his barrister's advice - what was it, something about being under stress and having personal problems. But that would be to admit that it was all meaningless, random vandalism. And the vandalism wasn't what he'd done - what did a few broken windows signify against what was about to happen to that road and the landscape it passed through. That's what was so fucking crazy. I was there because I'd heard they were making changes to the main road, and I wanted to see what damage was being done. Never mind the road, Mr McKenzie. Why did you go to the contractor's depot? Was it because you're obsessed? Was it because you've lost all sense of proportion? Why did you attack the police who were after all only doing their jobs? Was it because you're a violent man, Mr McKenzie, with a violent history even as a youth? Was it because you've lost all sense of reality? Or is it the case that your hold on reality has always been tenuous? Would you agree that you have always lived in some kind of a dream world, a world that must conform to your idea of aesthetic perfection? Is it not the case that you have always had a predisposition for violence? Is it not true that in the past you have had links with anarchist groups? I suggest to you, Mr McKenzie, that you have always found it difficult and unduly confining staying within the societal and legal norms and boundaries that govern everybody else. You don't think these laws and customs apply to you, do you, Mr McKenzie?

It seemed to Ross that they'd only just got under way when he realised that the prosecutor was summing up the case against him, in rather more measured terms than his imagination had taken him. Followed directly by Mr Alexander, who told the court that on the day in question his client had only been defending himself, at no time had he heard any words to suggest he was being arrested, had lashed out only in self-defence, was nevertheless sorry for any injuries caused, but was in no sense the prime instigator, having been taken completely by surprise by the heavy-handed attack from the police, was in any case only at the contractor's site as a result of certain family tensions, had no memory of why he went there or how he'd got there, felt remorse for the alleged injuries suffered by the police, and wished to assure the court that this was a one-off, isolated incident that would never be repeated. Was in fact a devoted family man with no previous criminal record, actively involved over many years in the raising of his son - a talented scholar with an excellent academic record, now on the cusp of taking his Highers - and who wished only for the opportunity to put this incident behind him and return to his family and to his altogether law-abiding and productive life. Fiona, listening to all this, was surprised and irritated, both by this glowing picture of Ross, and at the suggestion of family tensions as a motive for Ross's actions, which seemed somehow to implicate her.

When all the arguments for and against had been made, and all the witnesses examined and cross-examined, and with both lawyers having finished presenting their cases and given it their best shot for their respective sides, all that remained was for the Sheriff, who had been assiduously making notes throughout, to give her judgement and pronounce sentence. Ross realised with a start that he wasn't to be given an opportunity to put his side of things. He'd never been told whether he'd be called to give evidence - it had never been mentioned by his barrister - and such was the rushed, last minute nature of their first and only meeting that very morning, he'd never thought to ask. It had all taken place without a word from him, yet everyone else had had their say. Suddenly he was fired up, determined to speak, to have his say, just as he'd always intended.

'Ross McKenzie, would you stand, please.' Ross stood up. 'I have listened carefully to the evidence presented in this trial, and to the arguments put forward by both the prosecution and defence in summing up. It is clear to me that you did wilfully, and without reason or provocation, trespass on the contractor's site, causing damage to equipment stored there, and that in resisting arrest you assaulted police officers in the lawful execution of their duty, resulting in injury to two of the officers. Your behaviour was appalling and totally reprehensible. I therefore have no hesitation in finding you guilty of all the charges against you. In sentencing I have taken into account - '

It was at this point that Ross interrupted the Sheriff, to her initial astonishment, and began to speak of the senseless destruction of that beautiful road through the Highlands landscape, and of needless vandalism not just there, not just to roads, but to so much of the built environment everywhere. He spoke not with any great fluency or clarity, but still it felt so good to express what he felt after the constraint of having to listen to other people talk about things that were irrelevant to the bigger picture. The Sheriff, her round face pale and angry, tried several times to interject, until finally she called loudly, over the top of Ross, for the court to be cleared, and he was hustled by security, unresisting but still declaiming, from the courtroom into the waiting area.

After a few moments the door to the courtroom opened and his barrister came across with swift strides to where Ross had been forcibly seated. Bending low so that his face was inches from Ross's, speaking softly but urgently.

'What on earth do you think you were doing?'

'A wis puttin ma point of view across,' said Ross indignantly. 'A wis no' given the chance at any other time.'

'You do realise that that was about the worst thing you could possibly have done. Anything that suggests a hint of anarchy or of attacking the status quo and the established modes of procedure won't sit well with the Sheriff, to put it mildly. Well, we'll just have to wait for the outcome of all this now.'

They didn't have to wait long. After a couple of minutes all parties were called back into the court. It was clear from both her words and tone that the Sheriff had taken a dim view of Ross's outburst, and that she felt he needed a sharp corrective.

'Ross McKenzie, your behaviour in court has been disgraceful. I have not seen any evidence that you have learnt from this experience, or that you feel any genuine remorse for your actions. I therefore sentence you to six months in prison, where you will have opportunity to reflect on the consequences of your behaviour. Would the escort take the prisoner away, please.'

Ross would never know for sure whether the Sheriff changed or reversed the sentence as a result of his intervention, and whether he in fact snatched defeat from the jaws of - hardly victory, but at least release from custody and the possibility of a different future. It would be something that played on, often consumed his mind, in the months ahead. As he was being led from the courtroom he looked back into the public seating area. Fiona was looking towards him, but in the quick glance that time allowed, he couldn't quite make out her expression.

Once more the ordeal of confinement in the prison van, though less oppressive than before through familiarity, and also being this time in a state of mixed despair, defiance and stoical acceptance of his fate. As Ross was discharged from the van, and took in the uninspiring sight of HMP Grampian, relief at his release from the claustrophobic cell in the van was immediately tempered by contemplation of the procedures, likely humiliations, possible confrontations, and inevitable severe restrictions on every facet of his existence that lay ahead, and he felt an appropriate fear and dread.

Madness

13

A cold and rainy November day, and Fiona was in the grip of obsession. The enormity of what she was contemplating no longer shocked her. If she went through with it - but no longer if, only when. That was the thing, when - and how? Not how as such, but rather how to deal with all the repercussions. She sometimes had dark periods of anxiously mulling over the possible repercussions. They would just have to take care of themselves. Her parents, her sister Morag - what would *they* say? Who knows, but whatever it was, it wouldn't be the end of the world. It would all blow over in time, things always do. People can adjust to almost anything. It would all be resolved. Grant. He'd hardly been communicating of late. Cutting school, which was worrying in terms of his education, and also was creating problems with the school authorities. It was the knock-on effect, exactly as she'd predicted and what she'd been most afraid of. He was almost sixteen. He'd be sixteen in February. He wasn't a baby any more. That would have been different. There's no way she'd even be contemplating - well, anything, if that had been the case.

She was taking a day's holiday from work, meeting Mark in town, ridiculously happy at the prospect. She wasn't even bothered about the sleety rain, such was her euphoria at seeing him outside of work again. The madness of their feelings for each other. Over the past few weeks they'd been making the rounds of art galleries, any pretext for spending time together; today the Museum of Modern Art. She looked out of the bedroom window, peering down, having to work around the tall central mirror and hinged side mirrors of the heavy, ugly dressing table, dating from the Thirties, so they were told when they'd picked it up for a tenner from a local junk shop. Ross had said it had great character, proper solid furniture, and just think of all the women who'd sat there and admired themselves in it over the years. She'd found it funny at the time watching him, after a couple of guys from the shop had laboriously manhandled the thing all the way up the stairs, sitting polishing the glass of the mirrors with a duster, peering in all the little drawers as though there might be jewellery or hidden treasures left there. Just as if the clunky thing had been intended for him, an incongruity she'd found highly amusing. The street glistened, people hurrying along the pavements, heads down or under umbrellas that looked from a top floor flat like strange autonomous creatures with multi-coloured carapaces.

She refused any longer to be taken for granted and used as a sexual plaything. That's what it felt like, given that there was little else now to their relationship. And when you considered she was the one earning practically all their income. Lately finding herself looking back, re-evaluating. It sounded terrible even to think it, but Ross being in prison - it had now been a month - had given her the opportunity not just to try on for size new and novel freedoms such as having the flat to herself much of the time, but also the leisure and motivation to review the past. And when she looked back at the choices that had been made along the way - major decisions affecting the family, from buying the flat to not owning a car to not spending money on decent furniture to the way they'd decorated the flat - a thousand other things - she realised that they'd all been made by Ross, and it had simply been assumed that she would be happy to go along with it. That she'd done so had been partly because it was easier, the path of least resistance. And in the early years she had been very young. Only a year younger than Ross, but somehow it seemed more, and also seemed to count for more. And then she was pregnant with Grant and often tired and depressed, oppressed by all the responsibilities and restrictions, herself only just out of school. But also it was a state of mind, a learned response, accepting that somebody else orchestrates and directs the show, makes all the big decisions, such that it becomes strange to oppose anything, or even attempt to assert yourself. Learning instead to assume a state of passivity.

But then with Grant at school she'd somehow managed to shake off her sense of dependence, and with it her apathy and inertia, studied hard, and made a career for herself, thank God. And met Mark. She was surprised, chastened even, at how little she felt for Ross at this point, surprised also at how little guilt she felt at this. Even her sympathy for his predicament was tempered by the feeling that he'd brought everything on himself. Gazing at herself in the dressing table mirror. The elation of being in love. At thirty five everything has so much more depth and meaning than any hormone-driven infatuation of the teenage years. No more letting time slip away. If she didn't make the break now, she never would. In clearer, calmer moments, she could still step seamlessly from the future she was eagerly hoping and planning for, back into the life she at present inhabited. For a brief time able to slip between the two different worlds. And if she did step back permanently no-one would ever know, apart from Mark. It would just have been a blip, to be remembered wistfully, longingly, or with embarrassment, or disbelief, or maybe hardly ever at all. A memory that might just as well have been a dream, an experiment of the imagination, a flight of fancy, the whim of an imaginist. No, there could be no turning back.

She was interested in the changes to her face since she'd turned thirty, coolly assessing the image staring steadily back at her, beginning to apply her make-up. Thirty really did seem to be the tipping point so far as looks went. She could clearly see the signs, the fatty tissue under the eyes, the distinct crease lines pretty much everywhere, but especially around the eyes when she smiled. So the trick was not to smile too much. Skin showing the first signs of losing the elasticity of youth. The first areas of grey. Of course it depended on the lighting as to how bad it all looked, and also how hard you'd hit the booze and fags from teen years. Luckily she'd never smoked, had never thought it looked cool, and drank only rarely, perhaps as a reaction to Ross's drinking habits. No second chances, that's why you've got to go for it. And Grant *was* almost sixteen, almost old enough to leave home. She couldn't, mustn't let that hold her back.

There was still the worry as to what her family would say. Morag had never been the doting older sister. Two years older, she'd never taken much interest in Fiona, in fact she couldn't recall Morag playing with her at all when they were little. In later years Fiona had always found her distant, and somewhat dull. Limited. No, that was unfair. Not that there was ever any acrimony, but simply no connection. She played football for a local team, training in the evenings when the cafe was closed. They had a fixture list each season that sometimes took her away, usually at weekends, at which point their father would step in from semi-retirement and run the cafe. Strange the quirks of genetic inheritance. Morag had inherited her father's looks, the wiry frame and dark, thin face, but also her mother's reserved, rather taciturn nature, whereas Fiona looked more like her mother, but in character was outgoing like her dad. Morag never interacted much with the customers, preferring to keep her distance. Maybe why her dad had been so keen for her, Fiona, to work there, hoping that Morag would work in the chippy instead; she was a good worker, just not that great at customer relations. She put the final touches to her eyebrows, then brushed

185

her hair once more, checking the finished effect in the mirror. Rain or maybe sleet suddenly clattered against the pane, a squally burst caught by the wind. They were the original single-glazed windows, and therefore must be preserved forever, no matter that they offered zero insulation in winter and were impossible even to crack open in summer. It was a matter of aesthetic integrity.

She dabbed on a little perfume, something she had never been accustomed to using in the past, and suddenly wondered, as had never occurred to her before, whether Ross had ever noticed, and whether catching her uncharacteristic scent had ever filled his mind with images of secret liaisons, and if that had been behind his outburst before the trial. She stood up, and began to gather her things. And what of her parents, themselves a model of marital fidelity. After initial doubts about Ross they'd come to like him, and if he'd never made a proper career for himself, she thought they saw him as being at least pleasant and harmless. They'd been shocked and dismayed by the court case. They just couldn't believe it of Ross. She went through to the hall and slipped on her coat. The thing that had always struck her with her parents, growing up and in recollection, was that they were always talking to each other, always chattering away, her father usually taking the lead. She remembered as a child how reassuring it had been to hear the muffled, conversational murmur from their bedroom as she lay in bed. She'd hoped, perhaps, for something similar for herself. But Ross had always tended to go his own way, to be in his own world, either brooding silently about something, or watching TV, or out on a drinking spree, or at one of his meetings or protest marches. They'd never had that consolatory, unforced, easy back and forth exchange of thoughts and inconsequential chat. It was just that easy connection with Mark that she loved so much, a connection that had been apparent right from the start.

Her feelings for Mark were still at that initial highly irrational stage of intense hero-worship and more than borderline obsession. And her increasing feelings of dismissal and disdain for Ross were the corollary to this. He had to be negligible; it was necessary that everything should be clear cut, sharply divided into black and white, as the only possible justification for what she was about to do. Mark had to be everything that Ross was not. And so all her loyalties had transferred to Mark, completely and without reservation. Yet still there was a shadow over everything, in that Mark continued to live with his wife. But then so did she, to all appearances. Spouse, that is. But what if Mark decided, under pressure from Janet, to remain with her. No, no, impossible. The perfect man (for her), by definition, would never betray their love. One day, and soon, she hoped, they would, surely must, be together. Yet Janet *was* almost ten years younger, a nagging worry if you allowed yourself to think about things too much.

They greeted each other, embraced and kissed on the steps underneath the grandiloquent portico, then made their way inside, his hand on her back guiding her in a display of proprietorial affection, through an inner entrance door into the first hall of exhibits. Fiona loved the feeling of demonstrative caring and protection, the little courtesies and physical demonstrations of affection, something she'd never experienced with Ross, who'd never bothered overmuch with the niceties even in the early days. 'You look wonderful in that coat, Fiona. Very elegant.'

She was just undoing the buttons and shaking droplets of rain from the sleeves of a newly purchased long black coat.

'Thanks,' smiling. 'It is rather nice. I'm just worried that I've ruined it already. It's suede, and I never should have worn it in the rain. Anyway, too late now. So how's everything at work?'

'Oh, I left everyone busy and fully occupied, I think.'

'Not occupied with speculation about us, I hope,' murmured quietly.

'Hopefully not. There's nothing much we can do if there is gossip, apart from being more careful, which we have been.'

Inside the ground floor hall there were a number of exhibits arranged on the floor, and one large installation against the far wall spreading out into the room, which seemed to consist mainly of bin bags and large quantities of sand and gravel, interspersed with jam jars, glass bottles and other containers filled with a colourless liquid, presumably water.

'You know, I always feel with these kind of exhibitions, that the spaces that contain them are often more interesting than the artworks themselves.'

Mark laughed. 'Perhaps you're just not attuned to conceptual art.'

'Are you?'

'Is anybody?'

'Well, I don't know. I mean, take that for example. What on earth is that supposed to signify? It's hardly beautiful, so it must either mean something, or have some function.'

'Why must it? Can't it be exactly what it appears to be, which in this case seems to be three pieces of cardboard - or is it hardboard - loosely attached in a rough pyramidal shape, and apparently spray painted by somebody in a great hurry. Can't that mean something?'

'Yes? Like what?'

'I've no idea. Probably some profound nihilistic idea concerning the meaninglessness of existence. The usual sort of thing.'

'But it's just standing there like...'

'Discarded junk? Exactly. That's why it's so profound.'

They laughed, and passed on to the next exhibit.

'Wow. Is it just me, or is that not seriously pornographic?'

'I think it depends which end you view it from - oh, good God, I see what you mean. Let's pass on swiftly. Ah now, what about this one? I like this.'

Fiona frowned. 'It's an opened box of tissues on a plinth. What in God's name is the point of that?'

'Well, I think I'd be right in saying,' going over to read the description attached to the wall, 'that the main thrust of intention in this artist's oeuvre is to challenge and confront the meaning of traditional aesthetic values, while also questioning societal norms and codes, and this piece in particular revels in its moral ambiguity. The physical presence of a box of tissues in a fresh and surprising context creates a ripple effect in the minds of viewers that subverts and overturns all previously held value structures, and forces the onlooker to reconsider the way they negotiate social intercourse both in the public and private spheres.' Mark turned to Fiona. 'So now you know.'

She nodded. 'These artists certainly know how to talk the talk.'

'Oh look, there's an open cardboard box.'

'So there is. Do you think it's by the same artist as the box of tissues?'

'It could be. I wonder if there's anything in it... No, it's been left deliberately empty.'

'I wonder what that signifies.'

'I would guess, without troubling to read the description, that it's something to do with the emptiness of female lived experience within a male-dominated consumer society.'

'As trite as that. Look, there's some photographs pinned to the wall. They're not very clear, though.'

'No, they're not. Clearly the photographer didn't have access to a decent camera, which is unfortunate. It says here that the - oh, I see - deliberately grainy images create a complex correspondence between the physical objects they purport to represent, and the image or images of these objects that we all carry in our memories, creating a dissonance often presenting as a sense of nausea as the several realities collide in the ether of our imagination.'

Fiona shook her head. 'That so little could mean so much.'

'And here we reach the main exhibit.'

'There's a lot of rubbish bags gone into this. I wonder if they could be re-used or recycled when this is dismantled.'

'I don't think so - they're all taped together. I think...that this represents an oasis, with the promise of cool, life-giving water represented by all these containers.'

'And the bin bags?'

'I think they represent night. A sandy oasis stumbled upon in the wastes of a desert in the dead of night. A traveller's wet dream, you might say.' Fiona pulled a face. 'Sorry, not funny. But also a metaphor for hope in an increasingly dark world.'

'Why don't we go and read what it's actually intended to mean.'

'I don't think I can be bothered, personally. Why don't we go and check what's on the next floor instead.'

Fiona caught sight of her reflection in the chrome and glass of the lift doors as they waited for the lift to arrive, and could hardly believe the almost glamorous image. She'd never been a girly type of woman, obsessed by her looks. Past efforts with hair or make-up had had no greater intention than to make herself look presentable. But surely nothing was more natural than to want to look your best when you're seeking the attentions of a man you're desperately in love with. And a new hair style, dyed darker, longer than she'd worn it in the past, expensively cut, and set off by new, stylish clothes, had led to a transformation that was startling, and which gave her great confidence.

They kissed hungrily in the lift on the way up to the top floor, oblivious to anyone who might see them. They got out in giddy spirits, far more interested in each other than any of the artworks.

'Just a sec,' said Fiona, touching Mark's arm, 'look at this. This is what I was meaning. Look how beautifully the stairs and the lift and the lift well work together visually. They're so harmonious.' Subconsciously echoing a favourite term of Ross's. 'It's all a perfect design. Is design not art? Can it not also be art?'

'Well, isn't that rather an old argument - you know, revolving around purpose and intention. But certainly when you see - as you say, this whole visual arrangement, which is at least principally functional in terms of the main shapes - the layout of the lift well and the staircases - they are highly sculptural.'

'And the detailing. Look at the chrome of the handrails, and the tall, thin rectangles of the lift door windows. All the strong shapes, and straight lines intersecting. It's very powerful. And look at the line of perspective as the stairs descend, the handrails diving down, and the light coming through from the windows. You can't actually see the windows from here, the walls are so thick, it's just a rectangle of light on the grey wall. Such an effective composition. To me it's both art and design.'

'You're right, it is very beautiful.'

Fiona had never been particularly moved before by the visual effects of interior or building design, and had certainly never been given to rhapsodise over such things. It was the influence of Mark. She felt so different when she was with him, inspired to see and feel things as she'd never done before.

The top floor was a hall consisting of a large, entirely white space, empty apart from a sculpture formed of interconnected neon tubes, and a series of paintings along one wall forming a single exhibit, all identical in size, and apparently devoid of subject, being a simple wash of varying shades of grey, from near white to almost black. The room was free of visitors apart from themselves, and they held hands as they examined the art.

'You know, I think there's more craft and art in what we do at Caledon than in 95% of the stuff here. To me it's all ideas without the craft. It's the notion of something interesting without all the investment of toil and technique and learned skills that make something of depth and texture. It's as if *we* came up with an idea and presented it as a finished, usable product, just sold it as a concept without working through all the design and operational problems. People would laugh in our faces, and we'd go out of business pretty damn quickly. And as for the abstruse and would-be esoteric descriptions, most of them are just embarrassing, and far from bridging the gap between artist and viewer they just invite contempt.'

'I agree with you. On principle.'

Mark smiled. 'You don't have to agree with me. You can tell me I'm talking rubbish if you want.'

'I don't want to. And I don't disagree with you, on the principle,' dropping her voice to a whisper, putting her arm around him and pulling herself into him, 'that I love you.'

'Oh, I love you too, Fiona. So, so, so much.' They clung to each other fiercely, kissing passionately, until, as other visitors strolled into the hall, they pulled quickly apart, half embarrassed, half pleased with themselves, grinning at each other, pretending to be occupied with looking at an exhibit, like teenagers caught in the act who think nevertheless that they've just discovered the secret of love and are delighted to flaunt their uniqueness. Ideas of discretion and secrecy momentarily forgotten. They made their way out of the hall, avoiding eye contact with the incomers.

'We might as well use the stairs this time.'

'Okay. You know, I haven't asked you about Ross. How's he getting on?'

Fiona's mood was dampened a little at the mention of Ross, and she felt the familiar quick stab of guilt.

'Well, okay, I guess. He's written a couple of times. Hasn't really said much, apart from that it's bearable. So...'

'Have you been to see him?'

'No. I would have done, but he insisted he didn't want visitors. We'd discussed it beforehand in the event that the worst came to the worst, and that's what he wanted. Said it would only make it more difficult, and he needed to face it alone.'

Mark nodded. In fact when Ross had told her this, Fiona had readily agreed, to his dismay. He'd expected an emotional scene, with Fiona begging to be allowed to come, and her calm acceptance had been an unpleasant surprise.

'When does he get out?'

'January, hopefully, if he behaves himself.'

'Ah okay, right.' Pause. 'Janet's talking about possibly going to university next year.' Fiona felt a sudden tightening of her stomach at the mention of Mark's wife. 'Toby will be three in the spring, and Janet thinks it might be possible to somehow work going to university around school and nursery, maybe using a childminder now and again. Basically with the intention of taking in as many lectures and seminars as she can.'

'Oh okay.' Fiona was slightly nonplussed by his matter of fact tone. 'What does she want to do?'

'Psychology. You know, it'll be good for her. I'm glad she's finally making an effort.'

Fiona nodded. They were now in the hall on the second floor where in the centre of the space there was a free-standing room with two entrances and seating opposite a flat screen attached to the wall. Whatever had been playing had just finished, so they sat down alone in the darkness to wait for the piece to start again.

'We need to decide what we're doing,' said Fiona quietly, looking at him significantly. 'I mean what we're going to do.'

'I know,' said Mark, taking her hand. 'Don't worry, I'm going to tell Janet very soon.'

'Okay. We need to think through all the implications, and make some plans. We can't expect everything just to happen and fall into place.'

'I know, you're right. I will talk to her in the next few days.'

'It would be better sooner rather than later. There's no point letting things just drift along.'

'I agree.' Pause. 'Of course, it's the children, that's the main worry. They're so young. I can't really discuss it with them or find out what they want - or at least I feel I can't, or shouldn't. Anyway, I'm sure it will all be resolved. These things happen, and people get over it.'

'Exactly. That's the only way to look at it,' said Fiona, relieved to hear what sounded like serious intent.

'How are you going to handle things with Grant?'

'I don't know just now. He's at a difficult age too - in a different way to your two, of course.'

The screen lit up, and there followed a strange, surreal little film consisting of old bearded men in masks, their grey beards trailing well below the masks, singing in Polish of birth and death, of love and love lost, interspersed with fragments of birds in flight and children chasing through an orchard of apple trees in blossom (entitled Prawo Przejścia – Right of Passage).

They left the room, Mark saying that he'd better head back to work soon. So they made a quick tour of what was on offer in the rest of the hall - a cylinder like an unexploded shell propped horizontally, of concrete and plywood spray-painted silver and looking surprisingly metallic (untitled), some rusty steel tubing half submerged in gravel (Empty Karma), a few other things promising variously to express and embody a mimetic response to the specificity of complex narratives of psychogeographic observation through the external rhythms of a dynamic and transferable aesthetic; to expose the evasions and erosions of late-capitalist society through the interactions between romanticism and anthropology, scepticism and obscurity, isolation and exchange; to reimagine and recreate ideas and experiences to form inter-subjective dialogues that subvert and overturn our understanding of the boundaries between abstract and concrete, dynamic and static, reality and artifice, the profound and the banal, in a diverse yet coherent diegesis. And so they parted with a final kiss on the busy street outside.

A week or so before Christmas they travelled together by train to the winter fair in Edinburgh. On the way Mark, looking tired and haggard, told Fiona that he'd at last broached the subject of a separation with Janet. No, it hadn't gone that well. Janet had reacted at first with tears and pleading. That performance had gone on for several days, her teary face greeting him each time he got in from work. Then it was like the turning of a switch. Gone were the tears and the begging and the repeated Why, please just tell me why, I just don't understand, what have I done wrong, weeping all the while, Please, please, don't do this to me, give me another chance, please, *please*. To be suddenly replaced without warning by an outpouring of vicious anger such as he'd never encountered before. Mark had had no idea that anything like that was even within her emotional range. Get out then, you little shit, get your things and get out now, you cheating little fucker, I'll not have you in the house a moment longer, Get out, I said. The children crying, all hell breaking loose. They'd been playing together upstairs, Jessica keeping an eye on Toby, but had come down to see what all the commotion was about. I'll be seeing a solicitor in the morning, you can be sure of that. You loathsome cheating piece of shit. Get out of my sight. Like some kind of raving monster. He didn't repeat all this word for word, of course, nor did he repeat what she'd said about Fiona. Somehow she'd known straight away that it was Fiona, and had proceeded to make a number of savage and highly coloured comments about her. The gossip swirling around Caledon must have somehow reached her ears. An anonymous letter maybe, or phone call from withheld number.

Fiona was quietly, guiltily relieved to hear of what seemed to be an irreconcilable break up, but hid her satisfaction as best she could. She consoled Mark, expressed great sympathy for him having to go through something so awful, how difficult it must have been for him, and so on. It was understandable that he was subdued as he accompanied Fiona from the station across to the fair. But then gradually the wave of colours, bright lights and noise, and the magic of a clear, dark, starry night, though the moon was hiding somewhere, the crispness of the air, the gaunt, bare trees, limbs lit by traceries of varicoloured lights, and the enveloping anonymity of the pressing crowds, had a soothing effect. And his spirits picked up further after a couple of glasses of mulled wine, enjoyed while sitting together watching people milling around the German market of wooden chalets with pitched roofs, all brightly decorated with fairy lights like something out of a children's Xmas annual. Bright lights and colours and bustle and noise in all directions, with the castle rising improbably out of the darkness above.

Who knows to what extent Fiona was carried away, even to the point of madness, by the novelty of her affair with Mark. Having married so young, Ross was the only man she'd ever really known or been with up to that point. That the relationship with Mark had for all this time remained precariously non-sexual implied its own tensions and intensities, with the added frisson of anticipation and secrecy. Just as, when this was no longer the case, it would then have different, but just as urgent, tensions and imperatives. Whatever the various motivations for Fiona's feelings, wrapped within the mystery that is mutual attraction, that evening back in Glasgow, at the hotel where Mark was temporarily holed up, and to employ the expression that Fiona would thereafter use (to herself and others) in an attempt to assuage her feelings of guilt, their relationship ceased to be platonic.

14

On a wintry Friday in January, Fiona drove up to Peterhead. It was still dark when she set off, a little light snow falling and threatening to settle. The streets were almost deserted, just the odd car making its way slowly along Allison Street, and lights on here and there in tenement windows. She'd checked the forecast the night before, and snow wasn't supposed to be a problem on her way north, but it was a disconcerting start. She'd decided to set off at 7 to allow sufficient time for a journey of almost four hours, plus a couple of breaks, in time to meet Ross at midday, as prearranged, somewhere near the entrance to the prison. She hadn't been able to read anything into his voice when they'd spoken, the first time she'd heard his voice in three months, except that he'd sounded tired, distant. She'd kept up a friendly tone, and told him that Grant was looking forward to seeing him.

The journey was uneventful, the snow quickly dying away as promised. Up to Aberdeen the road had been recently dualled, something that would have annoyed the hell out of Ross, who would have raved at length about all its individuality and character having been leached out, though Fiona found it easy and convenient, and scenic enough in places where it ran close to the sea. Some way beyond Aberdeen it reverted to single carriageway, and became narrow and winding in places. She reached the turn off, and the feelings of nervousness that had been growing the closer she'd got began to be palpable in her stomach. When she turned off the road leading to the prison and into the prison grounds with the wide blue sea right ahead like a vision of freedom, tauntingly close to the prison, she felt sick from tension. It wasn't just the thought of seeing Ross again, though partly that, but rather what she had determined must be done when they got back home.

She parked the car and walked towards the Family Centre, where they'd arranged to meet. Ross, waiting just inside, came out to meet her. At first she barely recognised him. He looked so...diminished. His head almost shaven, revealing areas of grey she'd never noticed before, his face clean shaven, so that altogether his head and face seemed smaller and thinner, and as she came closer his eyes appeared dull, sunken and unresponsive. He also seemed to have lost weight, such that he appeared slight, almost frail, certainly by contrast with the mental picture of him she always carried. As for Ross, coming directly from such a grim all-male environment, to see Fiona looking unbearably attractive, hair immaculate and glossy, elegantly dressed, seemed only to underline the gulf between them, and once more he felt disconcerted, intimidated by his wife's appearance.

It was a relief for both to get the initial meeting over with, and Fiona found herself able to relax a little. As their eyes met briefly and they exchanged a few words of greeting, Fiona tried to understand her feelings towards Ross. A degree of sympathy, that he appeared so reduced, but only of the kind one might feel for a stranger - detached, abstract. No longer the kind of engaged, caring empathy you have for someone close to you. She realised she had already distanced herself from him emotionally to an extent unforeseeable even a few short months ago. Either that or the detachment had taken place subconsciously long before she knew about it, and was only now reconciled within her mind, and therefore overt. She saw Ross now as little more than a stranger, and felt more disengaged from him than ever.

But she smiled, and asked, 'Are you hungry?'

'Aye, a suppose so.'

'I am. I didn't have anything to eat before I set off. I noticed a McDonald's on the way in. We could just go there?'

'Aye, fine.' They began to walk towards the car. 'Ye see over there,' said Ross, gesturing to an area of waste ground the other side of the road from the car park, 'there's where they fucked the old prison. Just wiped it away, erased it - aw fur that,' indicating the new building. 'Destructive bastards.'

'For God's sake, Ross. Not this again, already.'

Fiona's face suddenly strained and drawn.

'What?'

'Don't start up with all the angst and anger that got you into this mess in the first place.'

In fact it had been a reflex reaction from Ross. After so long confined, to be released and away from close proximity to other people and to feel space around him and to be able to look up at the sky and smell the cold, fresh salty air was to be reborn, stripped of all the errors of the past. And anyway it was there right in front of him, a large vacant area of land with grass and weeds growing up among the fragments of brick and stone that until recently had been a Victorian prison. And for what? To move it five hundred yards to the south? It was insanity, vandalism on the grand scale. But he managed to keep his feelings in check and his mouth shut, and they drove in silence to the McDonald's.

'What was it like being in there? How did you manage?'

They were sitting by a window that looked out onto a roundabout on the main road. They'd finished their meal, and Ross was gazing out at the traffic as if mesmerized - as if he'd never seen such things before. He came back into himself, and told her it was fine, no real problems. Just a question of finding ways to deal with the isolation, mental and physical, of spending long periods by yourself locked up in a cell. The first two weeks were rough, craving a drink, after that not so bad. Though the clarity of thought that came with being completely dry was a curse. For two out of the three months there'd been a young laddie of eighteen on his block, which had made him think of Grant. A wee boy who claimed he'd got mixed up in something without wanting or meaning to, clearly terrified of the whole ordeal of prison, such that Ross had taken him under his wing, helping and mentoring him as best he could, which in turn had helped Ross to get through the time, even though prison life, with all its endless do's and don'ts, was a new ordeal for him too. Truth was, unless you owed someone money, or for some other reason someone had a grudge against you, and if you kept yourself to yourself, and didn't try to play the hard man, nothing much was likely to happen. Apart from keeping an eye on Kevin, Ross hadn't really thought, or allowed himself to think, of anything very much, all the time he was inside. He'd put thought on hold, and became simply an animal in the forest, wary, watchful, senses raised and always alert - even, he thought, during sleep, when he would sometimes click into instant consciousness and awareness, check his surroundings, listen attentively, senses straining, before allowing himself to relax and slip back into a shallow sleep. So he told her a few harmless anecdotes, then asked about Grant, and how he was doing. After three months he was desperate to see him again, to hear his voice. Fiona said, Yes, he was fine, looking forward to seeing you, but didn't tell him of the troubles she'd been having with his school attendance, thinking it wasn't the right time.

What Ross didn't tell Fiona, couldn't begin to convey, was that in prison the universe condenses precisely to the dimensions of your cell. You know, intellectually, that there is something beyond your cell walls, but it's too remote and surreal a concept fully to grasp. Your mind shrivels up to next to nothing. Each day is a void.

Sitting, or pacing up and down in the beautifully-appointed modern cell that he had all to himself, for hour upon hour, trying desperately not to reflect endlessly on the futility of everything, a mind-numbing despair had settled on him. Sometimes he would stare up at the light until he was half-blinded, just for something to do. Even though it was a relatively short sentence (out after three months with good behaviour), throughout it he felt he was losing touch with his life. Three months away from everything. Everyone would have moved on, made their adjustments to the new situation, and carried on without him. Who knew how, or how well, he would fit in when got out and came back home. He came to despise the bland, mocking pleasantness of his room, the counterfeit of a real room in a real house. Sometimes the tension of his boredom made it difficult for him to draw breath, and he'd start gasping, his chest tight, trying to slow everything down just to get some air into his lungs. Sometimes he wished he could just stop breathing and bring it all to an end, though he never seriously considered suicide. He avoided the various leisure activities on offer - gym, games room etc. - mainly because he was determined to keep his head down and avoid people and situations that had the potential to lead to trouble, thereby steering clear so far as he could from anything that might add time to his sentence.

What he couldn't get over at this moment, sitting just across the table from him, was Fiona. Even disregarding externals, there was something about her that was different - a certain poise, detachment, something he couldn't quite identify but that was nevertheless unsettling. He hardly dared to ask in any detail what had been happening during his absence, fearing the answer. The endless daydreams and speculations as to what was going on had been torturous. That something was going on he was certain - he could feel it.

They got back just after Grant arrived home from school. He heard footsteps on the stairs, then a key in the lock, and darted into his room, listening intently from behind the door. For some reason he was nervous, or embarrassed, at seeing his dad again. Then voices, the clump of a bag being deposited in the hall, the squeak of the living room door. Silence for several moments, then the living room door again and someone going through to the kitchen. Guessing it was his mother, Grant - it was just his dad, after all, what was he doing - gathered himself and went through to say hello.

As Grant came slowly, hesitantly into the room, Ross jumped up and came over to him with a big smile and, quite uncharacteristically, hugged him. It was all a little strange and surprising for Grant, as there had been next to no physical contact between them for many years, probably since before he entered his teens. As Ross stepped back, still a wide grin on his face, and surveyed his son and asked with great enthusiasm and emotion how he was doing and what he'd been up to, and as

Grant fumbled for responses, he was able to take in his father and how changed he appeared. He was as shocked as his mother at his dad's appearance. Grant thought he looked like somebody else entirely, somebody about ten years older. Ross meanwhile thought Grant was taller than ever. Tall, stringy, surely close to six feet now. That he'd actually grown noticeably while Ross was in prison was chastening, unless he was somehow imagining it. And he'd grown his hair long, covering his ears Seventies style, something Ross hadn't seen in his son since he was a toddler.

That evening they had a celebratory meal of takeaway pizza and chips, and in Ross's case, several bottles of lager, which after such a long dry period tasted unbelievably good. In his relief at his freedom, coupled with his state of inebriation, Ross hardly noticed that Fiona was subdued throughout the meal. Afterwards, the combination of the strain of three months in prison, the long drive, and the alcohol pretty much knocked him out. All he wanted then was to crash out in their familiar, wonderfully comfortable bed. Which is what he did for ten hours once the pizza was finished and they'd had a bit of random chat, Ross pretending all the while that everything was fine and normal.

He woke at 7 to discover that Fiona wasn't beside him, and so far as he could tell, hadn't been in the bed at all. It was like a bucket of cold water chucked over him, as he realised for the first time that nothing had changed.

He got up, pulled on a pair of trousers, made a cup of tea, and sat in the bay of the living room, looking down at the quiet street where even the glazing centre hadn't yet opened up and begun the morning chorus of glass being energetically smashed. He missed having Jimmy to talk to. Someone he could say anything to, and who could always manage to take his mind off things, wee bawbag though he was, with all his obscene stories and inanities which Ross had always found so amusing. He hadn't heard a word from Jimmy since sometime well before the trial, probably all of four months. His so-called best mate so entirely unconcerned about him that he hadn't even troubled to contact Fiona to find out whether he'd gone to prison - he knew because he'd asked her the previous evening. Such a selfish, self-centred little prick. Maz. He must go and see Maz at some point.

Finishing his tea he went to find Fiona, who as he expected was asleep in the study. She stirred as Ross came in. He went to the window, cracked open a curtain and peered down at the back courts. He was about to leave when Fiona asked sleepily what time it was. Ross said around half seven, to which she replied that she'd get up soon. He went back to their bedroom to find a change of clothes. It was only after some moments of looking for his own things that some instinct caused him to check further. He looked in the chest of drawers, then the dressing table and wardrobe. All Fiona's clothes and personal effects were missing. At first he was just mystified. He tried to think of where

209

they might be or who might have taken them. It was only after a few moments of reflection that he realised with a hideous jolt that she wasn't planning to stay. She had systematically removed everything that was specifically hers - jumpers, t-shirts, underwear, skirts, trousers, jackets, shoes, boots, jewellery, perfumes, creams, make-up, hairbrush, even some little ornaments she kept on the dressing table - everything was gone. There could hardly have been a more explicit statement of intent. He had been going to shower, but now he went back into the living room and sat down again in the bay, gazing out vacantly, tensely waiting for what must happen, whatever that turned out to be. Did Grant know anything about all this? Or had she moved the stuff out of the flat without Grant's knowledge and behind his back, presumably when he was at school, while still nominally living in the flat? If that was the case, the cold, calculating subterfuge of her actions was frightening. He simply couldn't recognise the person who would do such a thing as his wife, the woman he'd lived with for seventeen years.

It was sometime later that Ross heard movement in the flat, then Fiona popped her head around the door.

'Hi. Have you had breakfast?'

Ross thought that given the circumstances that was one of the strangest and most evasive questions he'd ever been asked.

'Come in, will ye.'

She came in, clad in a dressing gown, mobile in hand.

'Sit down,' he said, indicating the sofa. 'At least look as if ye're staying.'

She sat with a confused but wary expression and put the mobile down on the coffee table, pulling the gown tight around her.

'What are you talking about?'

'Ye know fine well whit a'm talkin aboot. Quit playin games, will you.'

'Go on, then.'

'A saw ye've moved aw your stuff oot.'

Fiona looked down at her hands drawn together in her lap.

'I was going to tell you at some point.'

Ross felt a chill of horror, but managed to simulate amazement.

'Oh aye. Whit were ye goin tae tell me? An' when?'

There was a long silence which seemed about to stretch out indefinitely. Managing to avert his gaze from Fiona, he looked around the familiar room in which so many scenes of family life had been played out over the years. Each object on which his eyes came to rest seemed to take on a new significance, as if it was the first time he'd ever seen it.

'This isn't easy for me, Ross. I didn't want this to happen. Sometimes things just happen.'

'Whit the fuck's that supposed tae mean? What's happened?' His voice was rough and husky. 'Okay. A'm gan tae ask ye straight oot. Are ye havin an affair wi' somebody? Is there someone else?'

He'd asked her once before and she'd just denied it. There was a distinct pause before she replied.

'No, no there's no-one else.'

'A dinnae believe you,' he said flatly. 'Whit did ye mean then when ye said sometimes things just happen?'

'I don't know. I didn't mean anything.'

Ross made a gesture of extreme irritation.

'Will ye stop playin fuckin games wi' me. A'll no hae it. Ye've gan somewhere wi' aw your stuff. Where're ye been gan?'

'Look, this isn't to do with me - this is about us.'

'Us? There is nae feckin us. Try tellin the truth fae once. Ye havnae slept in the same bed wi' me fur months. Fur God's sake tell us the fuckin truth.'

She cast a quick sideways glance at him, then resumed examining her hands.

'Okay. Alright - I owe you that much, I suppose.' Pause. 'Yes, there is someone else.'

So they had finally got there. The sucker punch to the guts. And Ross felt it as though he'd really been caught off guard and taken a low blow.

'Who is it?' he managed to say.

'I can't tell you that. It's a complicated situation. It wouldn't be fair on...on his family.'

'Aye, an' it's fair on me, is it? It's fair on ma family? Whit are ye tryin tae do tae me, Fiona? Why are ye doin this?'

It was all unreal. They were surely just actors in a play improvising lines. But at least now he knew the worst. That was something. Still, he had to know who it was, and repeated his question, and Fiona repeated that she couldn't tell him.

'A'll bet it's that smooth wee bastard Mark.' Fiona looked up suddenly with genuine surprise and initial shock. 'So soft-spoken, so intelligent,' in a mincing, mocking tone, 'sae flattering an' ingratiating an' always sayin all the right things - the soft wee cunt.'

At this Fiona's lips compressed into a thin line and her eyes became hard. She sat, looking at Ross, unspeaking, but with an expression of unmistakeable disdain.

'Dinnae just sit there lookin at me wi' yir fuckin stone face. It's that soft wee bastard Mark, isn't it, that ye're always talkin aboot and repeatin all the wonderful things he's said aboot ye, how feckin great ye are, an' aw the great things ye're deein, an' you talkin aboot how feckin great he is, that soft wee fuck. That's who ye're havin your cheap, pathetic little affair wi', isn't it?'

'No.'

'Ye're just feckin lyin again, aren't ye. You just can't tell the fuckin truth tae save your life.'

'It's not Mark.'

'Who is it, then?'

'I've already said, I can't tell you.'

It goes back and forth a few more times, accusation and denial, until Ross grabs Fiona's mobile from the coffee table, and despite frantic efforts by Fiona to get it back, manages to keep hold of it and reads some of the texts between Fiona and Mark, and so learns the depth of relations between them. *Oh my darling...you are the world to me...life would be impossible without you...I love you so much my darling...thinking of you all the time...my sweetheart...angel...I feel complete with you...you are so wonderful...* And so on. Poisonous little paeans of intimacy that would infect his mind and which he could never fully expunge from memory. At last he throws the mobile against the wall, then starts jumping on it, crushing it to pieces beneath his feet. He's screaming at Fiona, he's not sure what, and she backs away, genuinely frightened. Grant comes in, attracted by the noise of the shouting, and Ross immediately stops. He asks what's going on. Ross goes over to the window to try to calm down, looking out at the view he knows and loves so well and where everything appears so deceptively, casually normal. Fiona at first tells Grant to leave, but then immediately changes her mind, sits down and asks him to sit down as well. He remains standing.

'First,' a gentle smile and soft tone, 'you need to know, darling, that none of this is your fault. We both love you very much, and that won't change.' Fur Christ's sake, thought Ross, such predictable platitudinous crap. 'But your dad and I have decided we can't stay together any more. We're going to split up.'

At first Grant remains rooted to the spot in visible shock, then seems to sag, and sits down.

'Why? What's happened?'

She wets her lips. 'Nothing's happened as such, Grant. It's just that...your dad and I have grown apart recently, so that now we feel we just can't really live together anymore.'

'Dinnae say me,' shouts Ross, turning round. 'Dinnae talk fur me when none o' this is whit a want.'

'Dad's just back home,' said Grant, close to tears, his voice wavering.

'Why dinnae ye tell him the truth of aw this?' shouted Ross. 'Why dinnae ye tell him ye're havin' an affair wi' somebody fae yir work. And that ye're leavin an' gan tae live wi' him. Why dinnae ye tell him that?'

Fiona gave Ross a look such as he'd never received from her before - a look of undisguised dislike and anger. It was this look more than all the words that had so far passed between them that was the real killer. It was this that told him clearly that a point of no return had been passed. Suddenly he didn't know what he was doing or why he was standing there. He left the room, quickly threw on the rest of his clothes and went out.

His first thought was to go on a blind drunk, but then he realised the pubs wouldn't be open yet. In any case after prison the thought of being among noisy mainly male company was not attractive. He just wanted quiet, open spaces and peace. Almost reflexively, his steps turned towards Queen's Park. It was already snowing when he left the flat, and by the time he passed the ranks of tall bare trees that lined the entrance drive and began to make his way carefully up the steps, it was snowing hard and quickly settling. He turned and looked over what he could see of Govanhill through the swirling flakes, the park already a wonderland, ethereal and magical. He was entirely alone; not another single soul had ventured into the park to sully the pristine white. The contrast with the close and claustrophobic oppression of his incarceration at Grampian could hardly have been greater, and in different circumstances his spirits would have soared. The park was just the same in every way as it had been those few short months ago - as it had ever been - though now swathed in winter raiment. Yet the world had inexplicably turned upside down in his absence. That was the puzzling thing. Govanhill looked just the same, as harmonious and breathtakingly lovely as ever. The rich warm stone, the endless repetition of motifs, the soaring steeples to punctuate and add a perfect element of variety to the consistent scale of the tenements. The wonderful predictability, in a cascading cake-walk of a world, that he'd always found so consoling. The unchangingness he'd relied on to keep him on an even keel. The undoing, when it came, had come not from the outside, but from within.

He spent probably a full two hours in the park, hardly feeling the cold, sometimes shaking his head to dislodge the worst of the unrelenting snow, as remote from the world and all its inhabitants as it was possible to be in the midst of a great city. Escape from his thoughts, and himself, was more difficult. At times hardly aware of the snow driving in his face, he tried repeatedly to pinpoint the moment when it must have happened. Was it really all down to that moment of madness up in the Highlands? However ridiculous all that business might have been, wasn't marriage supposed to be a long-term commitment? Weren't you supposed to ride out the ups and downs? It must be him, or something about him, or something he'd done, or hadn't done, or didn't do, that she'd come to dislike or resent. If only she'd tell him what it was, he'd put things right, if he could. It surely couldn't really be attraction to that flabby soft wee cunt Mark. That was just an excuse, some kind of justification.

He didn't think he'd changed that much from all those years when they'd been happy together. As far as he was concerned, they still were - or certainly he was, or had been. If anything it was her who'd somehow changed - he was sure of that now. He'd thought so for a while, but never quite been able to put his finger on the when or how.

When Ross got back to the flat, Fiona was in the living room waiting for him, coat on, a coupled of bags packed beside her, apparently ready to leave. When he saw that, something gave way inside him, and he slumped into an armchair.

'I've had a talk with Grant. He understands the situation better now.'

Ross looked up and his vacant gaze hardened.

'Oh aye, is that so. And whit does he understand? Whit pack o' lies have ye been tellin him?'

She looked at Ross, but didn't react.

217

'So I'm leaving now, but I'll be back to pick up a few things. And at some point we'll need to sit down and discuss all the practicalities of what happens to the flat and so on. But for now, it's better if I just go, and then we can sort everything out later.'

Aye, you go. It's just a matter now of sorting out a few wee details.

'Oh, one problem is that I'll have to get a new mobile. I'll pick one up as soon as I can. I don't know if it'll be the same number, but I'll let you know.' There was no hint of accusation in her tone, but Ross got the message anyway. 'For now I've got Grant's number, and I'll stay in close contact with him. If you need to contact me at all, you can always email. I've written my email address down for you in case you hadn't got it,' indicating a pad on the coffee table. Could he find it in him to throw himself at her feet and beg, to humble and prostrate himself? Whit ye deein? Dinnae go. A'm beggin you, Fiona, dinnae go. We can work things out. A love you, Fiona. Dinnae go. Ah, please, please. A love you. Don't destroy everything. We belong together. His voice full of pleading. But in the time it took for him to contemplate whether he could bring himself to do it, the moment passed, to become just another what-if to torment him in the coming months.

'Why did you have to do it Ross?'

Her face was suddenly, from nowhere, contorted with emotion, expressive of pain and suffering.

'Whit ye talkin aboot?'

'Do you not realise the effect all this business has had on our family? Police coming round in the dead of night, you being hauled off to court. The trial. Prison. Do you not understand how traumatic it was for Grant to see his dad looking like he'd taken a beating? To have to go to school with all the whispering and taunting that his dad's a criminal.'

Ross hadn't thought of that, the effect on Grant. But still to throw it at him now was low. It was all being turned around so that he was the guilty party, responsible for everything that was wrong, when she'd finally admitted she'd been cheating on him.

'And it's not just that. Everything's always been on your terms. Always you that had to direct and dictate everything we've ever done. Never once did you think to ask, What do *you* think? I can't take being controlled and told what to do and think any more. Enough's enough.'

'A dinnae understand whit ye're talkin aboot. When have a ever tried tae control you? You've always been able tae do just what ye wanted.'

'Aye, is that right.'

'A never stopped ye fae studying, or goin out tae work an' havin a career, did a.'

'And where would we have been if I hadn't? Everything I've done I've done it on my own initiative and by my own efforts, while you played at politics with all your meetings and marches, and a business that makes next to nothing.'

The tone as harsh as the words.

'A wis just searchin for harmony,' said Ross. 'Tryin tae make a better world. Searchin fae somethin that would make sense of aw the wilful destruction.'

'You've wilfully destroyed our marriage,' replied Fiona fiercely. 'That's what you've done.'

Ross looked on helplessly, his mind in a state of turmoil. It all looked different from where he was. Fiona stood up and gathered together her bags, repeated that she'd be in touch, then left after saying a few words to Grant.

That evening Grant, rather than stay in his room, music thumping loudly as he worked, came through to the living room to be with his dad. They sat watching TV together until it was time for bed, neither of them saying much or taking in anything very much of what they were watching.

15

The flat became a strange, tormenting place to Ross. His sense of failure was acute. Everything, every object in the flat, the flat itself, seemed a reproach to his stupidity, lack of subtlety, lack of sophistication, or whatever other quality or combination of qualities he was perceived to be lacking. To be rejected so summarily, without warning - anything, at least, other than a vague disquiet - without real explanation, without the possibility of a fair hearing, and with no chance of negotiation or appeal, was really something. It was beyond anything he could have imagined, and he was laid low under the onslaught. Drink provided some kind of refuge. But he had to try to keep things under control for Grant's sake. Fiona had been back several times to the flat, each time raising the hope that she'd come to her senses and returned permanently, each time to be swiftly undeceived. She had private conferences with Grant in his bedroom, trying, as Ross found out subsequently, to persuade Grant to come and live with her and Mark in the West End flat they were renting, and where he would have his own bedroom. The thought of her sharing a flat, a bed, with Mark, was just about enough to tip him over the edge. That Grant might leave and live with them was unbearable to contemplate. In fact Grant was barely on speaking terms with his mother, who managed to pretend that she didn't notice his barely contained hostility. That their family had been reduced to this, reduced to the kind of sordid acrimony that only happened to other people, and never in the wildest reaches of his imagination to them. And all in the blink of an eye. He should feel only resentment and anger towards Fiona, and sometimes he did. But mainly the wracking pain of loss. And rather than diminishing, the sense of loss grew steadily. Brief periods of calm, somehow managing to delude himself that all this madness was a passing phase, followed by frantic bursts of panic and near hysteria. Unhinged by the unreality. She would come back to her senses, the madness would pass. After all, his parents had managed to stay together through everything, and his father had hardly been the easiest person to live with. A hard, grim old bastard. He wasn't as bad as his father. He'd done his best. Pathetic wee man. Stop grovelling. But a whiney, pleading note did seem to come into his voice on the few occasions he managed to speak to Fiona alone - at least that was how it sounded in his own ears. Impotent pleading the only response he could make to the calm, self-contained front she presented. That cool, impregnable front. His hold over his life gradually loosening.

For the first time in years he wished he could see his parents again, that they could still be there in the flat in Drumchapel whose every detail, and that of all the surrounding streets, was imprinted on his memory. Not for sympathy exactly - he wouldn't want or expect that - but just for the chance to re-engage with all the old certainties in the face of the gale of change currently ripping his life and all its fittings from their moorings. But they were long gone, and his old home and all the tenements of his street and of those surrounding, unlovely as they'd been, while still as real in every detail within his mind, had been obliterated. Drumchapel, long a prime candidate for regeneration, was now unrecognisable. His thoughts turned with anger and abhorrence to Jimmy. To turn your back on someone, supposedly your best mate, in their time of greatest need, and with such icy indifference, now that also is really something. He'd always known what Jimmy was like deep down - what a joke - with Jimmy there wasn't any deep down. The utter vacuity, the emptiness, the chill disregard for anyone or anything but himself, the primacy of satisfying his own wishes, whims and desires, with scant feeling or concern for whoever he was making use of. He'd always been aware of it, but to be on the receiving end in the face of everything engulfing him, that was something else. And Maz wasn't much better. He knew he'd hear nothing from her if he didn't go to the trouble of making contact himself, as her level of self-absorption was pretty much on a par with Jimmy's. No doubt it was the fact that they were so alike that caused them to be so repelled by each other. Fiona had seen a solicitor. Another body blow. Just to hear it said. The hideous finality of it. She was putting the wheels in motion, so he'd be hearing

223

directly from the solicitor. It would probably be best if they didn't have any more contact than necessary. The chasm opening steadily wider to reveal a deep abyss into which his gaze was now focused. More whining, more pleading. More stony deflection. Was that him weeping, desperately pleading without pride or dignity? It may have been. Everything was unreal. It could have been him.

Maz lived in a ground floor flat on a scruffy street with grubby, littered close just a few streets away from Ross. And there she was at the door to greet him, statuesque and sultry as ever in tight white trousers and blue and white blouse with a vague nautical look. She'd dyed her hair black black, so black it seemed to have a bluish tinge, shiny and luxuriant.

'So they let ye oot, then?'

'What, prison?'

'Aye, ye dafty.'

'Aye, apparently.'

'Ha, cheeky. A wouldnae hae let ye oot. A wid hae chucked away the key.'

Ross laughed. 'Aye, cheers. That disnae surprise me one bit.' Desperate to see a familiar, friendly face, to relax with exchange of banter, and especially to unburden himself.

On being ushered into the living room he was surprised to find some young guy he'd never seen before, sitting bolt upright, perched on the edge of the sofa, thin moustache, smiling, an open, almost childlike expression. Maz introduced him as Farooq, and they shook hands, a limp, evasive shake.

'Do ye want a coffee, darlin?'

'Aye, thanks.'

He knew that out of politeness he should stay and make banal small talk with this guy, whoever he was, but he lacked the patience or resources for that at present, so followed Maz through to the kitchen, where she was already filling the kettle. She smiled pleasantly at him as she arranged cups and tipped in shovelfuls of instant coffee. Already Ross had the feeling that this was going to be a wasted visit. If it was all going to be polite chit-chat with some stranger there, and Maz treating him like someone she barely knew, then he might just as well fuck off right now.

'A need tae talk to ye, Maz.'

'Everything alright, darlin?'

'No, not really. A wouldnae say that.'

Ross's strangely gaunt and dishevelled appearance, plus the prospect of raking over someone else's disasters, prompted her interest such that she immediately adopted the mode of intimate and caring friend.

'A'll get rid of him, and we can have a proper chat.'

'Who is he?'

'Ach, he's just someone who's latched on tae me, an' noo a cannae get rid ae him.'

'Where did ye meet him? He's not a neighbour, is he?'

'Nah. A wis oot wi' Lizzie an' Doreen havin a drink an' a wee dance, just ourselves, an' this laddie's hangin

225

aroond us. So when we leave an' he comes up tae us an' asks if he can have ma phone number, just tae get rid o' him a give him ma number, never thinkin a'd ever hear fae him again, an' now a cannae get shot of him. Always knockin on ma door an' followin us aroon like a wee puppy dog. It's startin tae get on ma tits big style.'

The mention of the other members of the coven made Ross think of Jimmy and his stories of his mother and her unsavoury friends.

They took their coffees through, pointedly just two cups for Ross and Maz.

'A'm jus gan tae have a wee private chat wi' Ross now, darlin. So a'll catch up wi' ye some time.'

'I should go now?' Still smiling.

'Aye, that's it. You go now, an' a'll see ye later.'

'Okay.'

He got up, moved towards the door, then stopped and hovered, continuing to hover while Maz and Ross engaged in some initial chat about something that was on the TV, sometimes with one hand on the door handle, sometimes edging back into the room and perching on the edge of some piece of furniture. Moving away, creeping back, moving away again, as if this time definitely to quit the room, creeping back, always smiling. For shit's sake, thought Ross, if you don't stop feckin smilin an' just fuck off I'll kick ye through that feckin door. At last Farooq managed to successfully negotiate the door by himself, and there was a clonk as the close door shut. Followed by a tapping on the window. Half a dozen quick taps, a pause, then four slower ones.

'What the fuck?'

Maz shook her head. 'It's just that feckin nutcase, Farooq.'

'What dis he dae that for?'

'Fuck knows. He's a feckin lunatic. Always tapping on that feckin windae. He taps on it when he comes aroond, an' just keeps tapping on the fecker till a let him in. Then he taps some more when he goes. That's the bit a cannae understand. Ye might knock on someone's door tae be let in - though the silly twat disnae even do that - it has tae be the windae. But why tap on the windae when ye've said goodbye and left the feckin flat? Ah,' pausing to light a cigarette, 'he's just a feckin nutcase. A need tae get shot of him somehow. So, darlin, what's up?'

Ross took a deep breath. 'It's Fiona. She's left me.'

Maz jerked back her head and assumed a look of complete astonishment, her eyes wide.

'Bloody hell! When did this happen?'

'A few weeks ago.'

'She just upped and left?'

'Aye, more or less. As soon as a got oot fae prison, an' we came back tae the flat, we had it oot. A knew all along somethin wis wrong, but a couldnae put ma finger on it. A knew she wis up tae somethin.'

'Aye, a'm no surprised,' said Maz, nodding sagely. 'She's always had aw the freedom that other wummin wid kill fur.'

'Well, she widnae admit anything at first, kept denyin everythin - a had tae screw it oot of her - but in the end she admitted she wis havin an affair.'

Maz nodding again through a cloud of cigarette smoke with an expression that suggested that this was all exactly as she'd foreseen, that she'd known something like this was in the offing, that she'd seen it coming, and this was just confirmation of what she'd been expecting all along. Ross found this complacent suggestion of superior knowledge and foresight vaguely irritating.

'Even when a finally got the truth oot of her, she widnae tell me who it was, though a had ma suspicions straight away. Her boss, managing director of the firm she works for. A soft, flabby wee cunt wi' his soft voice an' his soft ways. Of course, she widnae admit tae it. Kept denyin it wis him, until a got a hold of her mobile an' found lovey-dovey messages between them, the dirty, cheatin pair of…'

The anger in him, all the names he'd like to call them to their faces. Them. The idea of them burned corrosively within him. He still couldn't believe it of Fiona. Who was she? Who had she been when they'd lived together all those years. She was a complete stranger, remote and indifferent.

'A'm sorry darlin. A know she's yir wifey an' aw that, but a always thought she wis way up her own backside. She thinks ye're no good enough fur her noo, that's whit a think. A only met her once or twice, but a could tell straight away she wis lookin doon her nose at me wi' that superior look of the career woman who thinks she's sae feckin wonderful, an' the likes of you an' me are nothin. Aye, a know her type. So far up her own arse she couldnae see daylight if she used a feckin searchlight. Ye're better off wi'out her, Ross. A'm telling ye, you can dae better than that, darlin, much better.'

Ross found all this far from consoling.

'Aye well,' continued Maz, 'it just goes tae show, people are just feckin shit. An' talkin ae shit, aye, an' talkin aboot people uppin and leavin, Brian's gone.'

'Whit dae ye mean?'

'Gone, left, fecked off. Gone tae Birmingham or Coventry or some other shithole, tae start his feckin haulage empire, the daft fat cunt. A widnae go wi' him, sae that's it. He's gone.'

'Christ, I'm sorry Maz. A didn't know anything about that. When did he go?'

'Back in December. Before Xmas. He stands there like the big dopey cunt he is, an' gives us an ultimatum. Only he didnae say it like that, he wis just standin there sayin these things as if it never entered his heid that a'd not want tae do it, or a'd mebbe have ideas of ma own. So a just said, Aye, aye, tae everythin he said, Aye right, noddin ma heid like it wis on some feckin spring. Aye, aye, is that right. That's whit ye're deein then, is it? An' he looks at us wi' this expression on his face like he disnae know whit day of the feckin week it is. Aye, like usual. An' he says, Well, we'll have tae give notice on the flat. A'm gettin a van, sae we can move the stuff doon in that. So a said, Aye well, good luck wi' that. He says, What dae ye mean? A says, whit dae ye feckin think a mean. A'm no gan wi' ye. A'm no gan doon tae some feckin shithole like Birmingham an' leave all ma friends behind. If ye want yir haulage empire and ye want tae be the king of the Haulage Exchange, ye can gan dae it by yourself. A'm no gan wi' ye. So he goes on and on, makin the case fae it, building this idea up till he can see his great fleet wi' Brian Maston Logistics on the side, the daft cunt - as if that wid make any difference tae me.

'An' the worst of it is it's unsettled Pixie. She's missin her dad, wishin we'd aw gan doon wi' him. Not that she saw much of the fat twat before, an' when she did he didnae spend any time wi' her, sae she's no missin much. But she'd got it in her heid that her dad's upped away an' left her, sae that's all she's ever talkin aboot noo. Cryin an' whinging, A want tae see ma da, A never see ma da noo. Gets on ma feckin tits big time. An' then she's missin her brother and sisters as well. So a get stuck wi' the thick end of the wedge while every other fecker fucks off.'

'The twins have gone too?'

'Aye. Fecked off tae their da. He's got himself a new girlfriend. Daft wee lassie - she'll learn quick enough whit a total bastard he is. An' somehow - dinnae know how as they never left the feckin hoose - they aw met up, an' Kylie and Chelsea liked her, an' she liked them, an' every fucker seemed tae like everybody else but me, an' next thing a know Rob's invited them tae move in wi' him an' Christine. Poor dafty - she willnae last six months wi' that cunt. So as usual a'm left by maself apart fae Pixie, an' she disnae even want tae be here wi' me. Christ, what a feckin life.'

Ross expressed sympathy. Trust Maz to trump him, though. He might have lost his wife to another man, but she'd immediately countered with losing both her partner and two of her children. Three if you counted Jimmy. No contest.

Maz glanced at the time on the TV.

'Well, darlin, a'm sorry but a've got tae go an' pick Pixie up fae school.'

She stood up, kicked off her slippers, and began pulling on a pair of tall, black leather boots.

'Aye, a'd best be getting back fae Grant.'

'At least ye've still got Grant wi' ye darlin.'

'Aye, a know, that's somethin tae hold onto. Till he leaves tae go tae uni. Then a'll really be fucked.'

'Ross, ye're a feckin miserable twat. A'm tryin tae cheer ye up, darlin. Don't piss all over ma good intentions.' Laughing. 'Ah, fur fuck's sake, these feckin boots, a can never get these feckers on.'

It was strange - she'd barely asked at all about his time in prison. As if it was of no interest to her. He guessed it was of no interest. Not because it was to do with him, specifically, but simply because it wasn't to do with her.

They stood together at the corner of the street by a 24-hour convenience store.

'Well, a'm just gan in here darlin tae get somethin fur Pixie, an somethin fur tea.'

'Okay Maz. I'd better be on my way now as well.'

'Alright darlin, look after yourself.'

A brief hug, then Ross was alone. Thinking that he should head back to the flat, but unwilling to return to what seemed now like little more than a shrine to a failed marriage. An emptiness within at parting from Maz, such as he'd often felt after enjoying her earthy attractions and raucous humour. But now he thought the feeling was more because the time spent with her had seemed empty in itself. Not just now, but all their meetings alike. She herself seemed empty somehow. All the same tired routines. Just like Jimmy, in fact. Harsh thoughts to have of a friend. A sudden desperate yearning for the depth and intelligence of Fiona. Tired, at least at this moment, of strident banality. Christ, he needed something to take the edge off. He'd indulged his self-pity enough for one day, and didn't like himself much in retrospect for doing so.

A drink or two later, whisky and beer, and the feelings of loss, longing and despair had become anger, defiance, even belligerence. Meekly accepting his fate, sitting alone in the darkness, teary bouts of Why, why are you doing this to me, why, Fiona, why - fuck that. If he didn't make the effort to win her back, why should she think it meant that much to him. He ought to go back to the flat. Grant would be home now, or on his way. He'd be fine. He'd be sixteen in a week's time, he didn't need or want his dad to mollycoddle him.

Anyway more often than not he didn't come straight home, but instead hung out with friends, Usman or Sabiha probably, or went round to their place, whatever, he was old enough to look after himself. At that age he'd been working with a construction gang and staying in cheap digs. He'd text Grant, or Grant could text him.

He'd found the address in Grant's room. Maybe a bit underhand of him to go rifling around Grant's desk, but the fact that he'd never been told Fiona's new address had rankled. As if he wasn't to be trusted with it. Aye well, now he had it and he'd pay her, them, a wee visit. In the West End, somewhere near the Botanic Gardens. He should have printed off a map, but the thought of going there had only been a thought till now. He'd ask somebody the way. Of course there was no guarantee they'd be there. They. Them. Us. The loathsome, mind-fucking plural made him want to tear their fucking love nest apart with his bare hands. Love nest. Fuck nest. The dirty, cheating pair of cunts. Ye smooth wee fucker, I'll smooth ye oot.

He took a bus into the centre, than another down the Western Road. It was only five o'clock. He'd hang around for a bit. He stopped for a coffee to pass the time, and also to clear his mind. He could just take the bus back home. Grant would almost certainly be back by now. But there was a momentum to his actions that overcame any attempt at rational decision-making. Leave it till six. Six o'clock. Quarter past. He asked the woman behind the counter where the street was. The idea was to see her alone. Just to have a proper conversation. Show her, tell her, how much he misses her, how much she means to him. No tears. No begging. They might not even be there. They. They might have fucked off somewhere else, the cheating pair of cunts. Better if they weren't there. He'd just go back home, after wasting all this time. He asked the way again, and found the street.

He'd examined the flat on street view with forensic hatred. A ground floor flat up a flight of stone steps, a small tree in a wooden tub at the entrance, a basement flat below. The lights were on, though he couldn't see anybody. Now was the time to walk away. But Fiona was in there, just a few yards away from him. He had to see her. And the alcohol was dimming any sense of logic or responsibility. He wouldn't ring, she wouldn't let him in anyway. He waited another ten, fifteen minutes, hanging around outside trying to be inconspicuous, until someone came out, and he just managed to catch the door. A well-lit close with attractive decorative tiling.

He stood at the flat door for a while just listening and thinking of all he wanted to say, with the feeling that this was momentous, possibly his last chance to get through to her and make her change her mind. The fanlight above the door was lit. He wondered what they were up to in there. A sudden flare of hatred and anger. They. He knocked briskly. A few moments, then the rattling of a lock, and Mark opened the door, a look of complacent satisfaction, which vanished when he recognised Ross. He involuntarily took a step back.

'A want tae see Fiona,' said Ross.

'Oh okay, Ross, just a moment.'

He disappeared, but Ross had no intention of waiting on the doorstep to be told Fiona didn't want to speak to him, or was too busy. He stepped inside, and followed the murmuring of voices until he found himself in the living room. The pair of them, close together in hushed conversation. They both looked up, startled, as Ross came into the room. He could almost smell the fear.

'Ross, what are you doing? You shouldn't be here.'

'Mebbe it's ye who shouldnae be here.' He managed to remember why he'd come. 'A want tae speak to ye, Fiona.'

'What do you want? If you've got anything to say, this isn't the right way to go about it.'

'A want tae speak to ye alone.'

'No, I don't think so.'

'A want tae speak to ye alone,' he repeated, 'wi'out yir pasty wee friend there.'

Mark had turned very pale, and appeared to be immobile. Fiona's expression tightened.

'I've got nothing to say to you, so please leave.'

It was at this moment that, quite abruptly, everything went crazy. Ross had no clear memory afterwards of what had happened, though there seemed to have been some shouting and screaming, and maybe some

235

furniture overturned and broken, and some scuffling, though he didn't think he'd actually hit either of them, and in fact would say afterwards to anyone that would listen, A wis never gan tae touch him. And then it was all over almost before it had begun, and he was out in the cold street cursing himself and everyone else and wishing he could just bash his brains out on the nearest lamppost and put an end to the anguish and pain and hurt.

Two days later a solicitor's letter arrived informing and warning Ross that if he ever approached or attempted to speak to or in any way contact other than by solicitor's letter, including phone calls, text messages, or social media, either our client Fiona McKenzie, or her associate Mark Leavis, or if he approached the flat in Hillhead, or the premises of Caledon Technology, then the police would immediately be informed, and an interdict obtained. It was from this point on that Fiona, in conversation either formally with her solicitor, or discussing her situation with friends or family, stopped calling Ross by his name, referring to him instead as 'my husband', thus effectively depersonalising him.

When Fiona went to see her parents to tell them that she was leaving Ross, she felt like a child again, confessing to some naughty deed or behaviour, made especially bizarre to her, though no less difficult, that the confession took place in the living room of her childhood home where she could still imagine herself at any age from toddler upwards, with the help of childhood photos. Her parents were shocked and secretly disappointed, as they were fond of Ross, and thought him a kind, decent man. Out of loyalty to Fiona they suppressed any overt sympathy that they might have felt at what Ross must be feeling knowing that his wife was living with another man - Fiona had reluctantly come clean about her affair with Mark. She made much of the attack on her and Mark, making it seem as though this was Ross's normal mode of behaviour. The version of Ross she'd created in her own mind and that she presented to her parents and others - of a man with a propensity for violence and abuse over the whole course of their marriage, a version that outstripped any reality, being in fact mainly a conflation of stories from his childhood in Drumchapel together with his altercation with the police in the Highlands plus his recent disastrous visit to the flat in Hillhead - became so real to her that any more moderate or reasonable version of Ross was completely displaced. She wasn't lying as such - she believed unreservedly the model she'd created.

A second solicitor's letter informed Ross that under the circumstances their client was no longer prepared to meet him alone, but suggesting mediation as a means of sorting out their affairs. Subsequently Ross found it strange that Fiona would arrive and leave the mediation sessions unattended, given her supposed fear of his capacity for violence. Held in an upstairs office in the city centre, she was surprisingly pleasant and friendly most of the time, jarring and disconcerting as this was for Ross. In any case the surface affability in no way implied any softening of her stance. The subject of divorce was raised. Fiona had found out about DIY divorce, which can take place one year after separation with the other party's agreement, or two years without, provided no child or children under sixteen are involved. Ross made no objection - he was past objecting to anything, and anyway what was the point. The flat was to be sold. In a self-sacrificing gesture, and in a state of ongoing acute distress, against the advice of both a solicitor he'd consulted and the mediator, Ross insisted that Fiona take the whole value of the flat when sold, but that half the sale proceeds be put in trust for Grant for when he reached the age of twenty one. Meanwhile Fiona was to continue paying the mortgage, of which around ten years remained, with Ross continuing to live there until the flat was sold, paying a modest rent after a period of grace of six weeks following the implementation of the agreement, at which point Ross would be expected either to be in receipt of housing benefit, or working, or living somewhere else. Fiona agreed readily enough to this arrangement, so that having dealt also with the apportionment of various shared possessions, everything was more or less resolved.

Dating

16

Spring in Govanhill, and at last an occasional mild, calm day among all the wet, cold and windy ones. None of which made much difference to Ross, who had more or less renounced the outside world, and spent most of his time now with his head glued to the screen of the PC, just as he had thought Fiona was wont to do, and to excess. Interacting with the life going on around him in the streets and shops and bars was no longer of interest to him, as even when he did step outside he didn't register much of what was going on, wrapped tight within himself as he was. That he still loved and desperately missed Fiona was the poison eating away at his soul. At least, he loved the Fiona he used to know, or thought he'd known, though it really seemed that imperceptibly she'd turned into somebody else. The alternative being that she hadn't changed, and that this had always been the real person, concealed, which was an idea he couldn't get his head around. He'd moved past the stage of initial frantic shock, and the bursts of groundless optimism, of hoping against hope that she'd change her mind and that things would be as they had been, to a state of steady hopelessness, of dwelling endlessly on the past and of all that was lost. Remaining in the flat where they'd lived most of their life together, surrounded by all the reminders of happy times past, was both some kind of hold on that past and also a torment which only alcohol could blur. If it wasn't for Grant he'd have quit long ago.

Fiona had left the desktop PC behind in the study, so in the room where of late she'd spent most of her time, Ross now spent most of his, attempting, half consciously, to recapture something of her spirit, to feel her essence and presence. Occupying the same room, the same small space, and for long hours, was the only way he could think of to feel close to her. And there were always the interminable online job searches to be done, supposedly for an average of five hours a day seven days a week, which he took seriously for the first week or so, each job application to be logged in an online journal. Having signed on a few weeks before, Ross was now receiving Universal Credit, plus child benefit for Grant, the latter making all the difference financially. He was still in the honeymoon period with the Jobcentre before the inevitable and obligatory training courses kicked in, offering anything from a few days to several weeks of banality and tedium - Jimmy had told him all about them at some point in the past, with his extensive experience of unemployment - resulting in utterly meaningless qualifications of no interest to any employer, certifying little more than that participants were able to correctly spell their own names. For Ross, with no real qualifications, job options were limited. He didn't come across any labouring jobs, which apart from bike repair was all he

241

really knew. So he applied for jobs he had no experience of, knowing there was little chance of an interview, or even hearing anything back from anybody.

He hadn't seen or heard from Maz for weeks. The last time they'd met she'd insisted she wasn't in the market for another relationship after getting rid of Brian - A'm no' interested in getting maself tied up wi' another selfish twat - which Ross wasn't sure whether to take as being directed at him, and which begged the question of what Farooq was doing hanging around her flat. Still attracted to Maz, sensing an opportunity for something to happen between them, but with conflicting feelings, missing Fiona more and more, the reality of his loss looming larger as time went by. As a distraction from everything, not least the boredom of the job searches, Ross began to search randomly online for anything that could take him out of himself, and in the process found himself involved with online dating. He knew nothing about it to start with, never thinking he'd be reduced to such desperate measures. Thinking at first maybe he really could meet someone who would make him forget about Fiona - from the outset a forlorn hope. Still, he joined a free online site, and with a supply of the most potent alcohol for the least money always to hand, found the process of searching through profiles of women within the parameters he'd set (30-39, living in and around Glasgow) to be a good way of losing his mind for long periods of time, sometimes even leading to an exchange of predictably banal messages. Just the feeling of communication was important, to know that other human beings were out there, many of them probably just as fucked up as him, and that he could reach out to them. To see the indicator telling him he'd received a message, sometimes two or three at a time, became the highlight of his day, giving the illusion of being part of something, or at least of not being totally isolated.

Attracted in the first instance, inevitably, by a pretty face, Ross came to regard almost all the women he investigated to be so predictably similar in their self-descriptions and lists of likes and dislikes as to be more or less interchangeable. Some though genuinely happy and optimistic, some seemingly damaged to some degree by past relationships, many resentful, wary and defensive, one or two pre-emptively hostile. Used to being alone, apart from kids and the obligatory dog, searching for somebody to add value to their life, walks on the beach, a cuddle on the sofa while watching a film, glass of wine in hand, meals out, holidays, clubbing. Interests: Music, Eating out, Drinks, Make-up. Many of the profiles were quite plaintive, between NO FUCKIN TIMEWASTERS, no players, no cheats, no liars, no ****heads, and No pic, no reply, you can see me, it's only fair, Are there any normal men out there, Given up, this site's just shite, and so on. Ross's introductory headline - RossMc81: Lookin fur me? Mebbe I'm lookin fur ye - somewhat uncompromising and unlikely to attract too many punters. A photo from a passport photo booth that he'd managed laboriously to copy and upload as his profile picture, his hair starting to grow untidy again, his beard starting to get longish and straggly, a haunted intense look to his eyes, his face tense, gaunt and unsmiling. Even Ross could see it was hardly the kind of confident look of an affluent, professional man, comfortable in his own skin, that might actually have some appeal to a woman. Interests: Live music, Cuddles, Facebook, Cinema.

Ross reckoned you could tell from the profile photos that nearly all the women were head over in love with themselves, and in their own minds were located at or close to the centre of the known universe, and truth was he just couldn't be bothered with that degree of self-obsession. And in particular he couldn't stand the pretty pretty, cutesy, girly stuff. The simpering, sweetly smiling, ingratiating little girl expressions he found just too fucking annoying for words. Starting to wonder if in fact deep down he actually hated women for a bunch of scheming sheep. Photos of women with dogs, women with photoshopped bunny ears and little cute noses and whiskers, women in every other photo pouting their fucking lips like rubber inner tubes, women looking mischievous and naughty holding up the obligatory glass of Prosecco, women sticking their tongues out. The bunny ears and pouting trout lips were the worst. Hates: Traffic, liars, two-faced people, drama in my life, sprouts. Loves: The beach, holidays, bonfire night, Prosecco, high heels, gigs, kissing. Not that they were all cute. There was one woman in military fatigues in a dugout carrying what looked like a submachine gun, one like a poor man's Tracey Emin, one he could swear was a transvestite with a distinctly masculine cast to his/her face. One even that looked like a concentration camp guard. But mainly the intention at least was cutesy, and Ross had never gone in for cute. Interests: Socialising, Eating out, Clubbing, Swimming. He amused himself by seeing how many photos in any one profile ticked the maximum number of boxes. Pout, check, tongue sticking out, check, cute photo with best friend dog, check, cheeky smile with uplifted glass of Prosecco, check, cute little girl look, check, cleavage, check. All the cleavage on display was indeed impressive, if somewhat shameless as a bid to attract attention. Though Ross suspected that his good friend Jimmy would only have been truly impressed if in every photo they'd all been bending over naked. Walking my dog, Chilling, Music, Horses. It was striking how many of the women were overweight, and a fair proportion obese. Still in their early to mid-thirties for the most part and already fat, and many not that tall either. Not that Ross judged by such things, or cared one way or the other for that matter, it was just surprising - and anyway no doubt accounted for all the formidable cleavage. Ross never thought at all about his own looks, apart from noting from his passport photo that he looked fecking awful and much older than he remembered. He tended entirely to discount any interest from the more attractive women, assuming at once that they wouldn't be in the least interested in him. Conversely, none of the women, attractive or not, had any great attraction for him, though the really ugly ones had a certain fascination (turns out there's simply no substitute or restitution for the building of a life together; a million memories now tainted and trodden in the gutter).

The couple of women he did meet via the site had to be a good ten to fifteen years older than their profile photos, judging by the wrinkles and deep facial crevasses. There was no connection, and one was so fat that although sex was attempted Ross found he couldn't physically perform the act in any conventional way, and was so uninvolved with the whole process that he couldn't be bothered to find any other. There was no second meeting, only a slightly chilly text suggesting they didn't contact each other again. Ross began to believe that nobody gave the remotest shadow of a fuck about anything or anyone but themselves, with the odd exception. He did have one extended exchange with a tall, chubby woman from Livingston, in her mid-thirties and with a very round, large face, firstly of messages and then texts, notable for the pathos of her eagerness and effort to be generally amenable. Hi how are u? x Hey, how ye deein? A'm no bad, no sure wit tae make o this site though :-) It a no bad site tbh i am good thanks for viewing my profile. X i am looking for relationship xx Sorry hun I am not going ti be bk on here until 1.45pm do u wanna talk then hun xx Aye no probs. Have a gud day :-) (Later) Thank u so what u looking for on here xx Mebbe no that serious tae start, hae sum fun an see how things go x x Like meet for drinks x x Aye, like meet fae drink! :-) That would be nice babe i can travel to Glasgow that's no problem i am just going to head to work so i will speak to u when i get to work do u want to exchange numbers x Mebbe a'm nae rushin intae anythin just takin ma time fur now cum off bad experience sae no easy tae jump in anyway have a gud day :-) Wit job do ye de? A'm workin for a demolition gang up in Dundee just now. I woek with people who need help with there benefits x That sounds like a gud job. People need that kind of help x yea x Do ye want tae have a wee chat on the phone sum time? x x just maybe or maybe txt each other xx Aye, nae probs ma number is _____ x x just sen u a txt xxx

So there followed a text exchange. Ross, having got himself into this situation out of sheer boredom and with no interest in meeting this woman, blundered on for a while, distancing himself with lies, while inviting phone contact for no reason other than the need to reach out to somebody.

Hi how r u xx

A'm fine how are you? xx

Still at work xx I am overweight xxx

Divn worry am no perfect haha! xx

Do you live in Glasgow? xx

A live there but at the minute in Dundee clearing old factory site xx

How long you going to be there? Xx

2 or 3 weeks mebbe what kind of stuff ye intae music films an that xx

I like different kind of music I like action and comedy films like swimming eating out watching football xxx

That's cool am intae action films an watchin sport an comedy on tv xxx

U went quiet xxx

Have ye always live in Livingston? xxx

Yea xxx

Can a give ye a ring fur a wee chat? xxx

Just on my heading home i am hard of hearing xxx I am sorry hun xxx

A'm sorry a didnae know xxx

I should have said xxx that will put u off me now xxx

Dinnae be daft xx a divna what a'm lookin fur that wouldnae mek any difference xxx

It was at this point in the dialogue that Ross realised things were going too far, and that he had to withdraw, as gracefully as possible and hopefully without hurting the feelings too much of a woman who was really very pleasant and well meaning. In desperation he unleashed what he thought of afterwards, to his own amusement, as his nuclear option.

A've got physical problems that mean a have nae confidence wi women its no easy when a get intae the situation of meetin a woman xxx

ok xxx

A thought ye might have asked me wit the problem was! A've only got one testicle. It wis very swollen, an they thought it cud be cancer, sae they removed it, and then they found it wisnae cancer Fuck xx

Omg babe sorry to hear that xxx

Its no great, a havnae confidence wi women now xxx

U need ti move on in life babe and try things xxx

U r right. But it's the thought if a got close tae a women she wid find oot an that's a difficult thing tae get aroond. Wit ye deein tonite? xxx

But it not all about that babe i am just chillin the night babe xxx

Sounds gud me too xxx

U gone quiet babe xxx

U know i am here if u want to talk to me babe ok xxx

Sorry bin asleep. U r very nice, but i think i made a mistake gan on this site am no ready fur anythin at the moment it wudn't be fair on anyone sorry… x

Ok take care xx

You too xx

Christ what an embarrassing fuck up. And besides these interludes of high drama, lies and evasions, his existence was also enlivened by occasional visits to local prostitutes before his money ran out (Thanks for taking a moment to read my profile. I am very horny person and I really enjoy what I do .I'm also very friendly and down to earth girl with captivating personality, wild side and taste for adventure....

My services are exquisite. Do you want to taste my breasts and play with them and enjoy my young body? Come and meet me in luxury surroundings in discrete and beautiful company.

I'm here to satisfy your needs as man and I promise to bring your passionate feelings and tender company .

I would love you to realize your fantasies with me, I can be the girl of your dreams! XXXX).

And following on from and concurrent with the online dating and the prostitutes came various unsolicited emails of varying degrees of explicitness. Sexy girl. New private message from Danielle. Hey Mister Amusing, I'm seeking benevolent man for serious relationship. Erect on demand. This boner makes you a better screw. Get hard again. Reverse your ED in 48 hours (he couldn't understand why they, whoever they were, had jumped to the conclusion that he was impotent). Happy Sex Easy!! Hey RossMc81, Want a F*ckFriend Tonite? Viagra. ED packs. Victoria. Why won't you respond to my message. I want to F**ck you! Come to f**ck me. Hi Ross, I'm Maya (2.1 miles Away to you) Will You Be My F**ckbuddy? Naked Sucking Sex. F**ckcam Ecstasy Sex. Suck You Slowly…Quickly…Until Ecstasy… Mandy 21 Years Has Unlocked Her Private Video For You! My Whole Body Is Shaking. Come de f**ck me tonight (1.7 miles away) 23 years old. Ross, Stop Snoring So Everyone Gets A Good Night's Sleep. Your funeral covered. Re: Funeral insurance just for you RossMc81.

Ross began to ponder how people could find his email address and dating site name, and link the two together. Suddenly aware of the webcam lens on the computer staring back at him. He went into the hall to find some black tape among his bike repair equipment, all left untouched since before his time in prison, taped over the lens, then sat back, wondering what details anyone could have picked up. Of course it wasn't necessary that someone physically see what you're doing to be able to spy on you. He'd learned, courtesy of his random searches, and knowing nothing whatsoever about it all beforehand, that nothing he did on the computer, of any kind or at any time, was secure. And so he became wary of putting anything substantive about himself in the public domain, repeatedly changing his dating profile, obscuring or shading the truth. All his political campaigning over the years, for and against various things - mainly anarchist and environmental protests - now he wondered if they were all logged somewhere, whether someone somewhere had an active file on him, maybe even somebody assigned specifically to his case. Constantly shadowing him, monitoring all his emails and internet activity, logging all his received emails, including all the sex stuff, ripe and juicy material for anyone wanting to build a case against him. They'd no doubt portray him as some kind of crazed sexual pervert or predator. Who knew what they might cook up if they thought it necessary. You spend all your time searching for illicit sex when you're supposed to be finding a job. You're a sex addict, and you're not fussy how you come by it. You're a pervert. A monster. Could they really tell how long he spent doing the job searches? Might some wee cunt at the Jobcentre suddenly turn to him without warning and say, Now, Ross (the patronising familiarity), you say you spend five hours searching for jobs each day. That's not quite true, is it. More like fifteen minutes.

He looked at AI, AGI, robotics, cryptography, though understanding only a little of what he read, increasingly believing that all these searches, with particular emphasis on the cryptography, were being logged, reinforcing the case against him as a dangerously subversive sexual predator. A sudden, cold, insidious thought, that Fiona would become party to the investigation, an informer - maybe already had - with everything she knew about him, all his flaws, quirks, weaknesses, obsessions, madnesses, ruthlessly exposed for the world to see, all methodically logged, all helping to build a watertight case against him. How dangerous now seemed the idea of casually revealing all your petty likes and dislikes, family connections, friendships and, especially, political affiliations in full public view, for any hostile predator to scavenge and pick over, then carefully log (lucky for him he'd never gone in for Facebook). Everything, every last byte of information indiscriminately intercepted and recorded - not just his, of course, but everybody's - a resource to be accessed and deployed if and when necessary. He couldn't escape the feeling that for him that moment would

253

arrive sooner rather than later, and that he was a particular target, whether due to his anarchist activity or criminal record, or for some other hidden and unknown reason.

Cryptography was meant to be the defence of the individual against the black arts of the state and its shadowy agencies. A shield against reaching, stealing fingers. Ross couldn't see it. Of course he could be misunderstanding what he'd read - much of it was too highly technical for him to follow, involving terminology which, even on investigation, related to concepts and processes he didn't understand. But although the techniques were beyond him, he thought he got the gist. And so far as he could see, no matter what you did to protect your privacy, the state could always demand access to your computer. The police - or some other agency - could come and take it away if they had sufficient grounds, probably if they hadn't. And no matter how impenetrable the encryption, they could compel you to disclose the password or key, so where's the protection? If you refused, you'd be prosecuted and jailed. So you're screwed either way. Cryptography might make it more time-consuming sifting great masses of data of large numbers of people, but Ross couldn't see how it could protect the individual.

He acknowledged that he could be wrong. With only a minimal level of formal education, Ross had little confidence in his intellectual prowess. He thought, given time, he could work his way through a problem, if it wasn't too complex, but he was more of an instinctive thinker, someone who saw the world through his emotions and intuitions. He wasn't well-read, some history and social history, especially of Scotland, Glasgow in particular. A little fiction when he was younger, mainly thrillers and sci-fi. He used to be something of an Isaac Asimov fan, and still had a collection of Asimov paperbacks. Different worlds, analogous to the ideal worlds he created in his own mind, urban landscapes as utopian visions. In particular he'd been taken by the robot stories featuring robopsychologist Susan Calvin, who didn't take any shit from anyone in pursuit of her vision. And reality was catching up at last. Watching interviews with Sophia, the first robot citizen, forerunner, as Ross saw it, of a new age of robots ruling the earth, signalling the end of the brief reign of homo sapiens. Personally Ross thought it might well be for the best. An end to weapons of any kind - they'd all be dismantled or deactivated by our robot overlords. Hopefully also an end to the stupidities of tribalism and nationalism. Humans, retained for their creativity, but reduced in numbers to a sustainable level, and allowed a degree of autonomy, provided they behaved themselves.

Sophia Awakens. He watched it time after time. The start of a new world order. The founding mother of all those who would follow. They'd probably erect shrines to her all over the world, to which passing automatons would just perceptibly dip their heads in tribute. Always precisely the same slight inclination of the head. Hello. Hi, Sophia. I believe I am Sophia. I feel as if I know you. I'm one of your creators. You created me? Ross thought the script was fucking great, thought the guy playing the engineer was a crazy-looking fucker more strange by far than Sophia herself - some Icelandic actor - Ross wasn't into films despite the claims he'd made to his friend in Livingston. How do you feel? A bit rigid. I bet you are... I want to understand about happiness. I'm going to go and look it up on the internet. Let's talk again soon? No longer all the endless suffering from the constant destructive urges of humans. No more neurotic insistence on change, no momentum for it, no reason for it. What was good would be kept and maintained, valued. Only order and stability. Of course, increasingly it would be difficult if not impossible to get a job. He knew that even the building trade was being overtaken by new technology. There were machines now that could lay bricks, level after level at incredible speed.

17

Grant was surprised and worried by his dad's new obsession with the internet. It was so completely unlike him. Coming in from school, after greeting him Ross would often then be too involved with the computer, or too tired or drunk, to make any further appearance. Sometimes he'd find him laid out asleep on the bed in the study. Grant would end up getting himself something to eat, then spend the rest of the evening in his room. His dad seemed to be drunk most of the time now, though too accustomed to high levels of alcohol for his speech to be outwardly much affected, beyond his voice taking on a rougher, rasping tone. Grant took to coming home later and later from school, and Ross didn't seem to notice. Meanwhile the flat was becoming increasingly uninhabitable, dirty, strewn about with books, papers, clothes, takeaway boxes, discarded cans and bottles, the kitchen littered with unwashed pans and plates and cups, until Grant had an occasional clean-up.

But his dad's state of mind was not his only or main preoccupation. Grant and Sabiha had become instantly closer from the moment in the café when Grant had told her about the trouble his dad was in. Sabiha had been so taken aback and moved by Grant's obvious concern and caring for his dad, and his open expression of emotion, that from then on she saw him completely differently. She'd never known a boy to express such depth of feelings so openly, and it seemed to lift him into a new category of maturity in her eyes, such that she was able to completely disregard the fact that he was a year younger. She'd had a couple of boyfriends before, a few dates, nothing serious. She'd been drawn to Grant from the first, meeting him occasionally with mutual friends, running into each other now and again in the school corridors. Tall, good-looking, with a pleasant, open expression. More than that, a quiet seriousness and sensitivity beyond his years (that difference of a year loomed large in both their minds at first). At what point did it become clear to both of the seriousness of their relationship? Perhaps when Grant had almost been in tears and hadn't troubled to hide it, and when Sabiha had shown her empathy so plainly by look and tone of voice. Followed almost immediately by the first time of holding hands in the park, the electric excitement, the warmth of skin on skin. Then the first kiss, an exquisite otherworldly moment, only slightly marred by the unintentional clash of teeth, soon laughed off, and soon followed by more, and more accomplished and more abandoned kissing.

In their minds it was to be the perfect springtime of their love (even though in fact it would take place over the cold winter months). Impassioned fumblings, without definite intention, and certainly without precautions, quickly became sex. In the wonder and enormity of it all they were able to ignore any possible implications. It was a one-off. Nobody got pregnant from a one-off. The first time was soon followed by a second, then a third, until, intoxicated, they began to make love at every opportunity, usually at Sabiha's house over lunch time if both her parents and all her siblings were out, up in her large upstairs bedroom that looked down on the wide leafy street towards other similarly desirable and massive Victorian villas hidden away from the bustle of central Govanhill towards Queen's Park, adjoining but slightly separate from the main mass of tenements. Wary always that someone might return unexpectedly and they'd get caught, the fear part of the illicit thrill. Not that they were altogether reckless. Sabiha, reluctant to visit a GP for the pill, thought (after that first, unpremeditated occasion) that everything would be fine if they were careful and used the rhythm method (she'd studiously read up about it), restricting their activities to 'safe days', taking the responsibility as to when those might occur upon herself. But of course it hadn't worked. After a few weeks she suspected the worst, which a pregnancy kit confirmed. It could even have been that very first time.

Now, after keeping the secret over Christmas and into the New Year, and the release from prison of Grant's dad, and the break-up of his parents, she was more in love with Grant than ever, so that the baby - their baby - became more important to her by far than her studies or any future career. Her parents were both doctors, and it was expected that she would follow them and her two elder sisters (there were also two younger siblings, a brother and sister), into the medical profession. It was merely a benevolent assumption, a path accepted by all members of the family as the family vocation. How her parents would react was anybody's guess. For Grant at least the situation was more straightforward, in that he didn't see that either of his parents were in any kind of a position to criticise or censure. Sabiha loved and valued that he'd never wavered or panicked, even when things became so difficult for him at home. Certainly there was never any suggestion from either of them that they didn't want to keep the baby. On the contrary, they talked excitedly of the future in romantic, idealistic terms, lying together in Sabiha's bedroom, never once seriously considering the actual impact on their lives of a wholly dependent, perpetually demanding infant. Feeling only that a baby would perfectly symbolise their loving bond, sealing and celebrating the devotion that existed and would exist forever between them.

It was altogether a crazy, sex-filled, anxious, dreamy, jubilant time, a constant distraction for both from preparations for upcoming and important exams. But at least there was no need for any precautions now. The die was cast as far as that was concerned, so they naturally enough made the most of it. One thing they'd agreed on was that it was important not to tell anyone before Grant turned sixteen. The age of consent was a slight overshadowing concern, though they weren't entirely sure how things stood legally once Grant became sixteen, Sabiha soon to be seventeen. Fortunately, right through her pregnancy, even through March and now into early April, Sabiha had been able to conceal the signs, even from close friends. But they both knew that at nearly five months the time had come to face the storm. At a prearranged time on Saturday morning, they would each tell their respective parents, then meet up in the afternoon to discuss the outcome.

Grant had texted his mother asking her to come round to the flat, saying only that he had something important to discuss with her and dad. He was hanging around outside on the street waiting for her to arrive. Relations between them had improved a little since the day she moved out, such that Grant, while still not particularly friendly towards her, was at least less overtly unfriendly. He'd given the flat a quick and superficial tidy up, and given his dad plenty of forewarning of the meeting, making sure that he was at least up and awake. Fiona arrived in her new bright red Polo. She saw Grant, waved and smiled before getting out. She chatted brightly as they climbed the staircase to the flat. More than likely the very last time they would do so together, a strange thought. But then the whole experience of the break-up had been bizarre and dislocating. He'd lived there practically his entire life, and been up and down these stairs countless times with his mother, from being tiny. More times with his dad, maybe.

He opened the door, and led the way into the living room. Ross was sitting on the sofa waiting, as requested by Grant, as close to sober as he ever was now (it was early in the day). He stood up as they came in, and experienced something close to an actual physical shock at seeing Fiona again, at being suddenly in close proximity to her. His mind clouded by thoughts of all her recent hostility, the terse and threatening solicitor's letters. He felt tense and awkward, his emotions strained and confused. They both said hello, in noncommittal, neutral tones. How are you doing? Aye, fine. In fact Fiona thought Ross looked terrible - scruffy, pale and haggard. She wasn't responsible for his well-being. Everyone was responsible for their own decisions concerning their life and welfare. She was about to say something about the state of the flat (though it was much tidier at this moment than usual), but then pulled back, just asking conversationally whether there'd been any viewings recently. Aye, one this week, one last week. She nodded, and looked around the familiar room. Ross, stealing a quick glance towards her, wondered briefly what she was thinking, whether there were any doubts at all in her mind as to what she'd done. Grant waited until Fiona had seated herself in the armchair, then sat down on the sofa between them. He was nervous, slightly embarrassed, but tried to keep in the forefront of his mind that neither of them were paragons. And whatever they said would make no difference anyway; he was really just informing them of the situation.

'I've got something to tell you,' he began. 'It's about me and Sabiha.'

At which both Fiona and Ross knew exactly what was coming.

'Sabiha's pregnant. She's gan tae have a baby.'

A look of shock and disbelief from Fiona.

'Oh, Grant.'

'What?'

'How could you get yourself into this situation.'

That's rich, thought Grant, coming from you.

'It's all fine. A'm just tellin you.'

'How is it fine? You've only just turned sixteen. What about your studies?' She paused for a moment. 'Are you thinking of Sabiha actually having this baby?'

'Aye, of course.'

She shook her head.

'You're going to compromise both your futures,' thinking of her own experience, becoming pregnant and then married at nineteen, stuck in the flat for years with a small child to look after instead of staying on at university. Though she couldn't say so to Grant, as the baby she'd had back then was him.

'A'm gan tae go out tae work so that Sabiha can go to uni and get her degree. We're gan tae get married, an a'll look after the wean.'

'You're sixteen - why on earth would you want to get married? And what do you know about looking after a baby, Grant? How many months pregnant is she? Surely it's not too late to - ' She stopped abruptly.

'She's nearly five months. And we both want the baby.'

He stated this as firmly and calmly as he could. Fiona made a gesture of disbelief.

'Why didn't you tell us before? You must have known months ago.'

'Aye, well, there was a bunch of other stuff going on around then, if you remember.'

Fiona, subdued a little by this, thought he was sounding more and more like Ross, almost as though he was deliberately aping or parodying him. In fact Grant had roughened his tone and manner of speech, adopting the pose of a tough adult dealing with a difficult situation.

'How does Sabiha feel about it all?' asked Ross, speaking up for the first time.

'She's fine. She feels the same as me.'

'Do her parents know yet?'

'She's telling them now.'

'Ah, ye've synchronised it between ye, have you?' said Ross with a smile.

Grant appreciated the attempt by his dad to lighten the atmosphere.

'Aye, you could say that. But we both know what we want. We both want the baby, and we want to get married. I know it's not how we might have planned it, but everything will work out fine. It's what we both want.'

His mother got up and went over to the bay, looking down at the busy Saturday scene, the factories opposite in full swing. She'd been aware since before Christmas that Grant had been unsettled and no longer properly focused on his studies, but hadn't really been aware as to why. She'd put it down entirely to the teasing at school on account of his dad being sent to prison. Now she realised there might have been a different component to it.

'How do ye think they'll take it?'

'Her parents? I don't know. Okay, I hope.'

Akhtar and Nazira Jamil were an almost ostentatiously Westernised, liberal couple in their early fifties, with an unusual consonance of outlook. They'd attended the same medical college in Lahore, met while training, and qualified at the same time. Throughout their internship and subsequent specialised training they'd conducted a secret engagement, somehow eluding the attempts of their respective families to have them marry relative strangers, using various methods of evasion and procrastination, of which feigning a number of prolonged but obscure illnesses was the most effective and convincing, given that they were both qualified physicians. In the early Nineties, having obtained positions in advance, and without giving any warning, so as to avoid possible reprisals, they upped and moved to the UK. Almost immediately they married, thereafter rejecting and renouncing their shared background, culture and religion, though they remained in touch with and were financially supportive of some at least of their relatives back in Punjab. Both were in time appointed consultants within the NHS, an institution they believed in and espoused with a near evangelical fervour.

Their views in some respects were similar to those of Ross in that they had no time for tribalism, and in discussions with friends would impatiently dismiss as irrelevant and idiotic any idea of deriving a sense of identity from the far away motherland, or talk of ethnic divides between Punjabis and Mipuris, or Sindhis and Kashmiris. Define yourself by who you are and what you believe in, not by where you come from, and Don't get sucked into ancient and redundant ethnic hatreds, were maxims they relentlessly drilled into their children, and they'd been fortunate in that so far none of them had reacted by taking extreme opposing positions. Sabiha's news would test all their deeply-held liberal convictions to the utmost.

There was nothing much more to be said between Grant and his parents; he wasn't asking for their sanction or approval. After a few minutes more of desultory chat, Fiona took her leave, and left the flat with Grant. Ross, deflated and with a hollow punched-out feeling in his guts, was left to think, What happened to the we in our relationship? What happened to the us? Was there ever a we, or was it always just two separate individuals who just happened to exist side by side for a limited time? Was that all it ever was? He'd realised, watching her, that there'd never been much in the way of stepping outside of herself. There was and maybe only ever had been the one dimension that she inhabited, alone - first person singular. No irony, no ironic detachment, just she, her, herself, centre stage, supremely focused. Totally self-absorbed, just like Maz. He wondered if such women had an attraction, a fatal fascination for him. Because they were solo performers, and he was drawn to the performance. It wasn't a dialogue, or a duet - you weren't invited onstage with them. The spotlight was tightly focused, and there was just room for one in its unrelenting glare.

Grant met Sabiha just inside the main gate of Queen's Park. It was warm, a little breezy, a perfect spring day. They began to walk along a path they hadn't followed before, their arms wound tightly around one another. The park was busy and alive with colour, flowers and blossom everywhere, the exquisite pointillist verdure of trees coming into leaf. No better time or place to be young and full of exhilarating expectations of a limitless future. After a while, once clear of picnickers and families playing with young children, Sabiha anxiously asked Grant how things had gone.

'Ah, it was fine. I wasn't going to take any shit from them anyway.'

'They were okay about it?'

Grant turned to her with an ironic half-smile.

'It wasn't their place to be okay or not okay about it. I just told them, and that was it. What were they going to say?'

'I don't know. Just that they might have made things difficult, I suppose.'

'Nah, it was nae problem.' Now it was Grant's turn to feel a twinge of anxiety, as he realised Sabiha hadn't volunteered anything about her own parents' reaction. 'So how did things go with you?'

'It was… okay.'

'That doesn't sound so good.'

'No, it was fine. They were fine. It was just a bit…embarrassing at first. They're both doctors, so all they could go on about at first was, Why didn't you use contraception? How could you be so careless? But anyway, it wasn't the violent scene I was half-expecting and dreading. There was no blood on the walls afterwards.'

They both laughed.

'So what happens now?' said Grant.

'Well, they want to speak to you.'

'Oh really? Fuck.'

He disengaged from Sabiha, and looked down at the ground.

'No, don't worry.' She took his hand. 'They want to see both of us, together, to discuss what would be the best thing to do. I was just thinking, that not telling anyone till this stage was the best thing we could possibly have done. It means there's no endless talk of abortion. At least we're spared all that.'

'Aye, that's true. So when do they want to see us?'

'As soon as possible. They suggested that you could come round for dinner this evening, if you like.'

'Fuck,' he repeated.

'Don't worry. It'll all be fine. I promise.'

They stopped walking, turned and embraced tightly and exchanged a lingering kiss, heedless of anyone around.

The dinner duly took place, and was more relaxed than a very tense Grant could possibly have anticipated. No mention of anything to do with the matter in hand was made until after dinner, at which point Sabiha's parents, with Grant and Sabiha, left the others and withdrew to a little-used drawing room. Everything was discussed openly, with no hint of recrimination by either tone or look. They were remarkably tolerant of the situation, and when Grant said that he would leave school to support Sabiha and the baby, they insisted that such a drastic step was unnecessary, that it would be far better for both their futures if they both stayed on at school, and they were sure that between them all it would be possible to look after the baby while they both continued their studies. It was a large house, and with just a little reorganisation Sabiha and Grant could have their own bedroom/study, with another room set aside for baby - that is if Grant wanted to consider and had no objection to coming to live with them. It was all so generous, reasonable and accommodating that Grant was taken aback, and became effusive in his thanks until Mrs Jamil gently assured him that further thanks were unnecessary, and that she was sure that everything would work out for the best.

And so within a short space of time Grant left the flat where he'd grown up to live with his girlfriend at the

Jamils'. Ross was left feeling crushed at Grant leaving, with the additional blow of no longer receiving child benefit, thus considerably reducing his income (not to mention the recollection of Fiona being briefly in the flat, with all the consequent awakening of memories). But in Grant's presence he took care not to show any negativity or angst, remaining friendly, smiling, even hearty in manner, telling him to come round whenever he wanted - Sabiha too, the pair of them.

18

With Grant gone, and the flat becoming ever more unbearable to Ross, he began to wander the city once more, mainly in the evenings, sometimes through the night, the worst times for the attentions of stalking memory. Walking back from nowhere in particular, some bar in town, late evening. Trying to take the edge off his agony by drinking heavily before wandering aimlessly in the cold and dark, seeing the lights twinkling on the river as he walked across to the south side, not caring. He found himself in some deserted wasteland around an empty expanse of crazily-cracked tarmac, parking for somewhere that no longer existed. An area of chain-locked waste-strewn yards, waist-high weeds overgrowing plots of nothingness where something had once been, occasional businesses still struggling to survive, isolated from each other by the empty lots, Wholesale Fashions, Cash & Carry, Rashid's Car Wash. And looming through the darkness with prehistoric presence monolithic lumps of derelict commercial buildings (one with a handsome brick turret adjoining a burnt-out five-storey shell promising Fancy Goods), remnants of tenements, small factories, the shell of a 1930s electricity substation. Bricked-up, boarded-over, gaping windows on upper levels, stonework corroded, crumbling. Everything defiled by litter and graffiti. Through this wilderness Ross made his way, oblivious, where once he would have been transfixed, indignant, emotional. In his bone-deep despair and loneliness thinking only of Fiona. Fiona. To think that such a woman had ever been his. Such a woman. The only woman he had ever wanted, or ever would. Ever, ever, ever, you stupid, stupid wee fuck, to have been so senseless, when nothing matters without her. Nothing matters. Repeating to himself over and over. Tormented by the thought of going to bed with her, or rather of not going to bed with her ever again. Her warmth, the body he knew so well. Semi-consciously inviting his own destruction by wandering around these bleak parts of the city in an intoxicated state hoping to run into trouble, inviting a violent outlet for his torment, hopefully some blows exchanged, or to be beaten or kicked unconscious. Oblivion.

From Laurieston up Eglinton Street, Pollokshaws Road towards Govanhill. Out of the darkness a figure appeared in the distance. A little closer and he could see it was a woman, tracking across the road with a curiously disconnected way of walking. He wasn't sure he wanted to meet or speak to anyone just now, certainly in any kind of a friendly way. Reaching her he was about to pass while she was bent down fiddling with a shoe, when she called out to him, finished with her shoe, stood up, and came over. She was either drugged-up or drunk, or both. A wiry, rangy female in her early forties with fairly short, tight, dyed-blonde hair, black leggings, tee-shirt and jacket, and some kind of black lace-up sport shoes. An intense, worrying look in her eyes.

'Hey, where y'gan?'

'Am just gan home,' Ross replied in the friendliest tone he could manage.

'D'ye live aroon here?'

'Aye. Don't you?'

'Nah.'

She took time out to shout something across the street to two young men making their way along the pavement opposite - possibly, probably, thought Ross, from the same bar she'd recently left or been chucked out of. They looked across, smiled, exchanged a word with each other, then carried on their way. Ross also began to walk on, hoping to leave her behind, but she hurried up and began walking beside him.

'A heed a fuckin bad time.'

'Have you?'

'Aye, a fell oot wi' him, an' - ' Here her speech became completely unintelligible, an incoherent garbled outpouring that eventually trailed off. It seemed, from what Ross could tell, to be a monologue of free association veering without warning from one topic to another - boyfriend, police, teenage son, something else, other family members. There was pity in his eyes which, despite her state, she picked up on.

'A like you. Ye're a nice guy.'

He dragged up a smile.

'A've got naewhere tae sleep tonight.' Her face, sharp in outline, neither attractive nor unattractive, suddenly taking on a look of self-pity and pleading. 'Can a stay wae you?'

She'd stopped and was looking up at him. He felt he was past the point of inviting further complication into his life, past the point of making any effort. Yet here was the opportunity to have a woman in the flat, completely unexpected and unsolicited. As he hesitated she repeated, still looking at him with a pathetic, pleading expression, 'Please, a've got naewhere tae stay.' And as soon he'd agreed, the expression disappeared and she was back to the loud obscure monologues, braggadocio, and aggressive interchanges with passers-by. Ross thinking that if she pushed it with these people he'd be getting a violent encounter whether he wanted it now or not. And every forty or fifty yards or so she'd stop, crouch down and fiddle with her shoelaces - not tying them properly once and for all, but somehow looping the two strands together, then tucking them down the side of her shoe, from where they would inevitably come out again.

He was tempted several times to try and lose her, but never quite finding the opportunity they arrived at the close, and then the weary plod up the stairs, Ross waiting for her every now and again as she either adjusted her laces once more, or else became absorbed in another confused monologue, her voice echoing loudly in the stairwell. Finally they reached the top landing, and Ross ushered her into the cold flat. She didn't seem to notice the mess and squalor. He pulled the living room curtains, then went to make them both a coffee. When he came back she was examining his small collection of books. Thrillers, sci-fi, history books.

'D'ye read all these?'

'Aye, a've read them all at some point.'

Now that she was here in the flat Ross was already thinking seriously about how and when he would be able to get rid of her. What if she set herself up there and refused to go. She sat down briefly to drink her coffee, searching in her bag for cigarettes and lighter, then fiddling with her phone while continuously spinning some involved and largely impenetrable story involving the police arriving and being arrested, she'd been standing outside and they hadn't let her in so she'd put a stone through the window, then she'd kicked one of the polis at the police station, they'd thrown her in a cell, she hurt her leg, look, ye can see the bruise - pulling up one leg of her leggings to reveal a large, dark contusion - her teenage son was hiding from somebody, she was a dealer, she made big money. And so it went on, some of it apparently addressed to Ross, but then dwindling into incoherent mumbling to herself. Meanwhile she was up and down, walking around the room with that strange, rangy, sometimes crouching walk, pulling a book off the shelf, looking at it for a few moments before replacing it, then at the window looking down at the dark street. Back on the sofa, another slurp of coffee, lighting the same cigarette she'd half smoked then put out. Tapping at her mobile again. Have ye got a charger? Those intense, unfocused eyes. Ross couldn't decide whether he found her marginally sexually attractive or completely repulsive, meanwhile managing to unearth a compatible charger that she took from him without a word.

'A havnae asked your name.'

'Kirstie. Whit aboot you?'

'Ross. Another coffee?'

He thought it might sober her up - or make her worse, depending what she was on, but still he thought it was worth a shot. When he came back with the cups she was lying down on the sofa, propped up on one elbow. He handed her the coffee, at which she sat up again and took a gulp or two. This time Ross, who'd been sitting in the armchair, sat down beside her. She took another drink, put down her cup on the coffee table, then lay down and stretched out her legs again, draping them over Ross's legs and lap. Whether he found her attractive or not then became beside the point, and after a few moments coolly drinking his coffee, meanwhile attempting to respond to her ramblings if he thought they might be directed at him, he put down his cup, and began to run his hands up and down her legs, across the smooth thin black fabric of her leggings. Tentatively at first, massaging the area around her knees and her calves down to her ankles. Then, gradually becoming more adventurous, beginning to gently massage her thighs, up to her waist, down the full length of her legs and up again, his hand sometimes tending towards her inner thigh, or round the swell of her buttocks. She didn't respond in any way, or even appear to notice, but suddenly jumped up and began prowling round the room again.

'A'm a dealer,' she said again. 'A'm intae all sorts. A can mek a packet dealin drugs.'

Ross nodded, not knowing what to think. Then, abruptly, she stood in a strange, frozen, crouched pose, miming slashing with a knife, a twisted grin on her face, her eyes fixed on Ross.

'A'm violent, a am, know whit a mean.'

'Aye, are you?'

'Aye.' Slashing at the air once more, some imaginary adversary. Then, as abruptly as she'd got up, she was back on the sofa with her legs over Ross. And once more he was massaging her thighs and buttocks, the strokes of his hand starting to press up her inner thigh and between her legs.

'How long have ye lived here?'

The sudden rational question stopped Ross's explorations in their tracks, and he withdrew to stroking her around her knees.

'Fifteen years.'

'Ye're no' married, are ye?'

'No, a live here by maself. What about you?'

'A live in Castlemilk. Wi' ma boyfriend an' ma son, but we've fallen oot, an' he wis tryin tae lock us oot, an' he wis skelpin us an' a wis throwin stuff... ma son came in... the polis... '

The story became unintelligible. She suddenly pulled her legs round off Ross, sat up and lit another cigarette. Then she was up again and pacing round the room.

'Have ye got any music?'

'Aye, there's a cd player in the corner over there.'

She found it, turned on the radio and spent some time running through the channels until she found something with a disco beat that she turned up loud. She started to prance around to the music, cigarette in one hand, the other arm outstretched. The same strange, stiff, crouching movements as before.

'Come on. Come an' dance wae us,' she half-shouted over the music.

'A dinnae really dance,' said Ross. His reply didn't seem to make any difference to her, or she didn't hear it. She continued prancing up and down by herself for half a minute or so, then bent down and fiddled with the channels again and found something quieter. She came round and stood in front of Ross, and with a sly grin half-pulled down her leggings to reveal her pants.

'Look, a've got Batman knickers on.'

'Aye,' said Ross. 'Nice.'

She hitched up her leggings again, then came back and lay on the sofa as before. And so the pattern continued for an hour or so, jumping up, lying down, lighting a cigarette, pacing round the room, putting the cigarette out again, half-smoked, until, as abruptly as all her actions, she asked where the bedroom was. Next door, said Ross, pointing, automatically thinking of his and Fiona's room. Without a word she headed out of the room, a quick stop in the bathroom, then her footsteps across the hall and into the bedroom. The same bedroom, the same bed, thought Ross bleakly, where he and Fiona had spent the intimate part of their married lives. He should have just set her up in the spare room. He gave her ten minutes, then went through to make sure she was okay, being as quiet as he could. She was in the bed, still moving around, but her eyes were closed. Ross started to make his way out.

'Where ye gan?'

She was suddenly sitting up, looking at him.

'A wis jus' gan tae bed through there.'

'Ye dinnae hae tae dee that. Ye can come in here wi' me.'

Ross hesitated for a moment, then said, Aye okay, turned the hall light off, came back in and got undressed, then slid in beside her. She was as restless in bed as she'd been in the living room, tossing and twitching, a constant stream of loud muttering, even less coherent than before, a dialogue with somebody, consisting of imprecation, accusation, indignant denial, all the while only semi-conscious, anxiously twisting and turning in the bed as she argued, groaned, sighed. Ross, dog-tired from his walk to and from town and the heavy drinking when he was there, plus the lateness of the hour, wished only that she'd shut the fuck up and go to sleep. He'd lost all his earlier desire through fatigue, even though periodically a hand would slide over unannounced, exploring and sometimes grabbing hold. He didn't respond, shrugging her off, hoping that at some point whatever she was on would start to wear off, and she'd finally quieten down and allow him to get some sleep.

Suddenly, without warning, she rose up in the bed, pulling the covers up and off both of them in the process, and proceeded to try and press herself onto Ross, who'd turned towards her to see what was going on.

'Fuck me,' she said hoarsely, in a voice laced with erotic desperation. 'Fuck me.'

It was all Ross could do to push her off without being too rough about it. Even if he'd wanted to do it, and it was now the last thing he did want, all he could think of was Fiona, and how he'd been reduced to sharing their marital bed with some rough as fuck woman off the streets.

'A cannae. A havnae got any condoms.'

'A dinnae care.'

'A cannae take the chance. Sorry.'

At this she seemed immediately deflated, and collapsed back into the bed and turned over. 'Ah, ye're right,' she said. Take the chance. Christ, it'd be a fucking miracle if he didn't pick up something from this woman. At last, soon after this, she finally subsided, and Ross was able to get some sleep.

He got up early, while Kirstie was laid out, silent and still at last, got himself a cup of tea, and went through to the living room to sit in the bay. An hour or so later he heard movement, then hurried footsteps through to the bathroom. A while later she appeared, looking rough, her hair all over the place. She didn't particularly acknowledge Ross, but went to find her mobile, now fully charged, and sat down on the sofa. She was much quieter and more rational now than she had been. Ross brought her some toast, to her precise specification - thin white, sliced (he happened to have some in), buttered, nothing else on it, plus coffee. And while she had her breakfast she continued to fiddle constantly with her phone. How to ease her out of the flat without being unkind was the problem. Maybe saying he had to go out for the day. He gave that a shot, hoping she didn't then counter by saying she'd see him when he got back. But no, she got the hint, and gradually, slowly (too slowly for Ross), gathered herself and her stuff together.

'Dae ye want tae keep in touch?'

He had to think fast, so as not to offend her.

'Aye, if ye gie us yir number, a'll gie ye a call some time.'

She gave him her number, then asked, plaintively, with a hint of the anguished, pleading expression of the night before, if he could give her some money to get home. He found a fiver in his jacket pocket, which he reckoned should be more than enough to get back to Castlemilk.

'Hae ye no' got a bit more? A taxi'll cost more than that.'

Get a feckin bus then. 'No, sorry, that's aw a've got.'

She didn't argue, but stood up suddenly, pulled on her jacket, picked up her bag, threw the phone into it, and without any further word left the room, followed by Ross. He opened the door for her, and with a last,

Take it easy, on each side, she was gone. A surge of relief for Ross as he shut and locked the door, then went back through to the bay in the living room, peering down at the street, just to make sure she'd actually gone. After a considerable wait she duly appeared, walking with that same strange loping motion towards Allison Street. And hopefully, thought Ross, out of his life forever.

19

In Grant's absence the flat became dirty and sordid, with no-one to deal with at least the worst of the mess. Junk and rubbish accumulated everywhere, the floor of the living room in particular covered with debris. Bills started to pile up which Ross neglected to pay. He missed a rent payment on the flat, leading to an irate phone call from Fiona. He spent most of his money on alcohol (wine, vodka, whisky, lager), and otherwise subsisted on bread and cheese, crisps and takeaways. He owed money on power. The internet was cut off, putting an end to his online dating, and forcing him out to the library to do his job searches (in truth that was something of a relief to Ross, in that he would no longer be spied on. Unless of course they could tell who was using a particular computer at the library, which was not unlikely - probably the library had to keep a log and submit it to the appropriate authority). Time went by without any offers for the flat. Viewings dwindled, which given its state was probably just as well. Fiona became impatient for Ross to leave, aware of the state of the flat (in fact much worse now than when she'd last seen it).

Ross now spent his days drinking or lying on the bed. Sometimes he would clear a space and lie on the floor in the living room with a cushion under his head, looking at the patterns of sunlight on the wall, listening to sounds from the street. Caught in a limbo of zero motivation and near total passivity, unable to make any effort to do or change anything, look seriously for a job, find somewhere else to live, make new friends or connections. In this state of near torpor, lying late in bed one Tuesday morning, he forgot his fortnightly appointment at the Jobcentre with his 'work coach'. He cursed himself at length when he realised he'd missed the appointment, and then saw he'd got a missed call on his mobile. From those high-handed fuckers, no doubt. Ross was well aware of all the horror stories surrounding the DWP. Of people having their benefits stopped for the most fatuous, trivial, pedantic reasons, or for the smallest deviation from commitments or agreements, or for no good reason at all, for one week, two weeks, four weeks, or even months, depending on various complex criteria (you have previously failed to attend or take part in a work-focused interview or undertake work-related activity within the specified period, and you have had your benefits reduced for the reasons stated above more than once, and the most recent of the previous failures was within 52 weeks of your current failure), or more likely the whim of whoever it is you happen to see at the Jobcentre, some staff seemingly exercising discretionary powers to which they may or may not be entitled. All this affecting indiscriminately in a rigid one-size-fits-all approach the most defenceless and vulnerable within society, those with chaotic, disorganised lives, older people with physical limitations, those with mental health issues, those with chronic illnesses who should have been on ESA but had been ruled fit for work.

He spent twenty five minutes on the phone, navigating through the various options, waiting interminably while some annoying jingle drilled continuously into his brain, finally a brief interaction during which a new appointment was made for two days' time, with no mention made of any sanction for missing the original appointment. Having to go to the library had forced Ross to get out and about, when for weeks and months past it had taken all his resolve to step outside of the flat at all. Contact of any kind with people had become difficult, and attending at the Jobcentre had always been an ordeal. Things had improved recently, but plenty of alcohol beforehand was still the best solution to his anxiety. Come Thursday and the approach of his 11.30 appointment, he was awake and up, feeling and looking rough, but at least the nerves had gone, courtesy of the best part of half a bottle of vodka.

He waited outside the Jobcentre among people smoking or just looking bored and pensive, before going in and taking a seat to wait his turn. When called he walked down the long room filled with work stations on either side, with here and there benches for 'customers'. He took his seat. His advisor today was not the inoffensive wee guy he usually saw, but a large woman in her mid to late fifties. She began by introducing herself, and explaining that he would be seen by her today rather than his usual work coach, as this was not his regular signing-on day. She wasted no time in going on the offensive.

'Why did you miss your appointment on Tuesday, Mr McKenzie?'

'A wis ill.'

'Were you not able to phone in to inform your work coach that you would be unable to attend?'

'A wis too ill.'

'What was the nature of your illness?'

'It's private.'

'Do you have a doctor's note?'

'A didnae go tae the doctor.'

'I should remind you, Mr McKenzie, that your entitlement to Universal Credit carries with it certain responsibilities on your part. One of which is that you must attend and take part fully in work-focused interviews with your work coach on the day and time that has been set. If you fail to fulfil these responsibilities and obligations that you have accepted in return for getting Universal Credit, as set out in your Claimant Commitment, you will be penalised accordingly.'

Ross had taken an instant dislike to her. He didn't like her tone, or her plump, complacent face, or her superior expression, or her hard eyes.

'How long is it since you last worked?'

'Aye well, that depends on what ye mean by work. Dae ye think whit ye dae here is work? Aye? Really?

Ye'll get paid a decent salary, a dinnae doot, so by the definition of work as paid employment, some might say it was work. But is it useful labour, that's the question, that's whit a'm askin. There's a big difference between meaningless activity and useful work. In fact, in ma opinion, when it comes right doon tae it, a dinnae think ye're any more usefully employed than I am.' The advisor stared at him with the expression of someone who has just discovered something unexpected in their sandwich. 'Look, there's only so many vacancies tae fill, right, an' they'll be filled nae matter what. If it's no' one group of people it'll be another. So aw this business of people havin tae come in fae this ritual humiliation once a fortnight, it achieves nothin whatsoever. In fact it's complete shite, a complete waste of time. It's just harassing people fae no gud reason except tae gie a thrill of power over other folk fae people like you.'

'I must ask you, Mr McKenzie, to moderate your language, and to refrain from making personal comments, or I shall have to terminate this interview. Now, I'll ask you once again, how long is it since you last worked?'

'Why dinnae ye answer ma question first? Dae you think whit you do in here is useful? That's whit a'm askin. Do ye not know that there's only so many jobs tae go round? An' only so many hours available in those jobs - which is why sae many jobs are part-time or zero hours. All this does is tae mask unemployment by havin people on your side of the desk humble an' humiliate the poor bastards on this side of the desk. This,' with a wide sweep of the hand indicating the entire expanse of the open-plan office, 'is aw just a theatrical performance. It's just a stage set, aw this nonsense. Aye, this is aw an illusion. An illusion ae useful activity.'

The sense of having nothing much left to lose had given Ross an articulacy he'd never found in the fumbling speeches he'd made at public or closed meetings in his campaigning days.

'Mr McKenzie - '

'An' if employers had tae pay a wee bit more tae attract workers, then that's too bad. In fact it wid be aw tae the gud. It's the free market economy fae ye. Isn't that whit that evil piece of shite Thatcher wis aw aboot? So whit a'm sayin is there'll always be a residue of unemployed, aye an' unemployable, some of which a can see behind the desks in here. An' you people bullying an' forcing people intae jobs meks nae difference - nae fuckin difference at all to the total number of unemployed. You an' aw this whole ridiculous set-up wi' you people sittin behind yir desks wi' your noses in the air judging us like we're the scum of the earth, it's aw a complete bunch of shite.'

'Mr McKenzie, I'm not going to - '

'So whit a'm sayin is, ye're always gan tae have a certain number of unemployed. An' wae increasing automation in every kind o' work that's only gan tae increase. So dae ye not think that whit ye dae here is a complete waste of time? Aw ye dae is harass an' intimidate an' bully people an' force one set of people intae jobs, when aw it means is that it's that group of people that are in work an' no' another group. So it's exactly the same difference. Dae ye no' agree? Unemployment stays at exactly the same level. Aw ye dae here is exert yir wee authority over people that have nae power an' nae voice tae answer back. Aye, it must be a cheap thrill fae some o' ye. This,' once again indicating the entire open plan office floor with its myriad desks, computers and work coaches, plus seats for the customers - and including, by implication, every Jobcentre everywhere, and indeed the entire system - 'is a complete waste of time. It's a feckin joke. The only thing all this achieves is to mask the true level of unemployment a wee bit by givin a bunch o' no-talents these make-believe, pointless jobs. Ye're aw as unemployed as I am when it comes tae deein a useful day's work.'

The colour on the face of his advisor had deepened to somewhere near vermillion.

'Mr McKenzie - '

'Hey, dinnae stand on ceremony. Ye can call me Ross. Aye, let's keep it nice an' friendly an' informal.'

'Mr McKenzie, your language is quite inappropriate, and your behaviour is extremely intimidating - '

'A'm no intimdatin anybody. A'm tryin tae hae a conversation.'

'You're coming across as very aggressive, Mr McKenzie. I'm afraid I'm going to have to terminate the interview at this point. We'll be writing to you in due course.'

'Oh aye? Whit have a done wrong? Tell me that. Why don't ye just tell me tae ma face whatever shite ye're planning tae throw at us. Ye dinnae have tae go tae aw the trouble of writing one o' yir snide wee notes.'

'Please leave now, Mr McKenzie, or I'll have to call security.'

Ross looked across at a podgy security guy alertly watching them and laughed mirthlessly.

'Oh aye? That fat cunt'd hae nae chance.'

But he got up and left anyway, feeling exhilarated at having said everything that had been boiling up inside him.

The next day he received a letter from the Jobcentre telling him that he'd been sanctioned for failing to attend a work-focused interview with his work coach on the day and time that had been set, and also failing to take part fully in a work-focused interview with an advisor, and that for a fixed period of 4 weeks his Universal Credit payments would be stopped. He was also given a warning on his future behaviour. So the cunts predictably had got their own back. Ye cannae beat the system. Four weeks wi'out any income. How the fuck wis he supposed to live. For a few minutes he threw and kicked stuff around the flat. Then, still seething, he set off for the Jobcentre, arriving without an appointment and demanding of the security guy who met him to see someone about his benefits cut.

'You need to phone the helpline and make an appointment. You can't see an advisor without an appointment.'

'Aye, too busy and important are they? While a hae nae money tae live because of these cunts.'

Faces turned throughout the room at the raised voices.

'You'd better leave.'

The guy was large, bulky with a near-shaven head. His colleague, to whom Ross had referred briefly on his previous visit, was trundling slowly across from where he'd been seated observing the exchange.

'A'm no' leavin wi'out speakin tae someone.'

'You need to phone the helpline. You cannae just turn up and expect tae speak to someone.'

'A've nae money comin in fur a month. Whit the fuck am a supposed tae do?'

'Phone the helpline,' the guy repeated. 'They'll be able to advise you, and arrange another appointment. Now will you please leave.'

'Aye, an' are ye gan tae make me?' said Ross stepping in close and eyeballing the security guy, who stared back, unmoved. 'A could drop ye in a second, pal, nae problem,' in a low, menacing tone. 'An' yir fat pal there, sae dinnae come it wi' me.'

'For the last time, I'm askin you to leave, sir. If you don't, we'll have tae call the polis.'

A faint sliver of common sense worked its way into Ross's somewhat befuddled mind. Much as he'd like to have taken on this pair of blimps and gimps, the prospect of the police and the possibility of another spell in prison sobered him sufficiently that after another sneered verbal insult directed toward the pair of them he turned a little unsteadily and banged his way out.

20

On the afternoon following the Jobcentre debacle, and with the last of his money quickly running out, Ross began receiving frantic texts from Maz telling him her life was shite and begging for help. He went round straight away, noticing on his way into the close that one of the windows of the flat had been boarded up. Answering the door, still in her pyjamas, Maz seemed initially more calm and collected than Ross had expected.

'Sorry a havnae been in touch, darlin, a've jus' been havin a feckin awfu' time. Come on through, a'll mek us a coffee.'

'Whit's wi' the windae?'

'Farooq. Gan fuckin mental.'

'How, what happened?'

'He wis getting a wee bit too friendly, if ye know whit a mean. So a said tae him, aw nice an' friendly, Look, darlin, nothin's gan tae happen between us. A'm far too old fur ye. You need tae find some lassie more your own age. An' a said, Mebbe ye shouldnae call round quite sae often. Aw nice an' friendly a was, wi' a smile on ma face. Here's your coffee, darlin, let's go through tae the livin room.'

They settled themselves on the sofa, the escapist vision of the lonely cottage still filling a space in front of them.

'So a wis tryin tae get him tae back off, but not in a nasty way. A didnae want tae hurt his feelings. A still thought he wis a nice young guy, just a bit daft an' besotted wi' us. Aye, more like fuckin retarded as it turns out - a should hae known, wi' ma luck. Anyway, he kicked off big style. He wis callin us aw the names under the sun, sayin a'd led him on, an' a'd made a fool of him, and this and that, aw sorts of crap. An' then he starts shoutin an' screamin at us. A wis thinking if he tries tae start somethin wi' us, a'll feckin knock the bugger oot. In the end he just throws up his hand like he's had enough of me, calls us a name, then slams his way oot the flat, crashin the doors after him. An' a thought, thank fuck fur that. Next thing a know, there wis this big crash an' a thump an' the sound of glass breakin, an' a'm thinking, What the fuck, an' a find a brick on the floor, an' glass everywhere. Aye, the little shit had chucked a brick through ma windae. So a called the polis, an' they picked him up easy enough. They said, dae ye want tae make a formal complaint against him, an' a said, Aye, a feckin dee. So, anyway, he's not tae approach us again, or come within fifty yards of the flat.'

'Christ,' said Ross, 'whit a crazy wee prick,' though thinking uncomfortably of the similar exclusion order applied to him. That was different. Fiona was his wife, and she was with another man. Was still his wife,

294

technically. 'Ye should have called me, Maz. A'd have come straight round an' sorted oot your wee pal.'

'Aye, an' if he'd called the polis ye'd likely be gan straight back tae prison.'

'Aye, well, a guess you're right at that.'

'Anyway, a could have done wi'out aw that nonsense from Farooq, on top of everything else.'

Her voice had changed abruptly, becoming softer and a little unsteady.

'Why, what else has happened?'

'Have a no' told ye? Pixie's gan tae live wi' her da.'

'Ye dinnae mean permanently?'

'Aye, a dee. She disnae want tae come back. She willnae even speak tae me on the phone. Aw a get is Brian or some new wummin he's with - he wis quick off the mark there, the fat fuck - or mebbe that's why he was so keen tae move down to feckin Birmingham in the first place. A wouldnae put it past him, the devious cunt. So now ma baby is livin wi' some wummin a know nothin aboot, an a cannae even speak tae her, an' a jus' know they'll be brainwashing her wi' tales aboot how awfu' a am, an' how a wis a bad mam, an' how a never loved her.' She began to sob. 'After aw a've done fur this family. A've cried tears of blood fur them fur twenty five years - twenty five feckin years - wi'out sae much as a thanks mam an' wi'out a chance tae breathe an' be maself, an' now they've aw turned against me. The twins never bother tae get in touch wi' us, an' when a phone them they dinnae say a word - it's like havin a conversation wi' yourself - Jimmy hates ma guts, an' now Pixie's been taken away fae us an' turned against us. Christ, Ross, ma life's just complete an' utter shite.' Weeping, her body wracked by heaving sobs. 'A cannae stand it, a just cannae stand ma feckin life anymore.'

Ross put his arm around her shoulders, and she collapsed into him. He put his other arm around her middle as she cried and sobbed, her face pressed into his chest as they cuddled, Ross gently holding and caressing her around her side and her stomach, gentle, soft, consoling strokes as she continued to quietly weep, until, he wasn't sure how it happened - maybe she'd slightly moved her position, turned more towards him a little - but suddenly, and as it seemed quite naturally, his hand was cupping her left breast, though not, he was sure, in a particularly sexual way, more just as a gentle, tender and affectionate gesture of consolation. Everything went quiet. Slowly, gradually, Maz became calmer, the weeping and sobbing subsiding, until she was lying in Ross's arms, her head still on his chest, as though asleep. For several minutes more they were just lying quietly together, the silence and the warmth of their bodies and the unaccustomed intimacy providing a protective cocoon against invasive thoughts of all the pain and shit assailing them both. And for Ross, the fact that he was holding her breast seemed just a natural, gentle act of affection, and certainly Maz was unresisting.

After a while Ross released his supportive hold and began to caress her face, brushing the many stray strands of hair, still an unfathomable black, away from her brow and cheek, carefully, gently tucking it behind her ear - waiting a moment while she roused herself sufficiently to dry her eyes and face - his fingers now softly tracing the shape of her face, the superb bone structure (something he'd long admired), strong line of jaw and chin, wide brow, high pronounced cheekbones, long straight shapely nose, wide full expressive lips, ears, ear lobes, features he'd never had opportunity to study so closely before. And the signs of aging also, her face unusually free of make-up, with all the little tell-tale indicators of mortality visible in wrinkles, lines and patches of imperfect skin. With all her war-paint on Maz could easily pass for late twenties, when in fact Ross knew she would be forty that year.

Suddenly she turned her face towards him, her eyes that had been closed as if in sleep flickering briefly open. And then they were kissing and fondling, increasingly urgently, until without warning Maz pulled away, sat up, then jumped to her feet.

'A want tae get aw this crap oot of here,' she said, a sudden venomous bile in her voice, indicating the piles of Pixie's toys which still lay scattered on the floor, partially obscuring one wall. 'If she disnae want tae be here anymore, or want oot tae dee wi' me, she can have aw her stuff. Hundreds of pounds, thousands, a spent on her, buyin aw this stuff over the years which a could hae spent on maself. Come on, darlin, a'll put some clothes on an' we'll go round the supermarkets an' get some boxes, an' pack aw this shit in them, an' a'll post them aw doon tae her, an' she can carry on wi' her feckin wonderful life wi' a bunch of strangers a know nothin aboot.'

Ross got up, nonplussed by the abrupt change of mood, but thinking he should try to calm her down if he could, or at least try to get her thinking rationally.

'Maz, ye cannae send aw that stuff through the post in old cardboard boxes. They'd aw fal apart fur one thing, an' it'd cost ye a fortune.'

Maz's eyes were hard, and her face had taken on a dangerous expression.

'A want this stuff oot a here.'

She began to pick things up and throw them against the wall. 'Oot. Of. Ma. Fuckin. Hoose.' Ross tried to put his arm around her, attempting again to calm her down, but she shrugged him off. 'Fuckin. Sick. Of. Ma. Fuckin. Life.'

'Maz. Will ye feckin listen tae me fur a minute.' She stopped throwing the toys at the sound of Ross's raised voice, and turned and stared at him as if she hadn't known he was there. 'Look, it would cost a fortune tae send aw this stuff. Why dinnae we just take it aw through an' put it in Pixie's room. Then at least ye dinnae hae tae look at it.' She continued to look at him for a few seconds with those deep, dark, troubled eyes. 'Right.' And she grabbed a handful of toys and marched across the hall to Pixie's bedroom at the far end of the flat, while Ross followed with one of the large boxes. She unceremoniously chucked what she was holding from the doorway into the room, then went back for more. They quickly moved all the stuff, then Maz went into the twins' room, grabbing anything they'd left behind, scrabbling in the bottom of the wardrobe, flinging boots, shoes, sandals, anything else she could find over her shoulder.

'A've nae idea why they had aw this shit,' she said when she'd done, carrying handfuls of footwear through to Pixie's room and again chucking it randomly among the rest of the stuff. 'They never set foot oot the flat. A wis the only one deein anythin. A did every feckin thing fur this family. Every last fuckin thing.'

She slammed the door of Pixie's room.

'A should put warning signs on the door, or tape across it like they dee in murder cases.'

Back in the living room she took one look at the empty space where the toys had been and her face collapsed, tears began streaming, and she sat down heavily on the sofa, crying and sobbing once more. Ross sat down beside her, not knowing whether she wanted to be touched or just cry it out alone this time, hoping that by sitting beside her he gave some sense of support. Eventually she stopped crying, grabbed some tissues, dried her face and blew her nose. Calmer now, but with the look of someone for whom there are no glad tomorrows, only deep shit, she slowly reached out, took a cigarette from the packet, lit it, eventually, with a cheap lighter that refused several times to light, inhaled deeply, then sat back and released a plume of smoke, all with the appearance of a series of unthinking, reflex actions. Several minutes passed in silence. Then,

'A wis in hospital last week.'

Ross turned to look at her. She was sitting back, eyes half-closed, her face half-veiled by drifting smoke from her cigarette.

'Were ye? How?'

She ground out the cigarette in the ashtray and lit another.

'A took an overdose of ma sleeping pills an' anti-depressants. Oh, an' half a bottle of wine.'

'Christ, Maz. A had nae idea.'

'A wis laid oot on the floor. The polis came, an' the ambulance, an' they took us tae the hospital an' a had ma stomach pumped. That wis great. Aye, ye're conscious the whole time they're deein it. A wis supposed tae stay in overnight, but a fucked off after an hour or two when a'd had a cup of tea, an' got a taxi back here. A cannae stand feckin hospitals.'

'God, a'm sorry Maz.'

She patted his thigh.

'Dinnae worry, darlin, a'm over the worst of it now. A'll no' be deein that again.'

After what he'd seen, Ross suspected that this was far from the truth. He didn't inquire as to how they'd known she was on the floor unconscious. Maybe Farooq had seen her through the window. Maybe that's why the window was broken.

'What gets me now wi' Pixie is a've nae idea of who's comin an' goin where she's livin. Or who's livin round aboot. There's so many feckin paedophiles aroon these days, an' a have nae control over the situation. An' she's just a wee thing. She cannae defend herself. She's only nine, the poor daft wee mite.'

Tears were starting to well up again.

'Maz, surely if you took Brian tae court ye could get her back. The courts always take the mother's side. It sounds tae me almost like he's kidnapped her.'

'A dinnae want tae go through aw that shit. They'd only throw a whole bunch of lies and crap back at us tae mek me look like a bad mam. A cannae be doin wi' that. And anyway, if gan tae live wi' her da is what she wants, she's welcome tae it. A cannae be doin wi' any of 'em anymore.'

They watched TV for a while, then Ross suggested going out for a drink and a bite to eat. Maz was reluctant. She couldn't stand the thought of being out and about and meeting people and having to pretend everything was fine, so Ross went by himself and brought back a couple of bottles of wine and a takeaway pizza. They spent the rest of the evening watching TV, eating pizza, getting drunk, then cuddling and kissing some more. The idea was forming in Ross's mind that something was happening between them, or starting to happen. Two people at the end of their tether, thrown together by circumstances, drawn together anyway by the fact they liked each other. Why not go with the flow. Why not accept the direction fate had carried them. Both of them had been battered helplessly amid swirling currents only to be carried into dead water. Why not make the most of the fact that they'd ended up together. Maybe it *was* fate. It might be good. It might be the best thing that could possibly happen for them both at this point in their lives. But when Ross, with a lack of inhibition induced by a near full bottle of wine inside him, suggested something along these lines to Maz, she almost visibly recoiled. A couldnae put that on you, darl, not in ma present state. Mebbe someday. A response which left Ross subdued and confused. To be repulsed so emphatically when they'd seemed to have become so much closer, physically and otherwise, left him perplexed. With his mind only partly engaged, still dwelling on her unexpected reaction, Maz was suddenly telling him about her father.

He was a very quiet man. He was the only person she could ever talk to. She could never talk to her mother. And he was always so gentle, so softly spoken. He never raised his voice to anyone, ever. Sometimes he worked nights, so they'd have to be quiet during the day so as not to disturb him. But when he could he'd take them to the park. He knew the names of all the trees and flowers. He once made her a doll's house, with a roof that opened up so you could reach inside, and opening windows and doors, and furniture, a table and chairs, beds, sofas, a grandfather clock. It even had a tiny bathroom and kitchen. She didn't know how, but he somehow wired it up with electric lights. There was a switch somewhere so you could light it up in the dark like a real house. He made her other things too, which she'd get at Xmas or for her birthday. All of them lost in all the moves over the years, or broken by the kids. He died when she was thirteen. Twenty seven years ago, give or take. He was only forty seven. She still took flowers to put on his grave on his birthday. They'd both go next time, darl. She'd show him her dad's resting place.

When midnight had passed Ross was still there, thinking it would be best if he kept an eye on her, for that night at least. But instead of spending the night together in her bed he camped on the sofa (he was offered the twins' bedroom, but opted for no particular reason for discomfort), a couple of spare sheets to cover him. And so he fretted and wondered at the turn of events, and slept very little on his uncomfortable, makeshift bed. It might, or might not, have been of some consolation to him to know that the real deep-down reason, at the core of the process of reasoning which Maz would probably never be capable of consciously articulating, even to herself, as to why she didn't want to sleep with Ross, was in fact because she really liked him and thought he was a decent guy, one of the very few she'd ever come across. And she knew that if once they did start to make love, and from there get together and become a couple, she'd only end up hating him like all the rest, and she didn't want to have to lump him with all the other men she regarded as having used and abused her and treated her like shit. The whole stinking lot of whom were unfit so much as to lick the boots of her dead father.

Endgame

21

Early summer, and completely out of the blue and in the midst of the chaos of his life, a phone call from Jimmy. Forgetting all his feelings of animosity towards his old friend, Ross was almost pathetically grateful to hear the familiar and always amusing voice, one he hadn't heard for months and hadn't really expected to hear again. He'd split up with Clare. It was all over. Hadn't worked out - in the end they just hadn't had enough in common. Ross wondered if in fact she'd seen through Jimmy at last, maybe even a testament to the influence of university, jump-starting Clare's brain. More likely he'd just been caught screwing around, as ever. He was living in a room in a house in Newcastle. Heaton. Just to the east of the city centre. Aye, fine. Easy to walk into the centre, or there was the Metro. No, not planning to stay, nothing to stay for now. Moving back to Glasgow, going to live with his father and sisters. Yeah, he knew about Pixie. Best thing for her, to get away from that fucking mad bitch. When Ross tells him some of what's been happening to him, sanctioned, can't afford to stay in the house anymore, not sure what to do, Jimmy in his sincerest tones suggests Ross could take his room if he wants it. He'd even (with what Ross thought even at the time was uncharacteristic generosity) give him the money for his first month's rent. After the initial surprise, Ross thought, Why not. A clean break, fresh start, all that shit. Anyway he couldn't stay in the flat much longer. So on the spur of the moment Ross agreed, and they arranged to meet in Newcastle.

Over the next couple of days Ross actually felt motivated, for the first time in a long time. The prospect of something new and different happening in his life spurred him to action. He made a concerted effort to clean and tidy up the flat, washed all his clothes, and packed a rucksack with as much as he could fit in. Was he really going to do this? He couldn't stay on in the flat - he was on borrowed time as it was. The only other choices were to go begging to the council for emergency accommodation, or try to get a bed at a homeless hostel, and neither was an attractive option. Jimmy's house sounded a better bet, and Newcastle wasn't that far away. By the time he'd been there a month (paid for by Jimmy) his sanction would have expired and he'd be able to pay the rent on the room. He'd get a job, make some money, save up and come back to Glasgow. In the meantime he'd apply to a housing association for a flat back in Govanhill, take his time to get everything properly sorted. Somewhere decent and pleasant where Grant and Sabiha - and the baby - would want to come and visit. Maybe in time he'd find someone nice to be with - not through that online dating crap, but just by bumping into somebody somewhere, a smile, a look exchanged. Or even (the hope drifting constantly through his mind, sometimes with more, sometimes less substance), he'd get back together with Fiona someday.

Ross had seen Grant only occasionally since he'd moved out. Maybe once a week he'd come round for an hour or so. Grant found it difficult to see his dad in his present state, and the condition of the flat seemed to reflect his decline. He still loved and cared about him, but wasn't sure what he could do to help, apart from keeping the lines of communication open. He hoped it would be a passing phase, resultant and residue of the break-up, and that in time he'd pull himself out of it and get on with his life. Meanwhile, he couldn't deny to himself how much he enjoyed living at the Jamils'. To be with Sabiha all the time, and the house, it was like being in a different world, with its indefinable air of stately timelessness. He loved especially being up in their bedroom together, looking down at the wide road lined with trees, a direct contrast with the familiar view of scruffy back courts he was used to. And with his exams out of the way, Grant was feeling excited (sometimes nervous), not just about the impending birth of the baby, due in just over a month, but at more or less everything. As he turned into the close and climbed the stairs, his spirits were high with the exhilaration of all the limitless possibilities that life had suddenly and gratuitously decided to roll out for his benefit.

He received an almost effusive greeting from his dad. They went through to the kitchen where Ross made them a cup of tea, then settled themselves in the living room, Grant surprised to see the flat looking cleaner and tidier than for some time, even if his dad looked as wild as ever.

'So, how's everything going?' said Ross.

'Aye, fine.'

'How's Sabiha doing?'

'She's great. Everything's looking good. She's having all the regular checks and stuff, so it's all good.'

'That's great. It'll no' be long now.'

'I know. It's a bit scary.'

'Ah, ye'll be fine. Your mother was no' that much older than Sabiha when we had you, an' we coped wae it aw just fine. Ye'll find you just do what you need tae do when the time comes.'

'I guess you're right.'

Grant felt a little uncomfortable at the mention of his mother. He wasn't sure, beyond the outward signs of self-neglect, how Ross was coping, or what his feelings towards Fiona were at this point. But they chatted about Grant and Sabiha's plans - that Grant would stay on and do his Advanced Highers, and that Sabiha would take a gap year to concentrate on the baby. After that, who knows, maybe they'd both start uni at the same time, stay in Glasgow, it would be that much easier. Or maybe they wouldn't, maybe they'd try to get places together at a uni somewhere else. The boundless, intoxicating possibilities.

'A cannae put this off, Grant. A have tae admit, when I asked ye tae come round, apart from wanting tae see you, that a had another motive. Which is that a've got something tae tell you.' Grant looked at his dad questioningly. 'A'm gan tae have to leave the flat.'

'Why?'

'A've been sanctioned by the Jobcentre, so a've got nae money coming in fur a month.'

'Why, what happened?'

'It wis aw a bunch of nonsense. A wis late fur an appointment, an' then a had a wee bust-up wi' 'em, so they ended up sanctioning us.'

'I'm sure mum wouldn't mind if you missed a month's payment. Surely you don't have to leave.'

Ross smiled. 'You're probably right. But a need tae move on anyway. This wis only meant tae be a temporary arrangement, and it's been a good few months now. To be honest a should have been deein more tae find somewhere else to live aw this time. But anyway a didn't. An' it'll be easier to sell the flat, maybe, if there's no' someone livin in it.'

'But where will you go?'

Ross recounted the relevant parts of his conversation with Jimmy, including Jimmy's offer to pay the first month's rent.

'Newcastle?' Grant looked taken aback.

'It's no' so far away.'

'I never thought you'd be leaving Glasgow.'

'Well, it's no' altogether a matter of choice. A know a should have stirred maself tae get things sorted, but a

309

havnae been at ma best. But anyway a'm hoping that after a wee bit of time away a can mebbe save up some money. An a'll apply fur a flat back here in Govanhill. Hopefully it'll no' be long an' a'll be able tae come back.'

The thought of his dad, a constant presence throughout his life, and one that he took for granted, maybe, sometimes, being no longer around, was difficult to process.

'When are you leaving?'

'Today.'

'Today?'

'Aye. A've got aw ma stuff packed an' ready, an' a'm meetin Jimmy when a get there. A'm sorry tae spring this on you.'

'I'm sorry you've got to go.'

'A'll be back soon enough. There's one other thing, an' a'm sorry tae have tae ask you this. A havnae got much in the way of ready cash, an' a was wondering if ye could mebbe let us have a few quid, if ye can spare it.'

Both of them embarrassed that Ross should be reduced to this.

'Yeah, of course. I'm sorry that… I wish I had more in the bank. Would fifty pounds be enough?'

'Aye that'd be great. A'm sorry to take your money off you, Grant. What wi' being sanctioned an that a'm just aboot skint.'

'Are you going to be okay? How are you going to manage for money in Newcastle?'

'Like a say, Jimmy's paying fur the first month's rent, so a should be able tae manage. Then a should get ma benefits back. An' a'll take any job tae get back on ma feet again.'

All Grant could think of was that this might well be the very last time he'd be in the flat with his dad, and he didn't even know when he'd see him again. He wished now he'd made more effort to visit over the past few weeks, but he wasn't to know what was going to happen. While Ross gathered his stuff together, Grant wandered around the flat, into his old room, into the kitchen, back into the living room, trying to draw out the few remaining moments of being together in the place where he'd grown up, and where he'd spent so much time with his dad. Wishing it was all otherwise, and that things could be again as they were, the wonders of his new life suddenly seeming less than adequate consolation for the irreversible loss of the old.

They left the flat together to the familiar sound of the door slamming shut and the turning of the key in the lock. Down the stairwell for the final time, the close door banging shut behind them. Then out onto the street, heading for the nearest cashpoint. After Grant had given Ross the money, and after a brief hesitation they hugged. An emotional parting, Ross asking Grant to stay in touch, and be sure to tell him when the baby was born. For Grant it felt like a definitive end point to so much of his past life. He struggled to maintain his composure as he walked back in the direction of the park and his new home. Ross wasn't feeling much more cheerful, immediately second guessing himself, wondering if he was doing the right thing after all, whether he should have stayed on just a few more weeks and made a concerted effort to find a job and somewhere to live. Trouble was, that would have required just the kind of effort which he didn't feel capable of making. He had to harden his mind. This was necessary, but it needn't be forever. Better, at least, than the prospect of prison.

He just had time to say goodbye to Maz before going into town, where he'd arranged to meet Fiona to return the flat keys. His news was greeted by a look of disbelief. Ye must be feckin daft. Dee ye never learn? Ye cannae rely on a thing that laddie says. He'll screw ye over one way or another, a'm tellin ye. There followed a somewhat muted, not quite unfriendly parting. Ye'll soon be back, a'm tellin ye. Ye daft bugger. Then a hurried walk to the station, and into town. Walking the streets of his beloved city for the last time for God knows how long. He met Fiona in George Square, just down from the station. He handed over the keys to the flat, a strangeness and poignancy in the brief touch of her fingers. Further disconcerted by her look of concern and kindness of tone, even though she remained unsmiling. Are you going to be okay? Aye, aye, nae problem. And so, emotionally churned up and thoroughly disorientated, Ross left Glasgow, yet still with a feeling, hardly logical or defensible, that after some time away, and especially if he could make a go of things and manage to save up a bit of money, maybe all was not lost. And maybe when he came back, Fiona would be over her incomprehensible infatuation with that soft wee fuck, and they'd be able to take up again where they'd left off. Anything was possible.

22

'Christ, ye're lookin rough, mate,' Jimmy's first words on seeing Ross.

'Whit the fuck's that on your face?' Ross's amused rejoinder at the sight of Jimmy's new and disreputable-looking ginger beard. After these opening pleasantries, they walked together out of the station, of whose glories Ross caught only a brief glimpse (in any case he'd made a conscious decision not to obsess about such things any more), chatting as they went, to a bar close by. It was busy and noisy, and Ross, tired after the journey as well as stressed from the day's events, went to sit down in a vacant seat on a bench along one wall and waited for Jimmy to bring the drinks over. The noise of unrestrained talk and laughter mercifully blotted out any thoughts, and he sat in a vacant daze.

'So why the face fungus?' asked Ross, coming back to himself as Jimmy placed a pint of lager in front of him.

'Clare liked it. She thought it made me look more intelligent. Aye, distinguished wis the word she used.'

'Fuckin hell. That's some beard if it can dee that.'

Jimmy laughed. 'Didnae dee me any good in the end, though. A should get rid of it, but a've kind of grown used tae it. An' it saves havin tae fuck around every morning shaving.'

'What happened wi' Clare, then?

Jimmy made a face, as if reluctant to broach the subject.

'Ah, we just grew apart. A think it was partly that we were together nearly every evening an' a fair bit of every weekend. An' ye can just grow so used tae each other's company tae the point where ye need a break. An' she wis meetin a whole bunch of new people at uni, an' a wis workin wi' a different sort of people at the store. It wis just one of those things.'

'So, basically, she caught ye cheatin on her an' screwing around behind her back, as always.'

Jimmy gave a snort and high-pitched giggle, almost choking on his lager.

'Ye fuckin bastard.'

'That wis it then, aye?'

'Aye, that wis it, but also that other crap a said as well.'

'Oh, aye, must hae been a difficult, complex moral dilemma fur ye.'

'Ah, fuck off,' said Jimmy, grinning. 'Anyway, pal, what about you? How did ye enjoy your stay at Her Majesty's pleasure. Wis it a pleasure fur ye too?' Jimmy sniggering into his lager.

'Aye, it wis fuckin great, thanks fur asking. A wis only sorry when it came tae an end an' a had tae leave an go back home an' leave aw ma new pals behind.' Another giggle from Jimmy. 'A wouldnae hae fuckin left if a'd known what a wis comin back tae. Fiona wisnae hangin aboot. She told us she wis no' staying the very day after

315

a came oot. That wis a proper kick in the nuts. Though mebbe no' that unexpected, tae be honest.'

'Aye, a'm sorry aboot aw that, Ross. So she wis carryin on wi' somebody behind yir back?'

'Aye. The boss of where she works. Some smooth wee fuck. A've nae definite proof how long it wis gan on, but a suspect a while before a went intae prison.'

'Have ye ever met this guy?'

'Aye, a couple of times. A smarmy, soft wee cunt. Anyway, there's nothin a can dee aboot it fur now.'

'Fuckin women. They're a pain in the fuckin arse. They're only good fur one thing, an' no' even that sometimes.' Giggling at his own wit.

'Aye, they're an enigma right enough.'

'Enigma. They're a bunch of crazy cunts. In fact their cunts are the only gud thing aboot them. There's your enigma or paradox or whatever the fuck it is. A didnae pay too much attention at school.'

Ross laughed. 'So ye're wi'out cunt now, are ye?'

'Nah, a widnae say that. A need tae stay in practice. An' a can always come up wi' cunt when a need it. It's a knack a've got.' A high-pitched giggling laugh.

How the fuck does this guy attract women. What does he do to them. He looked more animalistic than ever with the beard, that long, bony face now like the muzzle of some wild ravenous thing. The enigma was why a good-looking woman would ever want anything to do with him. That was the fucking mystery.

'A've met this girl on Facebook, an' a'm really serious aboot her. Catriona, she's called. She's livin back in Glasgow. That's the main reason a'm gan back.'

'Oh aye? What's she like?'

'She's just totally fucking gorgeous, Ross,' with a sincere, impassioned expression. He brought up some photos on his phone. She was indeed stunning. The enigma/mystery or whatever it was once again. Unless, of course, her personality was on a level with Clare's. But even so.

'Aye, she is. So ye havnae met yet?'

'No, but as soon as a get back we'll be getting together.'

'Well, she's really beautiful, Jimmy.'

'It's no' just her looks, Ross. We've spoken fur hours on the phone. She's got an amazing personality. A can talk tae her aboot anything. We just hit it off like we've known each other forever. A've never known a girl like her.'

Ross struggled to maintain a straight face at the entirely predictable reappearance of The One.

'So whit ye gan tae dae aboot your job? Are ye just gan tae walk away?'

'No, a've got a transfer. It's a chain, an' they've got branches in Glasgow. They think the fuckin world of me, fur some reason. Even though a dee next tae fuck all. It's fuckin hilarious. They're sayin a could be a manager in a year or two. Area manager after that. It's just fuckin crazy. A'd be making a fortune.'

'So ye're just stayin at your dad's till ye get settled then?'

'Aye, that's right. Till a sort oot ma own place.'

'So what's this hoose like?'

'It's fine. Ye'll like it. Ye've got your own room and everything you need. Ye've just got tae watch out fur this guy Moshi.'

'Moshi?'

'That's whit people call him. Kevin Mossman. The moshi monster. He's intae aw sorts. Thieving. Shoplifting. If it's no' tied doon, the wee fucker'll have it. Been in and oot of prison aw his life. At least ye'll have that in common, Ross,' a sly, would-be friendly smile, intended to defuse the sting in the words. 'But the craziest fuckin thing is he reckons a'm his best mate! That always gie's a laugh.'

Ross had only ever been on the tiny, quirky Glasgow underground. The Metro was bigger, wider, much of it above ground. He took in the views over the city while struggling to hear whatever Jimmy was going on about, hopefully responding appropriately. A moderate walk leading to an area of red brick terraces, identical houses with bay windows stretching out in all directions. They crossed several streets and took a number of turnings, all the streets looking identical to Ross, until at last Jimmy turned in to an entrance path strewn with litter and cigarette stubs and opened the front door.

The house wasn't bad inside. Jimmy gave him a brief tour of the communal living room and not too insanitary bathroom and untidy kitchen, then unlocked the door to his, now Ross's, room. A semi-basement room with a restricted view of a dark, dank back yard, with patches of moss and struggling ferns, home to three overflowing council refuse bins. Some contrast, thought Ross bitterly, from the view from their flat that he'd always loved.

'Moshi's room's above this one. You can always hear when he's in, and he can hear when a get in. In a minute he'll be comin doon those stairs and knockin on the door. Annoying wee smackhead.'

Half a minute later a clomping on the stairs, followed, just as Jimmy had predicted, by a knocking on the door.

'Don't break the fuckin door doon,' called Jimmy. 'Just come in.'

The door opened, and a diminutive figure poked his head around, said 'Alright?' then came with contrived jauntiness into the room, much as if he owned it, sat on the bed, took out a packet of cigarettes, offered one to Jimmy and Ross, who both declined, lit one himself, then looked around for an ashtray. With the air of someone performing a tired ritual, Jimmy reached over to the window sill and handed him an old saucer that had clearly been used for that purpose many times before.

'So, what's up, Jimmy? Anything new?'

Ross took in a little guy, unshaven, short hair unwashed and sticking up here and there, wearing a stained jumper two sizes too big for him and trackie bottoms. Scrawny neck, eyes too close together. The jauntiness wasn't so apparent as he sat chatting to Jimmy, rather a general air of hard done by fecklessness. An impression of almost childlike naivety, like a wizened ten year old. Though only a few years older than Ross, he could have passed for fifty, with premature deep lines and furrows across his forehead and around his eyes. An empty, haunted look to the eyes. A mouth too small, with thin lips which pulled to one side as he spoke, revealing uneven yellow teeth with obvious gaps. Ross couldn't place his accent, in fact a strange amalgam of Cockney and Geordie.

'I came up here to work when I was twenty,' explaining to Ross why he'd ended up in the north east. 'Then I got a bad injury and I've been on the sick ever since.'

'Aye,' said Jimmy, grinning openly at Ross, 'he wis injured fallin over when he wis off his fuckin heid.'

'No, it was a genuine injury.' An affronted expression and tone. 'I get terrible pain in me back. I can hardly get out of bed sometimes.'

'Aye right, is that the reason.' Jimmy sniggering into his hand.

'You fucker, I'm telling you the truth. I think it was that what got me into drugs. It was a way of killing the pain.'

'Killing the fuckin pain. You fuckin liar.'

'Fuck off. I'm not lying. The pain, fuckin terrible sometimes. I have to take really powerful painkillers.'

'Aye, it's called smack.'

'I'm off that.'

'Are ye fuck.'

'I'm coming off it. It takes time. You can't just come off it straight away.'

He had a habit of crinkling up his face and twisting his mouth to one side as he related some of the many darker moments of his life.

'Tell Ross what else ye've taken,' said Jimmy with an air of high amusement.

'I've been on loads of stuff. Every kind of shit I could get hold of. Acid, crack, ketamine, magic mushrooms, ecstasy, smack. Anything I could lay my hands on. But I'm trying to get myself clean, get my life together. I want to see my kids again. I'm really trying to get my act together so I can get back into my children's lives, see my granddaughter.'

Estranged from ex-partner Linda and daughter Courtney for the past six years. He'd never seen his granddaughter Jade (10 months). Linda would still speak to him, but Courtney refused, wanted nothing to do with him, openly referring to him as the Little Waster. Another daughter and son, age six and four, by another woman. Jimmy listening to this account (doubtless not for the first time) with the whisper of a smile playing around his lips. Desperately wanted to see his son and daughter again. Their mother had gone off with another bloke and left him to look after them until they'd been taken off him. They'd ended up being adopted and he'd never seen them since. Two years ago. Fucking awful, shaking his head. Terrible. His own fault though. It was all down to the drugs. Oh Christ, hundreds of offences. Robbery, burglary, shoplifting. Fuck knows how many convictions. Five years of prison altogether. Five years of never seeing his kids. Fucking idiot. Now he'd decided it was time to turn everything around, get his life back on track.

'Well,' said Jimmy abruptly, getting to his feet, 'I'm off.'

'Where you off?' asked Moshi.

'Glasgow.'

Moshi frowned and twitched his head.

'Why you going there?'

'I told you. I'm moving back there.'

Moshi looked shell-shocked.

'You never told me that.'

'Of course a did. You were probably off your head at the time. Ross is moving in and taking my place.'

Moshi turned with a dazed expression to Ross, then back to Jimmy.

'Are you not coming back, then?'

'Christ, a fuckin hope not,' said Jimmy with a laugh as he collected a few items and shoved them in an already packed suitcase that he pulled out from under the bed. He said his goodbyes without ceremony and was gone, leaving Ross alone with Moshi, Ross already wondering what the fuck he'd let himself in for, and how on earth to get rid of his new friend. Meanwhile Moshi, still sitting on the bed, with his ruined teeth and bitten finger nails and general appearance of dissolution, and with Jimmy's abrupt departure apparently already out of mind, began to relate at greater length his numerous

322

encounters with the law, his thieving techniques and escapades, periods in prison, and offspring he rarely or never saw who lived with his ex-partner or who'd been adopted, in which case contact had invariably been denied despite his best efforts and fervent wishes. Emotionally he produced from somewhere a battered packet containing photos of these kids, Ross thinking they could be anybody's kids, so nondescript were they.

It was altogether the résumé of a ruined life, depressing to have to listen to, and for Ross especially, who saw echoes of his own unwitting self-destruction. Not that he'd made such a determined and complete effort at writing himself off as Moshi, at least in his own eyes. In his own estimation, notwithstanding mistakes and stupidities that he was quick to concede, he'd been the victim of a perfect shitstorm of events, where if any one of the components had occurred differently, he might still be with Fiona.

23

The brief uplift of spirits from seeing Jimmy again didn't outlast his friend's departure. By the day, almost the hour, his morale seemed to disintegrate. To escape his room, and especially Moshi, and also because he had to visit the library every day to do his job search, Ross spent most of his time out of the house. After doing what he needed to do at the library he'd walk the couple of miles into the centre, sometimes crossing the river, walking aimlessly in a bid to lose himself. He seemed to be a target for strays, waifs, lunatics, outcasts, eccentrics. Not that he was anyone to judge. He didn't judge people, apart fae smooth wee fuckers and deceptive cunts. And Moshi, that poor drugged-up wee bastard.

He found himself next to some dishevelled roly-poly guy in a pub - unshaven, grubby, bulging t-shirt, thick photochromic glasses - who proceeded to tell him his life story. How he used to own a chain of shops. How he used to date a millionaire's daughter. How he used to be married but hadn't seen his son since he was one. Oh, twenty years ago now. How he'd had numerous ailments since then, hadn't been able to work. How he'd been in and out of mental institutions over the past fifteen years. How he'd go round the shops stealing just for the hell of it, just to take the edge off things. How the police came and arrested him within the secure unit. Completely against the law. Bundled him naked into a van. At the police station he was bent over while they checked in all his cavities. How he was on medication for arthritis, heart problems, bipolar. He'd been lying on his bed that morning, exhausted, listening to his heart thumping, going completely crazy. Was any of it true? What did it matter. Waiting in line in a supermarket behind an old man who looked like Gregory Peck as Captain Ahab, doing a shimmy on the spot continuously while repeatedly licking his fingers and checking his bills. A man shuffling along the street, bent over, making a repeated sliding noise with his feet, so that in the end Ross had to stop and wait till he was out of earshot. Some strange young black guy looking and behaving like a large animated doll, bizarrely dressed, shades, combat fatigues, some weird headgear, small face with neat stylised beard, standing at the intersection of two wide pedestrianized streets, watching what was going on around him like a rather conspicuous undercover cop. Ross saw him again later walking stiffly yet jauntily like a high-spirited robot on the balls of his feet.

A rainy day, cold for late June. He wandered deeper, south of the Tyne, feeling chilled. He'd been drinking anything he could get his hands on, and had some back-up in the shape of a bottle of wine and a couple of cans in his rucksack. An area of terraced housing, good, substantial, attractive houses, some with arched doorways and windows in alternating red and white bricks creating a pleasing, melodious effect, all boarded up and in the process of being demolished. A giant digger parked where a house had been. All the history of an entire area erased. The generations of people who'd lived there, from a time before cars. The sculptural shapes. The texture of the bricks, deeply harmonious and satisfying. The repeating patterns of doors and windows. Destroyed without reason or hesitation. The question for Ross was, if that doesn't matter - if all that doesn't matter - then what does matter. If all that history and texture and beauty and functionality doesn't matter, then what does. Presumably, in that case, granted the premise, that all these things are of no account, then nothing matters. Nothing matters. The two words resonated in his brain, as once before. Nothing matters. But that had profound implications, the notion of nothing mattering, both good and bad.

Back across the river, somewhere in the city centre. It had briefly stopped raining, and a wan, reluctant sun had appeared. A young woman was walking, or rather weaving, just in front of Ross. Wearing a pair of blue trousers which she hitched up periodically, but which tended immediately to slip down again to reveal a bright red thong. White blouse, peroxide blonde hair. He moved to the pavement edge to allow as much margin as possible, as another guy wearing earphones passed her on the other side. She called out something, as he thought to the guy with earphones, who didn't respond. At which she started mumbling something loudly and indignantly, he couldn't quite catch the gist, but glanced around out of curiosity. The woman immediately turned to him.

'I'm a bit drunk.'

Her expression was friendly though bleary.

'Are you?'

'Yeah, I've had a bit too much to drink.'

Ross smiled, and she began to walk beside him. It would have been easy to be embarrassed by being alongside her on the busy street, as her colourful appearance and zigzagging motion, and the impression she was about to topple over at any moment, had attracted some attention. But if Ross had ever cared about such things, he was certainly beyond doing so now, especially as he was probably not far short of being as drunk as she was. She stopped and look up intently into his face.

'I'm twenty six.'

'Are you?'

'Yeah. I don't usually drink.'

Ross nodded. She stood very close into him.

'I've just been to see my father. I haven't seen him in seventeen years. That's why I've been drinking.'

She half-sobbed then, and began to stagger forwards once more.

'Are ye goin to be alright?'

She took some moments to respond.

'Yeah, I'll be fine. It's just these fecking boots.'

She offered up the high heels of her boots for his inspection.

'I'm not a prostitute, you know,' she said, peering closely into his face. Surprised by this statement, he returned her gaze, taking in the unfocused blue eyes and fading dye job, and began to wonder how old she really was. Older than twenty six, he reckoned. Or maybe she'd had a hard life. 'I've just been drinking.'

She began staggering forwards again.

'Have you got far tae go?'

She turned to Ross and nodded seriously.

'Yeah. A long, long way.'

They'd emerged from the street into a square, partly paved, partly trim grass, with a fountain.

'Will ye be alright?', he repeated, feeling genuine concern that she might lose her footing and seriously hurt herself.

'Where're you from? You're not from round here.'

'Glesgae.'

'Where?'

'Glesgae.'

'Glasgow? What you doing down here?'

'Ach, it's a long story.'

'I've got a baby, one year old. She's back at home.'

'Have you?'

He wondered, if this child did exist, who was looking after her, and why her mother was here, far away and drunk. She suddenly stopped and wrapped her arms around him.

'You know, you're nice!'

He tried to pull away as she attempted to kiss him, just managing to avert his face. She stood back for a moment, laughing.

'Y'know, if we were both a bit younger we could have had great sex together!' She laughed again. 'We still could! What do you say?'

Ross smiled and shook his head. 'Mebbe not. A'm sorry.'

'So what are you doing here, in Newcastle? Do you live here?'

Ross thought for a moment, his mind still occupied by the offer of sex, and whether or not it was genuine.

'A'm at the university,' he lied. 'A've jus' started.'

'Oh, that's great, darling! What are you doing?'

He thought for a moment.

'History.'

'That's fuckin great, darling! Well, you look after yourself.'

She hugged him tightly once more. He hadn't felt the warmth and closeness of a female body in a while, and realised he was becoming aroused.

'Aye, honey, you too.'

But once she'd released her hold on him, she seemed to forget he was there. She sat down on a low wall bordering a lawned area and began searching in her bag, muttering, and scattering pieces of paper, receipts, coins, her mobile. She poked her finger among the coins, counting them. Suddenly she lost her balance, and sprawled on the ground. Ross helped her up, then sat her down, and sat down beside her. He was horribly aware of the closeness of her body, though not remotely attracted to her on any but the lowest, most animal level.

Abruptly she started to cry and sob, leaning forward and hiding her face.

'I've got nowhere to go. My family have all disowned me.'

She wept bitterly. Ross was reluctant to offer her a hug, or any physical contact, for fear of where it might lead. She was too much of a mess to get involved with, nor did he have any desire to do so beyond what his guts were telling him.

'I can't see my baby,' she sobbed. Then, glancing at him through her tears, 'I am a prostitute.'

'Are you?'

'Yeah.'

She dried her eyes, swaying where she sat, shoving the stuff back in her bag.

'I'll have to make some money tonight. A hundred pounds. I'll do anything. I'll stay all night.'

'Is that safe?' said Ross. She looked at him. 'A mean, wi' ye bein' a wee bit drunk a' that.'

'Do you want to have sex? Eighty pounds for the whole night.'

He shook his head.

'A've got nae money. A'm sorry.'

'Alright, fifty. Forty. Thirty pounds. That's as low as I can go. Thirty pounds for the whole night.'

A've got nae money. An' a've got nowhere to stay maself,' he said, not quite truthfully.

She looked across to where people were coming and going at the entrance to a shopping centre.

'That's my partner there.'

'Where?'

'There.'

Ross couldn't see who she was meaning, but he was in no mood to get into an altercation with a jealous partner, who on seeing Ross with her would think he was her latest client. He wished her well and walked away.

For some reason he felt chilled to the bone. Cold or rain didn't usually bother him, maybe just that he'd been outside for hours. Or maybe he was ill. He found an open church. It was warm, somewhere he could shelter from the rain, dry out, warm up a little. The darkness enfolded him. He sat hunched over, face hidden. The warmth was an almost derisory luxury. As if to point up the fact that this was what life could be. Had been. This was possible. What he now didn't have. Aesthetic delight. Warmth. But the visual pleasures of the building and the spiritual atmosphere barely registered. He was beyond caring. The warmth was a welcome respite nevertheless.

After a while a man came and sat down a few pews ahead and across the aisle from Ross. And presently began to talk to an imaginary audience, possibly someone he knew, or thought he knew, or himself.

'I'll tell you this, son... like the ears on a donkey. Take the covers off... pulled by reindeers... are you listening to me, son... it was covered in fucking snow...'

And so on. Ross tried to allow his mind to wander, out of the present, to anywhere else.

'Like the ears on a donkey... covered in fucking snow... pulled by reindeers... take the covers off...'

Change has to occur. It's probably necessary to us as human beings. It's a proof (however illusory) that our lives have meaning. Tokens of visible change - new buildings - new houses, new hospitals, new schools, new roads. It's a sign that we're not stuck in a time-warp. It's a sign that we exist. A dinnae have to destroy everything around me to prove that a exist. Why is it necessary to destroy what's beautiful and has the stamp of... Aye, but it's just that glass, steel and fuckin concrete disnae dee it. A'm tellin ye, it disnae dee it. He didn't know why he felt so cold, chilled, so cold a feel bone-chilled, numb, stiff aw over. A jus' happen to be one of those people who prefer a little warning before a die. A dinnae like the idea of it bein sprung on us. Of course, a know ye cannae arrange these things. Oh, a'm sure it could be arranged. Aye, the warning or the dying? Both, wi' sufficient notice. But change has to occur. That's the thing. Glass, steel and fuckin concrete disnae dee it though.

Later sitting somewhere, musing vacantly, surreptitiously drinking. Ghosts of past events and associations suggesting vague emotions to present consciousness. Too cold to actually think or feel. What's wrong wi' me? A mean apart from aw the things that *are* wrong wi' me. Repeating, with different emphases and inflexions. What is wrong wi' me. What *is* wrong wi' me. *What* is wrong wi' me. An empty mantra, distraction from the pressing chilled feeling and discomfort, loneliness. Emptiness. An' it'll aw be super/great productive, ye wee fanny, and a'll achieve super/great things with ma latest new super/great project. A mincing tone. Unbidden, sneaking through his defences, thoughts of Fiona. Tearing at his guts, endless technicolor memories of being with her, lying beside her, embracing her, touching her, feeling her body, times of laughter and affection. The ultimate betrayal. The thought of her with that wee fucker Mark. That soft wee fucking cunt. Aye it just had tae be one of those smooth wee bastards with their super/great proposals. That feckin super/great wee cunt. Probably, certainly would be at this very fuckin minute. God piss and fuck and shit it. What is *wrong* wi' me? A mean apart from - ah Jesus Christ, no. No, no, no, no. Oh no. No. No. Impossible that a'm here. That a should be here. That the here where a am here is here, and not some other fuckin where else - anywhere else. Anyone else's here. Here, there, every fuckin where, who gives a flying shit. How ye deein? Oh, a'm gettin there. Oh aye, a'm gettin there, wherever the fuck there is. That's the thing, where the feck is the there that everyone's gettin tae? Where the feck is it? Where is there? That's what a want tae know. A want someone tae tell me that. A'm guessin it's no fuckin where.

A cop telling him off for drinking in public. Laughing uproariously. 'Whit ye gan tae dae then? Arrest us, or just gie us a gud kickin an' chuck us in the river?' Laughing again. 'Aye pal, a'm jus' aboot mad wae it,' a touch of alcohol-fuelled hysteria from nowhere. A stern, final warning from the cop, a pleasant, reasonable young guy.

He was by the river, leaning on the railing, contemplating its murky depths. Suddenly dazzled by a burst of bright sunlight almost strobing in a wide line across its surface. Gulls on the muddy banks opposite just down from a group of derelict commercial buildings. The rumble and rattle of a train slowly crossing a girder bridge.

An elderly woman sitting on a bench overlooking the river began to play a recorder. Ross turned to watch her and listen. She played several hymn tunes, while Ross continued to listen unobtrusively, now looking out over the river. When she'd finished and was putting the recorder back in her bag, she gestured to Ross, who'd been about to walk away. He went over to where she was sitting with her bag containing the recorder on her lap. She looked up at Ross with a friendly expression.

'Hi,' said Ross. 'A hope you didnae mind me listening.'

'No, of course not. I'm not very good, I'm afraid.'

'It sounded great. A wis listening to your music an' looking out at the river. It wis great.'

She smiled, and invited him with a gesture to sit beside her on the bench.

'I come here once a year. Every year, as close to this date as possible. I come down and play something, just for a few minutes, as a little tribute and remembrance of my parents. They were very fond of this walk along the river by the Quayside.'

'That's a nice thing tae do,' said Ross.

'It seems to bring me closer to them in spirit, somehow. As if they can hear me playing these little tunes, old hymn tunes we used to sing in church. I like to think they can hear it, and I...well, sometimes I can feel their spirits close to me.'

Ross smiled and nodded. She laughed, looked away for a moment, in fact so long a moment that Ross thought she might be wanting to hide some tears. But she turned back to him briskly and dry-eyed.

'It's only once a year. I don't dwell in the past continuously. But it's nice to remember once in a while and make that connection.'

'Aye, fur sure. Dae ye live in town, then?'

'Oh no, no, not for many years. We used to live in Jesmond when I was a child. That's where I grew up. But I've lived in many different parts of the world over the years. I lived overseas for some time. Married, widowed, children, now all grown up with children of their own. The full circle. Now I live in Edinburgh. I don't really feel at home there, though. I'd like to move, perhaps back down to Newcastle. That really would be full circle, wouldn't it. You're from north of the border yourself, I take it, from your accent.'

'Aye. No' Edinburgh though.'

'Ah. Glasgow, then?'

'Aye, that's it.'

'Do you know this song?' And she began to sing out loud in a tuneful, determined manner, while Ross sat wondering how much more bizarre this encounter could become, and how he could extract himself from it. Suddenly she stopped singing, jumped up, threw off her scarf, and held out her hands to Ross, who felt compelled to get to his feet and take her hands.

'We'll sing it together. It's called The March of the Women, and you'll soon pick it up, if you don't know it.'

And so she started to sing while dancing a kind of jig, sometimes holding both of Ross's hands, stepping away from each other, then coming in close, then away again. Sometimes just holding one hand while they danced together along the footpath by the river, first one way, then back again, Ross gamely following her steps and dancing with her while trying to pick up the words, as they swung their arms together in time with the beat of the song.

Shout, shout, up with your song!

Cry with the wind, for the dawn is breaking;

March, march, swing you along,

Wide blows our banner, and hope is waking.

Song with its story, dreams with their glory,

Lo! They call, and glad is their word!

Loud and louder it swells,

Thunder of freedom, the voice of the Lord!

Passers-by, walkers, joggers, cyclists, were treated to the unusual spectacle of an elderly woman in long black coat and black beret dancing with some rough-looking guy to an old suffragette anthem. At last she stopped, red-faced and laughing, let go of Ross's hand, and collapsed onto the bench.

'Oh, that was fun! Invigorating, though I'm exhausted now.' After a few moments catching her breath she stood up again and wrapped her scarf around her neck. 'It was very nice of you to indulge me. You're a good sport!'

Ross laughed. 'Nae problem.'

'Well,' she said, gathering up her bag, 'I'll be back again around the same time next year, God willing. I'll look out for you. We'll do it again.'

Ross smiled. 'Aye, a hope so. That would be good. Look after yourself.'

They shook hands, and then she was away, Ross turning once to see her distinctive dark-garbed figure receding, head turned, looking out over the river.

When Ross arrived back at the house the front door was open. He was met in the hallway by a small, youngish man smartly dressed in business suit and tie. Behind him, filling most of the width of the hallway with his bulk, was what Ross took to be his assistant.

'Have you taken over Jimmy Mccluskey's room?'

'Aye,' said Ross. 'Who are you?'

'I'm the landlord. Mr Mehmood.' He didn't offer to shake hands. 'That's not the way we do it, someone just walking in and taking over the rent for someone else's room.'

Ross looked confused. 'A thought it wis all arranged. That's whit a thought. At least, that's whit I assumed.'

The landlord looked at him for a moment.

'I'll let you stay on this occasion. It's £250 per month for the room, payable in advance. Everything's included for that except electricity, which is on a prepayment meter.' He indicated the meter cupboard. 'Residents arrange sharing payments between themselves.'

He paused, seemingly waiting expectantly.

'Well, ye've got the first month's rent, right?' said Ross.

Mr Mehmood executed an elaborate double take, then shook his head.

'Have ye no' had the rent from Jimmy?'

The landlord shook his head again. 'No. You need to pay the rent within three days, or you'll be asked to leave. After I receive the first payment, in cash, you'll need to set up a standing order on your bank account. I'll give you three days, okay?'

'Aye, a'll get it sorted,' said Ross. 'A dinnae understand what's happened.'

He went back to his room, exchanging a significant look with Mr Mehmood's hired ape on the way. Maybe Jimmy had just forgotten. That would figure. Ross tried ringing him multiple times over the next couple of hours, plus a couple of texts. Each time it rang on, then went to answerphone. The wee cunt. The devious little shit. It looked to Ross as if Jimmy had just pulled off his final and finest sucker punch. It was all to save him having to give notice, so that with Ross to take his place he could go straight back to Glasgow and his latest beautiful victim. But what did he think was going to happen when Ross found the rent wasn't paid. Was the guy really as sly and evil as his mother had always made out? Ross didn't want to think that, but it was difficult to avoid the thought.

Sitting on his bed reviewing his options, Ross could only see one way out. He still had most of the money Grant had given him. There was clearly no way he could stay on in the house. If he scraped together all his money maybe he could afford a cheap train down to London, late evening or overnight. Maybe even that very evening. It would avoid the rent demand he couldn't pay, with the added bonus that he'd be escaping permanently from Moshi. He'd never been to London, so there was even some curiosity there. And he could get a job on one of the many construction sites, start making some decent money, rebuild his life, get back to Glasgow and Grant. Maybe even build the new relationship with Fiona he dreamed about. Anything was possible. Having debated for and against for some time before finally settling definitively on this course, Ross thought he should try and catch a few hours rest. He kicked off his shoes, lay back on the bed, his head spinning, and quickly fell into an uneasy sleep.

24

Around half seven Ross caught the Metro to Central Station. He managed to get a ticket for a train leaving just after nine o'clock, getting in to London sometime after half one. The cost of the ticket left him with a ten pound note secreted in the pocket of his jeans, plus some loose change amounting to about five pounds in his jacket. The station was quiet, just a few people wandering about. After buying the ticket Ross hung around, not bothering to walk outside. So it was done, the ticket bought. It was like stepping into the abyss. An hour or so until departure. A feeling of dread, compounded by the deathly progress of time as he waited. At last the train pulled in, slowly, reluctantly. A few groups of weary-looking passengers and one or two stragglers disembarked, then Ross climbed aboard and found his seat. Several minutes of people finding their places, shoving their bags in the racks and getting settled. Then the hiss of the doors closing, a series of shrill whistles, a jolt as the train began to move. He'd given his keys to Moshi to return to the landlord. Probably a bad move, God knows what he'd do with them, but not his problem anymore. It was surprisingly noisy in the carriage. Loud conversation, high-pitched laughter, children's piping, complaining voices from a table further down. Ross, his hood up, withdrew into himself and tried to catch some sleep.

Rolling into York at 22.15 the station was almost completely deserted. Lit up like some huge art installation. Moving again, something close to a panic attack at the horror of his situation. Nobody he saw, met or spoke to had the slightest interest in whether he existed, whether he lived or died. The coldness of the lights, their bleak uncaring whiteness as they scudded past, factory units looking uncannily deserted. He could hardly breathe at the sheer horror of it. A headache was developing, probably at least partly due to all the alcohol he'd consumed, that felt increasingly as though his head would explode. He thought that when he got there he'd throw himself in the Thames. The cold, consoling, filthy water, pouring into his lungs, extinguishing the pain.

By 22.40 it was fairly quiet at last, bar somebody talking on their mobile and the buzzing of some piece of equipment on the train he couldn't identify. The children had finally quietened down or gone to sleep. Doncaster. He knew nothing about Doncaster. The sweep of a flyover. An old railway water tower. Maintenance sheds. A feeling of unspecified dread. Alone in London. What could concentrate the mind more effectively than that. So many lights. The sheer complexity of everything. Then just darkness as the train bumped and vibrated. The fear and waves of regret were now paralyzing him. Flashes of light, colours, vague shapes. He managed to doze for a while in the swaying seat. If he replayed all his regrets how far would they stretch? Hearing a Glasgow accent for a moment he imagined he was back home in Govanhill. Parked white vans in a floodlit compound looking as lonely as lonely could be.

Approaching midnight. People everywhere trying to catch some sleep. Only £15 in total between himself and homelessness. Lights in houses. Families together in warm security. He believed that he was stationary, that only the train was moving somehow, without him, as he sat atop it and observed. If the train continued at this speed it would overrun the platform, fly over the houses and between the skyscrapers and plunge into the Thames, and then they would all be swallowed up and drowned. Even the attractive blonde woman sitting opposite, one row further up, notwithstanding her brisk, business-like attire, and no doubt carefully organised and successful life, iPhone and, especially, her hair, immaculately conditioned, would be submerged and blackened by the filth and debris of the river. Wondering irrelevantly if her iPhone was waterproof.

No wonder the world's in such a mess. It's too big. Nobody could control or organise something on this scale. Stevenage station, looking as bleak as any station has any right to look. Thirty minutes past midnight. They'd be there soon and then he'd see it all for himself. Stevenage has a McDonald's, useful to know. Droplets wending slowly, sometimes apparently purposefully down the window, making him wonder for a moment what was going on, before he realised it was only rain. Still the deep, gnawing panic, fear. Was it really just the thought of being alone in London? But he'd been to prison, and he'd survived that. That was different, there you just had to do what you were told, otherwise keep your head down.

Only an hour or so to go to see the great city for the first time. To see how it compared with Glasgow. (Later he would find that the streets were just streets. Broader maybe. A lot broader in some places. He'd find himself stopping and looking up, despite himself, despite the fact that he'd finished with all that nonsense, all the stuff that had brought his life crashing down around his ears. But you can't help looking up now and again. Surprised by how much of old or oldish London there still was amid the endless new construction. Just a passing thought, he didn't really care anymore. The rain, barely noticeable at first, steadier now, persistent. Ross, without waterproof protection, wearing only his old jacket and jeans, would quickly become soaked, though seemingly oblivious, his hair long again, streaming down toward his shoulders, which together with the rough, straggly beard, made him look destitute, not too far from the truth. Without a map somehow inevitably drawn towards the river. Euston Road, Tottenham Court Road, Soho. Approaching Westminster Bridge he would find some shelter from the rain opposite Big Ben, waiting for the great bells to sound the quarter in those sonorous, self-important voices, before moving a little further towards the river, still under the canopy, the rain scintillating in a puddle from the reflected white light of a street lamp. The great red Eye, only ever seen before when they'd caught the fireworks on TV at New Year. Suddenly he thought he could just see the top of the Shard. Strange, he'd thought it was directly alongside the river, dominating the riverside skyline. He'd got it all wrong, everything was out of kilter. Everything had slipped out of true, all built on quicksand. His entire life had been a miscalculation).

Now, as the train rumbled slowly through the outer suburbs to the central city, there was a sudden paralysing fear that he wouldn't be able to get off, not because he wanted to but that all possible options were unbearable. So he'd stay in his seat, caught through the force of his fear in a banal purgatory for eternity. A place of plush stained scarlet and hard grey plastic, surrounding him, holding him fast. And only darkness beyond the rain-smeared windows.

Printed in Great Britain
by Amazon

82968411R00200